Praise for *The Witness Tree*

"Amy Pendino brings to life characters who matter to us as they take and lose chances, flee or stay, and dare to love despite the consequences. This is a deeply satisfying, character-driven novel. It contains mystery, suspense, and a long-held secret that, when finally revealed, offers hope and reconciliation to those who most deserve it."

—Lorna Landvik, best-selling author of
Once in a Blue Moon Lodge and ten other novels

"We love how *The Witness Tree* pairs strong, resilient women with unsolved mysteries. . . . Lush descriptions of the rural landscapes and the characters' inner natures will capture both thought and emotion."

—Lori and Julia, cohosts of MyTalk107.1
Lori & Julia Show St. Paul, Minnesota

"In this accomplished debut novel, Amy Pendino portrays two independent women born decades apart—strangers whose lives are bound together by a curse set in motion when a tree in rural Iowa bears silent witness to an unspeakable act. Over six decades pass before the curse finally exacts its retribution on this farming community, which is depicted with all of its small-mindedness and big-heartedness. . . . The characters display a depth of honesty and a deep understanding of the human condition. The ending is satisfying, yet leaves the tantalizing possibility of a sequel. *The Witness Tree* is a page-turner that is insightful, compelling, and wonderfully well-written."

No Ordi

D1484528

"From its opening pages, *The Witness Tree* absorbs the reader in a gratifying tale of friendship, love, and betrayal, uncovering long-buried truths and characters learning to be brave in a world with its own designs on their destiny."

—Greg Dahlager, Writer's Digest award-winner
and contributing author of *Dark Side of the Loon:*
Where History Meets Mystery

"From the first paragraph, I was captured by Amy Pendino's eloquent and descriptive writing style. The story follows two women, generations apart, who are compelled to leave their old lives behind for new adventures. . . . Two thumbs up for Pendino's *The Witness Tree.*"

—Christine Husom, author of the
Winnebago County Mysteries and the
Snow Globe Shop Mysteries

THE
WITNESS
TREE

A NOVEL

Amy Pendino

AMY PENDINO

ISBN 13: 978-1-63489-145-5
Library of Congress Catalog Number: 2018950324
Printed in the United States of America
Second Printing: 2018

22 21 20 19 18   6 5 4 3 2
Cover design by Liz Forester
Interior design by Patrick Maloney

Wise Ink Creative Publishing replaces every tree used in printing their books by planting thousands of trees every year in reforestation programs. Learn more at wiseink.com.

"Our souls are tethered by the love
of things that cannot last."

—Louise Erdrich

Dani

I

AT LEAST THIRTY hooks covered the red and white wall in front of the counter, one for every regular at Susie's Café. Each ceramic mug that hung there, embossed with its owner's first name in thick, black letters, made the loop from wall to table to dishwasher and back daily, sometimes twice. Several mugs had collected grime around their rounded handles; some had drab brown stains around their lips. Most of them faced the same direction, their openings tipped to catch the news from the local color congregated around the tables nearby.

Dani didn't have a mug with her name on it. She sat on the last stool at the counter, a "Crestview Farm & Feed" mug in front of her. Swiveling around, she could see all the way through the café, the small square tables in orbit around the big round one filled with local farmers and small-town businessmen. Except for her and Donna, the waitress, every other patron was male, dressed in denim and cotton, their bristly cheeks and forearms pink from spring sunshine.

The morning, damp and gray, had given Dani a reason to drive to town. Last week she'd planted her first crop ever. Until it sprouted, she had two choices: try to spruce up the rundown farmhouse included in her lease, or continue learning the twisting county roads that transected Howard County. She thought about picking up a window fan for her upstairs bedroom as she waited for Donna to return and take her order.

The café's screen door banged open and Jacob Dorn strode in. He eased himself around the counter, reached in front of Dani, and grabbed his mug off the wall, the "j" and the "b" almost invisible from use. He didn't so much as nod to Dani as he filled his mug from the carafe in front of her, his attention occupied by the loud voices emanating from the big, round table in back.

Jacob finished pouring and took the carafe with him, nodding to his neighbors and acquaintances as he passed. He claimed the empty seat left open for him, the one in the back that looked out on the rest of the dining area. The other men there had been drinking coffee and exchanging stories since before Dani came in.

"You go to the funeral?" the one they called Bud asked.

"Nah, sent Barbara. It was her day to work the Guild, so she was there anyhow." He took a quick sip. "She said not many came, other than the usual. Said it was a quick deal, over in less than half an hour."

Dani turned and watched Jacob place his cup back on the Formica-topped table with a flourish. He cleared his throat and picked up the threads of a conversation she'd overhead earlier but had not understood. "So, I'm planning to take that tree down this week. Old Swenson was the last one left, you know, so it'll be safe now—"

"Isn't that tree supposed to have a curse on it?" Dani recognized her own voice as the one that interrupted. Almost without being aware of it, she'd transitioned from her stool to the step that separated the counter seats from the dining area below.

Jacob's blackbird eyes turned and bored into her scarlet face. "What's your name again?"

"Uh, it's Dani," she gulped. "Dani Holden." An older man at the round table coughed into his hanky. Dani felt her heart drop to hide down near the floor.

"Dani, sure it is." Jacob's voice held no warmth. "You're renting that lot off of 8, aren't you?"

She nodded and told herself to be brave.

Jacob sat himself up to his full height, still an inch or two lower than the hat brims and shoulders of those around him. "You never farmed before, is that right?" Silence formed a barrier around his pack. Donna, carafe in hand, was a deer on the side of his high beams.

The roses drained from Dani's cheeks, but she kept her eyes fixed on Jacob's and tried not to blink. "Well, I—"

"Once you prove yourself at that little place you got, come back. We'll save a seat for you." He barked out a laugh, looking around the table to gauge the other men's reactions. A chair squealed across the linoleum, someone pushing himself out of Jacob's range.

Dani took a step back, but didn't return to her stool. She'd been in Crestview for a month and a half so far, and no one, save Donna, had put forth more than a tight smile in her general direction. Getting someone to talk to her, she was finding, was as difficult as navigating through the feed store without losing her way. She decided she might as well continue.

She stepped down near the round table again. The men had resumed their conversations. She caught the eye of a man next to Jacob and directed her question his way. "That tree, the one you're talking about, is that the one that's supposed to be cursed?"

"That's what they say." From the chair to the right of Jacob's, Bud broke the silence. He tossed a glance her way. "Story says the curse stays put 'til the last one alive from back then passes on."

"But no one knows for sure if old Swenson was the last one left or not." Lloyd took off his Frontier Seeds cap and swiped at his face, his smooth, pale forehead a startling contrast to his tanned and wind-creased cheeks.

A blond guy named Chuck finished up. "Anyone living here during that time was afraid to touch that tree, from the fear of that story. My folks said a criminal of some sort, some fella from Texas or somewheres, was killed there, hung, from that tree. Everybody knew about it. The story's just continued on."

Jacob cleared his throat. "Fellas, you know there's no truth to that. My dad told us the same thing when he wanted to put a scare in us." He reached forward for more coffee. "It's nothing but BS."

3

Bud switched his toothpick to the other side of his mouth. "That may be, Jacob, but are you willing to risk it?"

"Don't see why not. It's in the way, every time I steer near the edge of that section. I aim to take her down this week before we spray." He clapped his empty mug onto the table's surface. It clattered but did not tip. "Anyone got time to help?"

The other men mumbled a litany of machinery to grease, cattle to sort, supplies to pick up and deliver, everyone too busy to lend a hand to this particular chore.

"Dani, you must have extra time, that little place you're running? Know how to run a chainsaw?" Jacob drove these words at Dani with more volume than he needed. She knew that he was reminding her of her place and reasserting his own as the head of this table.

"I've got time." Dani waited for Donna to finish pouring top-ups. Steam shook like scolding fingers from each thick ceramic mug. If she helped Jacob, maybe the others would be more open to her, a woman, farming on her own. She stepped down into the dining area and stood to the side of their table. She told herself to ignore the tree stories and look past Jacob's arrogance. "What are you thinking?"

The others chimed in with their recommendations. They compared the use of chains to dredging; they debated cutting the tree there before removing the pieces versus dragging the trunk out whole. Every man spent hours by himself each day, ruminating over rainfall and wind speed and cloud formations. The way the leaves at the edges of the windbreaks unfurled could tell the story of the season ahead, if a person watched carefully enough. They'd obviously had the time to consider Jacob's dilemma, for each man spoke with his own firm confidence that his way would be the best and the cheapest.

No one actually volunteered to help, though, Dani noticed. She wondered how Jacob would deal with her without his audience nearby.

"I'd compensate you for your time, fellas." Jacob gave it one last shot. "We can get it done early tomorrow. It's supposed to dry out, and it'd be nice to have that thing out of the way for when I pass through with the sprayer."

The men started pushing back their chairs, patting their pockets, shifting about looking for change. Several gave their goodbyes and rose to make their way back to work.

"Bud, how about you and your boys? It'd give them something to do, other than riding around making dust on those four-wheelers you got them," Jacob said. It was dawning on him, Dani thought, that she'd be the only one with him out there in the field.

Chuck cleared his throat from across the tabletop. Lloyd snickered. They were the last ones at the table, lingering to see how Bud would respond.

"Normally that'd be fine, Jacob," Bud started, "only I promised Missy I'd take her and Jenny up to Rochester to do some shopping." He stood and carefully laid a single wrinkled bill at his place, tucking it under the edge of his empty cup. Adjusting the belt that protruded sideways from under his round belly, he pushed in his chair and turned to go. "You can pick up the boys at the corner, though. Tell me when. I'll have 'em there waiting."

Jacob was the last to stand. Usually there was a buzz of conversation and ribbing when the men left, but today, Dani noticed, their exit was like the departure from St. Nicholas's after Mass: quiet, contemplative, eager to get back to the familiar.

She made her way back to the counter up front, wondering what she'd gotten herself into.

Lilly

2

June 1939

LILLIAN BRADSTREET SCOWLED into the oval mirror above her dressing table.

She knew she'd find no answer there, but kept searching anyway. Her hazel eyes, quick to dart and sparkle, narrowed. She wrinkled her nose in disgust. Leaning forward, she pulled a wayward strand of hair flat. It stubbornly kinked again, causing Lilly to lose her grip on the last threads of her patience. She clapped her hairbrush back onto the table. A cut crystal perfume flask jumped and clattered.

Lilly pushed away from the mirror and crossed the wide pine floorboards to the other side of her room, scolding herself to worry less about her looks and more about important things. Things like her college course options, or the self-imposed reading list of "important books" that she still hadn't started.

She jerked open the tall wooden doors of the wardrobe. Her mother insisted on calling this her "armoire," but no matter the name, it wouldn't hold anything light enough to stave off the day's humid embrace. She shuffled through the cotton and linen shifts hanging there. Nothing seemed cool enough to be worn outdoors on a warm, sticky day in the middle of Iowa. Frowning, she pulled out a sleeveless yellow print.

Lilly left the top two buttons of the dress open. She slipped her bare feet into flat shoes, hoping her mother wouldn't notice her missing stockings.

Before the day grew more stifling, she wanted to meet her friend Elaine in town. They'd parted the night before on uneasy terms, after Elaine confided that she didn't think she'd be attending classes in Ames this fall with Lilly like they'd planned. Before she could question her more, though, Ned had interrupted and called Lilly to his side, warning that the end of the night was fast approaching. He didn't want to anger her father by getting her home on the dark side of ten o'clock, her curfew.

Ned. Another situation to settle, Lilly mused, tossing her purse over her arm before leaving the house through her front door. The air outside enveloped her like a moist washcloth. She felt through the purse for her sunshades and slipped them on, clambering down the concrete steps to the sidewalk in front.

Nathaniel Edward Wagner. His mother had been a childhood sweetheart of her daddy before he went into the service. He'd returned to town some years later with a college degree and a wife named Mary Margaret. Ned's mother's chilly regard had not yet melted.

Before returning to Crestview, Gene Bradstreet had finished his college coursework and was hired to sit at a commodities desk in St. Paul. He had a knack for knowing and setting the best prices for cattle and crops even though he was "book-learned." He'd spent weekends driving across the Midwest, meeting old-timers and dust-busters and guys who didn't think much but planted just what their own dads and uncles did. He'd whiled away the hours without sunlight reading books like *Cattle Production: Modern Methods* and *Grains for the New Age*.

By accident or foresight, when he'd returned to Crestview he'd purchased some acreage in Howard County, on the northern edge of Iowa. The land was bordered along one side by Beaver Creek, a spring-fed stream that ran, at least in some form, most every day there wasn't snow on the ground. He'd used this plot of land to experiment with the hybrid seeds his friend in Ames had been promoting, taking careful measurements and getting the information back to Iowa State College on a regular basis. Mr. Bradstreet taught an agronomy course twice a week in Des Moines at the university there.

He and Mary Margaret bought a bungalow in town, a few miles from his land. They waited many years for a family. By the time Lilly, their only child, arrived, the Great War had ended and people were rebuilding their lives and planning for their futures. In Howard County, tensions eased between those who were able to stay through the hard times and those who were forced to sell their land.

Lilly grew up as the town stirred back to life. The hotel reopened and a new gas station was built along Main Street. The streets rang again with neighborhood picnics, daily games of street baseball, and even a few new automobiles parked along the front yards. The section of houses east of Main Street stayed occupied during the war, Ned's family's brick enclave perched on the first corner past the Catholic church. Now, new homes, painted bright, cheerful colors, sprouted up on the west side too, near the Burlington rail line, green tufts of slender grass poking out from the dirt covering their front lawns.

Lilly lagged down Maple Street toward Elaine's. The mature trees along both sides of her street cast down slanted shadows from their outstretched canopies. Having walked this stretch more times through the years than she could count, she didn't notice the journey itself, her mind shuffling through questions related to Elaine's change of heart.

Elaine waited in a slim slice of shade in front of her family's tidy white house. "You're late!" she called, toying with a printed chiffon scarf she'd placed over her hair to keep the set. "I thought you'd be here earlier." Noticing that Lilly's hands and hair remained bare, she snapped her gloves into her purse. She looped her arm through Lilly's, and the two turned toward Main Street and Susie's Café.

"Lilly, I know you're surprised about what I had to say last night, but—"

"You're darn right. Lainey! We've been planning our getaway for years." Lilly pulled her arm away from the moist press of Elaine's skin. "What changed your mind?"

The conversation ebbed as they approached two little girls having a tea party on the lawn ahead. Evidently, both girls wanted to pour. Passing the small tea table, their footsteps sounded discordant and arrhythmic on the sidewalk. "Lilly. You know my family doesn't have the same . . ." She hesitated. ". . . benefits that yours does. My parents think I'd be a better help here at home."

"What?" Lilly's eruption stopped Elaine's words but her feet continued ahead in the same firm, steady pace.

Lilly pushed to catch up. "What about your plans? What about teaching?"

Elaine steadfastly plowed on.

"How can you give up so easily?"

Elaine didn't answer. Her lips, carefully rouged in "Sunset," pressed into a thin line.

"Can you convince them to change their minds?"

This time Elaine stopped. She turned to face her oldest friend. "Lilly. You aren't listening." Her features relaxed into a smile. "We won't stop being friends." Elaine's patience would have been a blessing to a classroom of energetic children. "I'll visit you. We can write."

Lilly sighed. She wasn't convinced. Past her friend's shoulder, Lilly watched the two little girls bend together over their tea set, their friendship restored, serving with grace and delicacy a frumpy brown bear and a rag doll wearing a kerchief instead of hair. "I suppose you have to listen to them," she grumped. "Let's get out of this sun so you can tell me what you really think." They moved in unison again toward the café. "I hope Susie has iced tea—it's too blasted hot for that swill she calls coffee."

"Amen to that," Elaine agreed. Of course, she would agree. Her desire to cause the least harm and to solve disputes quickly were the qualities that would have made her an excellent teacher.

They climbed the cement step to Susie's door. Their chatter perked up the postures of two silver-haired gentlemen sitting in the shade in front of the Crestview Farm & Feed across the street. Their movement had also been tracked by a young man crossing the alley opposite them as he strode toward an old blue truck. He wore a creased summer hat, his eyes hidden in the shadow beneath it. His boots were shiny despite the summer dust. He looked comfortable, moving easily through the smothering humidity and the broad-bosomed slant of the sun.

Dani

3

Dani steered her Ford truck onto the shoulder of County Road B. The double-headed tree before her languished in the open space between two adjacent sections of farmland. Its huge green globes stretched majestically up and out from the thick center trunk. Two boys were arranging a towing chain around the oak's lower branches like a necklace, encircling the thick, stunted elbows. Gray clots clouded the sun's rays, but yesterday's rain hadn't returned. A hot wind blew up from the south, humid and throaty. Dani eased off the road and drove between the two sections toward them, about thirty yards in.

The boys by the oak were known locally as Tater and Tot—alike as two spuds plucked from the earth, likely to stay together until it was time for them to be replanted again. Tater was the older, but not much distinguished him from his brother. They were lean and reedy. Both wore dingy T-shirts, the neck stretched out on Tot's to allow his chicken-boned clavicle to poke through. Their sneakers were full of holes. They worked as a single unit, efficiently, without speaking.

Dani balanced her steps between the planted rows as she neared them. They were intent on their task and didn't respond to her "Hello." It didn't matter, her greeting was cut off by Jacob's diesel engine bustling up from behind.

"Came to help after all, did ya?" he called down from the tractor cab. Dani got the feeling that Jacob liked making his audience have to look up to find him.

She denied him the pleasure. Instead, Dani turned to the boys and gestured with her right hand. "How do you think you'll topple it—um, her?" The last word in the question stuck in her throat. Folks in this area universally referred to their machines and other inanimate belongings as female. She wondered if it would ever feel natural for her to use feminine pronouns this way herself.

Jacob responded over the noise of the engine, which he'd slowed to a gravelly purr. "Thought we'd pull her over and cut up the pieces once she fell." A sudden, solid clank from the chain made him and Dani both turn back to the tree.

This oak had been a local landmark for ages. While her sisters lined up properly on each boundary of the cleared land, she stood defiantly alone in the middle of two fields. Her location bore witness to the property line that once existed between separately owned sections of land. Her trunk was knotted and bunched like a lady's slipped stocking, scarred from brutal encounters with steel and machines. They had brushed by her for as long as she'd stood, proudly holding her ground, refusing to bend or yield. There was no other tree around to match her proud grandeur, towering as she did to overlook her domain. Passersby often did a double take, noticing the eerie way her trunk, halfway up its length, split into two equally balanced sections, each a mirror in size and shape to the other.

Dani moved closer to the green Deere, grasped its silver rail, and hoisted herself up to speak at eye level with Jacob out of the boys' hearing. "I've been wondering. Why is it called a 'witness tree,' anyhow?"

"Used to be that a farmer would have to pay attention to the land when he'd plow or harvest," Jacob said. "Trees like that one there"—he pointed to the double-headed oak—"were planted on the property lines between sections. Then you'd know where yours ended and the neighbor's began." He stopped for a second to work the chew in his mouth. "The witness tree gave you something to aim for so's you'd have a straight line." He turned his mirrored sunglasses back so Dani could see her reflection in the lenses. "Don't need 'em anymore, what with the GPS and all."

"So why is this tree still standing?" She watched his glasses turn away.

"You know, you were there at Susie's." Jacob was antsy. "But there ain't nobody left from back then. Even if that story was true, which it ain't."

Dani waited in case he'd say more, but he didn't. She backed down the metal steps. "You know what you're doing, then." Her words were more a statement than an inquiry.

Jacob tugged the brim of his cap, narrowed his eyes, and shifted to a topic he was more sure of. "You sure you know how that saw works? It ain't no bitty chainsaw like you probably seen there in the city."

"I spent enough summers on my grandpa's farm to learn what I need to know." Dani turned away to hide her distaste. Geoff used to tell her that she could never be a doctor or a politician—she wasn't built to keep her feelings hidden behind a false front. Jacob's arrogance made her back teeth clench. She yanked her work gloves out of her back pocket and snapped them on.

Tater and Tot, standing in the bed of Dani's truck, had hoisted that long chain about a third of the way up the tree's length, as high as they could reach. Tater held the chain in place in the back; Tot had come around the front to hold the length taut for when it was time to pull. Waiting, neither said a word. Dani wondered if it was patience or plain stupidity that kept them silent. Either way, best to get this done and over with, she thought, and moved toward the saw beside the tree.

"You can start by slicing real low so she falls this way," Jacob ordered, dropping the engine into low gear. "You sure you know how to use that thing?"

Dani didn't reply. She bent to switch on the choke.

"You boys, mind, stay out of the way in case that chain busts." He turned forward and touched the gas pedal. The chain slinked tight, slipping just slightly against the weathered bark before catching hold of a gnarled joint.

The tree groaned. Fibers shifted in her body. She called out in a low moan. The chain dug into the bark, pushing wrinkles of her gray skin aside as they bit into their task. The tractor's engine responded with a snort and a black, angry plume of diesel smoke. For a moment, the opposite forces held equally.

Dani pulled the whip-start of the chainsaw—it squealed to raucous life, eager to join the parting. She cautiously began to insert the waving tip into the midsection of the trunk, but Jacob's strident holler stopped her short. "Shit, girl, dig into the roots with that thing! We don't want to have to pull the whole stump out!"

Ashamed, Dani pulled away. The tractor eased into a steady hum. Dani kicked some dun-colored leaves and dead grass out of the way before inducing the saw to a higher speed. She dug in, slicing a quarter-inch gap along the dirt line. A half-circle formed on the side closest the road.

A solid crack shot through the cacophony. Dani darted back, the chainsaw bucking up into the air; she kept hold of it while Jacob stomped on the gas.

The huge oak shuddered before cracking vertically, open space ripping from her midsection up to the sky.

The larger piece with the twin globes fell in a graceful arc toward the road, toward Jacob's chain and tractor, the falling leaves mimicking the hushed swish of ballet skirts. The bottom section remained defiant, though, proudly attached to its roots, an upraised ledge along the north side shaped like the backrest of a chair or a tombstone.

"Gol dammit!" Jacob cursed. He pounded back down the tractor's steel steps, his stacked boot heels ringing. As he joined the trio on the ground, his ranting continued. Dani did nothing to still the whine of her chainsaw. Tater and Tot looked on, passive and silent.

"How the hell are we going get that shit piece out of there now?" He stomped around the stump and kicked a wayward branch out of his way. "We can't leave her like this. I got to be able to get nearer to them rows."

Then he turned to face Dani, placing her at the center of his ire. "Turn that damn thing off!" His angry gesture toward the saw matched the fury in his tone.

She flipped the saw's safety switch. Jacob pivoted back to the stump, hands on his hips, to consider the tree's remains. Birds began calling again from the windbreak behind them. A breeze whirled through some of the escarpment that had been collecting at the tree's base for years, freeing it to continue its interrupted journey.

"Boys, tell you what: you get them shovels out of my pickup and see what you can do with this stump." Jacob wheeled to look at Dani again, his face composed and in control this time. "See if you can figure out how to cut that trunk out, and we'll haul that in with the bigger part. Hurry it up, now, I got an appointment in Decorah this afternoon and I can't spend all day out here." Jacob returned to the tractor's cab. He pulled a leather-covered cell phone case out of the glove box and started in on someone new.

Dani yanked the saw back to life and went to work on the far side of the trunk, her opinions tucked safely inside. She had volunteered to help, after all, and she supposed Jacob had a right to make the decisions here. She sliced the wood carefully along the earth to try to meet the marks she'd made on the opposite side. She thought she might be able to join the cut underneath somehow, if the boys could jimmy the other side up and off the blade. This idea was aborted when the oak's massive bulk refused to pry up.

Tater took the idling chainsaw from Dani's grasp then and started making vertical cuts into the trunk from the top, slicing sections the way you'd slice a pie. The other brother levered these smaller pieces out as they circled the stump's circumference. Neither boy said a word. Dani watched them and hoped Jacob's phone call continued so that she wouldn't have to face his dismissal of her abilities or intellect.

By the time he disconnected, they'd managed to shorten the stump to about hip-height. They'd also hacked off the biggest joints from the fallen tree. These and the stump slices were stacked atop the leafy branches still attached to the part they'd toppled, prepped for a tow out to the ditch.

Dani stood next to Tater while Jacob outlined what he wanted to happen next. "I'll pull her back to the road. You load up the tools and take the pickup; we'll shave off what's left in the ditch there and cut it up for firewood this fall." He adjusted his cap more firmly on his head and returned to the tractor. "We'll have to figure out something else for that stump, but at least we got the most of her out of the way. Good day's work, I'd say!" His voice was cheerful and buoyant again, ready to tackle the next task on his list.

Tater and Tot threw their shovels into the bed of Dani's pickup and climbed in after them. "Don't you want to sit in the cab, guys?" Dani called. No answer, not even a glance in her direction. She started the Ford and followed the moist tracks gouged into the earth by the arms and elbows of the downed tree. Pale green, diamond leaves littered the sides of the path like folded tears all the way back to the gravel road.

Lilly

———

4

Stepping inside the cooler interior of Susie's Café, the girls continued their conversation.

"Tell me more about what you're planning to do, once I leave for college," Lilly began. She dropped her pocketbook to the floor below her and pushed her sunglasses up to the crown of her head, like Hedy Lamarr in her *Picture Play* magazine. Elaine demurely placed her headscarf onto her lap and folded her hands on top of the table.

"Well, you know I've always had a good head for figures and sums," Elaine started, but Lilly wasn't looking at her; she was trying to capture the waitress's attention. Elaine continued anyway—Lilly picked up more than she liked to let others believe. "My father thinks that I could be a big help to him, staying home." She waited for her friend's reaction.

Lilly didn't respond.

"He wants me to keep track of his books for him." Elaine paused as a young waitress dumped two paper menus in front of them. She raised a smile, but the waitress ignored her and returned to the kitchen. "That way, they can save. It's important to Dad that—"

"Wait a minute, wait a minute," Lilly broke in. She leaned forward. Elaine blinked at the hazel eyes so intensely focused on her own.

"You're going to work in your dad's shop?" Lilly's body was rigid, her mouth a thin line.

"Shh," Elaine cautioned. "It's not really my decision to make."

Lilly harrumphed and slapped open the menu that lay in front of her.

"You know it's arranged for Stephen to take over for Daddy, when he's ready. And it won't be too long before I hope to be married, myself." Elaine's voice trailed off, either from a lack of enthusiasm or because of the waitress's reappearance at their table.

"What'll you have, girls?" she asked, snapping her gum. Her apron was dingy; the corner of one pocket hung down, torn. *Carole* was written on her name tag, but no one really needed to read it—Carole was pretty well known throughout the back rooms and tavern parties around town.

"Two iced teas, please." Lilly ordered for both of them. She handed the menus back to Carole. "If you have a lemon, we'd—"

"You want them sweetened?" the waitress interrupted. "We're out of lemons."

Elaine caught Lilly's eye and shook her head. "That'll be fine. Thank you."

Carole snapped her gum and sashayed away once more. Lilly turned from the waitress's display and settled herself onto the red leatherette seat. "Lainey, are you sure about this? I mean, we've planned this since we were little girls."

Elaine smiled gently. "Sweetie, I'm sure." She reached across the table for Lilly's hands. "We'll always be friends, you know that. This is what's best for me, for my family."

Lilly briefly returned Elaine's squeeze—her pearly nails were so ladylike and fine—but quickly pulled away again. "I don't want to go without you. Who am I going to walk to classes with? Who will eat dinner with me, tell me I've got gravy on my chin?"

Elaine chuckled.

"No one knows me like you know me, Lainey. I'm . . ." Lilly's voice trailed away. Her spine slumped. Her greenish eyes were suddenly darker; they seemed unable to meet Elaine's. "I'm afraid to go away without you."

"Oh, Lil, you'll be just fine." Being a supporter was a role in which

Elaine could shine. "You'll find new friends and you'll learn new things, and . . . I don't know . . . you'll be so much, well, bigger than you would be staying here."

Lilly looked up to meet Elaine's gaze. "I know what you're trying to do, you know."

Carole returned and sloshed two slippery glasses onto their table. "There's sugar over there," she drawled. "Let me know if you want pie to go with that." She turned and waltzed back into the kitchen. The silver zipper at the back of the uniform's neck wasn't closed, and Carole's tangled hair had come out of its bun.

"Looks like Carole's found some 'sugar' of her own!" Lilly snorted. The girls dissolved into laughter they tried to muffle with their paper napkins.

The café door behind Lilly jingled open. Elaine snapped straight up and snatched the napkin from her face, all amusement wiped away.

Lilly turned in her chair to see who or what had caused this drastic reaction. Spotting no one she knew, she rotated back to continue their fun.

Elaine was not in the mood. "He can't be in here," she hissed. "He should know better."

"What do you mean?" Lilly attempted to swivel around again to see what she'd missed, but her friend's hand stopped her. "What happened? Who's there?" This time Lilly's whisper matched Elaine's somber tone.

Elaine leaned forward. Her perfectly arched eyebrows were pinched together. "That, that *Mexican*, or whatever he is." Elaine's disdain for the man had sharp edges. "They have their own place to go. He doesn't need to eat here." She'd increased her volume so the man would be able to hear. "Maybe he can't read the sign."

"Lainey. For cat's sakes." Lilly sat back and folded the edge of the damp coaster under her glass. "What harm can one man cause?"

"There are rules about this. This is our town, and we need to be vigilant about who we welcome here." Elaine lifted her sweating glass and took a dainty sip. "We can't be too careful, you know." She patted her lips with her napkin and settled back into their conversation, though she kept glancing over Lilly's shoulder to monitor the stranger.

Lilly toyed with her coaster. She thought about what Ned had told her, about the workers at one of the nearby farms. They were upset about the lack of sanitation by the river and wanted to move their camp up onto the highlands, into the evening breezes. Before Ned had mentioned this, Lilly hadn't thought about where the summer workers slept or did their business; until recently, she hadn't really even recognized the workers at all. They'd always blended into the backgrounds of the fields and outbuildings, quiet and hurried, here a few days or weeks before moving on to the next field, the next harvest. Ned didn't think they had the right to ask for anything other than the wages they were paid. It wasn't like they were permanent hands, after all. They should feel lucky to get what they got or move the hell on, he said. If there was one thing he knew, it was that listening to those migrants would only make them think they had something important to say. Lilly didn't know if she agreed with him or not.

Carole came strolling back, smoothing down the front of her skirt, and noticed the new customer. The only parts of him that could be seen from her angle were his shiny, dark hair and his broad shoulders. "Hello there," she called, grabbing a menu and flouncing over with a toothy smile.

As the stranger looked up to meet her, she stopped, inches from his booth. Her face froze. "Oh! Well, um—" she stammered, the menu hovering in midair. Her faded blue eyes, widened past the point of a polite stare, didn't blink.

"I'm, I'm sorry, but, well . . ." She took a big step back and clasped the menu tight to her bosom.

From their table, Lilly and Elaine waited to see what would happen next. Lilly was turned completely around in her chair; Elaine, hands clasped under her chin, lips a tight line, looked to be staunching her words.

"Sir," Carole continued, "we're a family business here." Her voice petered out. She pointed to a sign by the front door with her menu: WHITES ONLY.

The café was silent. Even the kitchen, which usually spewed forth clanging metal and steam, had gone mute.

The stranger's deep voice, measured and calm, broke the impasse. "That shouldn't be a problem, miss." His voice relayed deep and confident assurance. There was absolutely no hint of an accent—no Mexican, Texan, nor even the local German inflection—in its timbre. A river ran through that voice, an intoxicating current that pulled you closer, that invited you to bend in, to pay attention.

He turned his head toward the girls, and his countenance was just as riveting as his profile. Lilly was astonished to see that in the stranger's smooth, dark skin were set blue eyes the shade of faded denim, visible even from her side of the small café.

"I'd like a cup of coffee, miss, and a slice of whatever pie you feel is best today." His even, white teeth were framed by a calm, confident smile.

Carole pivoted and strode back to the kitchen.

At their table, Lilly's eyes sought Elaine's. Neither girl could think of what to say next.

Dani

5

ONE OF THE things Dani liked best about living out in the country was the sounds, especially after the sun fell. Things you didn't or couldn't hear during the busyness of daylight hours came to life in the dim and the dark. When the sun was high, you couldn't hear the whispers of the rippling corn stalks as they shushed each other; you'd never notice the chirps and calls of the birds in the tree line over the mechanical growls of farm machines. Some people, Dani knew, grew edgy or even frightened by the vast space and the open, edgeless sky, especially during the nights when the stars didn't shine, but she had spent enough time on her porch now to appreciate the solitude for what it was, not what might lurk inside it.

The sun was close to setting, stretches of purple crowding the orange and rose hues ever closer to the horizon, before Dani came in from her field. She took a quick shower and carried a cloudy water glass, half-full with whiskey and two ice cubes, back out to the front porch. She settled herself into the lap of a rough-hewn rocker and put her stocking feet up on the peeling wooden rail. Her sweatpants were a buffer against the scratchy woven seat; the small of her back arched perfectly against the chair's slats. She took a careful sip, swishing the gold liquid through her teeth before she swallowed. Others complained about the whiskey's burning fire, but Dani enjoyed the combination of its heady, brassy ripeness and the ice's cool rush.

Holding the base of her glass, she whirled her drink around and thought about that double-headed tree. The cursed tree. Dani had never seen a tree like it, not during her growing-up years in town, at her grandparents' farm, or even during college or her internship way up in the Rockies. The way the trunk branched off into two perfect spheres, each a mimic of the other in shape and scale, was almost otherworldly. But since its fall, no one had suffered any misfortune or consequence due to the alleged curse. Not as far as she knew, anyway.

Dani could understand how that tree would inspire fearful stories, but she was having a hard time putting the whole curse thing into its proper mental storage slot. She wondered who would curse a tree and why. On the other hand, when they'd pulled at the trunk and it began its separation from the earth, the groan it had made had been eerie, almost human.

Her cell phone rang from inside. Her startled inhalation sent her sip down the wrong tube. Choking, Dani tried to place her glass on the porch rail, sudden tears screening her vision. Through her swimming eyes, she saw the phone's lit screen glowing from the old, round-topped table in the entry hall. Normally, no one interrupted her evenings. She'd broken up with Geoff months before leasing the farm, and her parents mostly called on the weekends. She hurried inside, grabbed the phone before it could shrill again, and pressed the green button.

"Dani? Is this Danielle Holden?" The deep voice, vaguely female, suggested late nights and too many cigarettes.

"This is Dani Holden."

"Dani, I'm sorry to call you at home. I should've waited 'til the next time you dropped in, but . . ." The voice petered out.

"Who did you say was calling, again?" Dani asked.

The gravelly chuckle from the phone sounded forced. "I'm sorry, this is Donna. Donna Lund? From Susie's Café?"

It took Dani a minute to process the greeting. She wondered why Donna would be calling or how she even found the number—there wasn't a land-line at the farmhouse, and most cell numbers were difficult to locate. "Hi, Donna." Dani looked past her reflection in the cloudy-edged mirror to the dark room behind her. She hadn't done much by way of decorating when she moved in; it helped that the farmhouse's owner had left the furniture he didn't want, because Dani had nothing with her when she moved but her pickup and the clothes in her suitcase. "What can I help you with?"

"It's none of my business, I know, only . . ." Dani heard the other woman take a drag of her cigarette and could almost smell the burn of the smoke she released. "Only I overheard what you all were talking about the other morning? I wanted to know if you know anything at all about what you've gotten yourself into."

Dani brought her phone back to the porch. She sat, picked up her whiskey, and asked Donna to explain what she was talking about.

"I know you're a newcomer here and all, and while I sure don't mind you're being a woman, there's others that'd use that to their own, you know, advantage."

Dani heard sharp yips from the other line. Donna offered a brief " 'S'cuse me a minute," and covered the phone to scold a puppy. Dani took a sip of whiskey. "Look, I know it ain't my business, but you, you don't want to get mixed up with that tree you and Jacob was talking about."

Dani lowered her glass. "Donna, I appreciate your call, but you're a little late. We took it down yesterday."

The voice on the line stayed quiet. The dog, though, started up again.

"I guess I don't understand why there's so much to-do about this tree. First of all, how can there even *be* a curse on a tree?" Dani sighed. When Donna still didn't answer, she tried again. "It came down pretty easy. We got all the branches off, and most of the trunk we sawed into firewood for next winter."

"I wish I would've called you sooner," Donna broke in. "I was just . . . embarrassed, I guess, or afraid that you'd think I was poking around where it wasn't my business to." The strike of a lighter, then another strike, were followed by a quick intake of air. "Didn't anyone explain the curse to you?"

Dani picked up the ripe, throaty mating calls of the frogs from the ditch at the front of her property. They sang all night long, especially early in the summer season, according to the farm's owner. Since she'd been here, Dani had come to recognize the sound as a "good night" of sorts. Hearing it now, she felt herself growing more relaxed and sleepy. "Donna," she said, "I don't know much about anything, as the guys at your café keep reminding me."

Donna's muttered "Well . . ." sounded polite rather than positive. At least she didn't seem to be one of those who said one thing to your face and the opposite behind your back.

"All I know is that the tree has or had some sort of curse preventing it from being cut down." Dani pushed her toe on the porch floor to get her rocker going again. "Other than that, I've heard Bud say he's seen a 'haint,' whatever that is, out dancing under the tree on bright nights, and Lloyd swears his dad will cross a section or two out of his way in order to avoid driving next to that piece of land."

"That's about right," came the voice from her cell, "but you haven't got to the worst of it. You know what they say about the hanging, don't you?"

Dani sighed; Donna appeared to be in the mood for a late-night talk. "I don't, no. Can you tell me what you know?"

The rest of Donna's hesitation must have been released in the rush of air Dani heard before she continued. "Folks say Jacob's daddy, old Jesse, hung a man from that tree, all those years ago. No one knew who the man was, but he wasn't from around here." One more exhalation whooshed out—then both lines grew quiet, Dani pondering that outsider's fate. After a span of silence, Donna inhaled, then continued. "They say the fella swung up there for a full day before anyone cut him down, to make a point, and by that time, with the heat and all, they needed to get him in the ground real quick. They're supposed to have buried him right there at the foot of that double tree."

Dani's breath quickened. The dwindling ice cubes in her glass sloshed against her top lip when she tossed back what liquid remained. After the World Trade Towers had come down a year ago, her recognition of impermanence had started jumping up regularly. These piercing, unwanted visits were part of the reason Dani left the city to seek a different sort of life for herself. She wondered if she'd used up an extra allotment of heartbeats every day she'd ridden the bus, worked, shopped, lived in Minneapolis. Since she'd moved to Crestview, though, her heart had found its normal pulse again. Until this tree business, anyhow.

She heard a male voice from Donna's side of the line.

"Gotta go, honey," Donna whispered to her. She used a bright voice to answer someone else. "Just a minute, I'll be right there!" Returning briefly to Dani, her tone once again lowered. "We can talk more another time."

The call disconnected.

Dani's shoulders slumped, her pulse outpacing the frantic calls from the nighttime chorus of frogs in her darkened yard. Instead of offering their usual calming reassurance, their sounds became jeering admonitions.

Their warnings followed her when she left the porch and went inside. She heard their cautions trailing her down the hall, echoing from the corners of her room, forbidding sleep.

Lilly

6

LILLY PURSED HER lips to add an extra dot of lipstick to the center of her mouth. She slipped the slim silver compact, which also held a tiny powder and pad, into her square evening bag. Grabbing a lacy cardigan from the back of a chair, she swept out of her bedroom, dancing with light footsteps to the jaunty tune in her head.

Nearing the top of the staircase, she slowed to listen in on the voices below. Ned spoke in his low tone without much pause. Lilly's father was chuckling. She could also make out the tap-tap of her mother's heels nearing the bottom of the steps, which she took as a signal to get moving again. Lilly carried herself in what she hoped would pass for a graceful descent, squinting her eyes and drawing her lips into a cheery smile. She hoped she'd be able to fool the others, because she wasn't fooling herself. But, as was often the case, she didn't have time to work through her own reaction—not with the three strongest influences in her life standing expectantly before her.

"Hello, Ned." Lilly kept moving, crossing the landing toward the front door where the men stood. She hoped Ned wouldn't try to kiss her cheek in front of them, as he'd been doing lately. She put her hand on her father's forearm and scolded him. "Dad, I hope you're not boring him again with your statistics. I'm sure a banker like Ned doesn't have any interest in what you and Mr. Borlaug have been dabbling in."

Mr. Bradstreet pulled his pipe out from between his lips and smiled indulgently at his only child. "Lillian, Ned has more than an average man's interest in the new ideas that Norm and his fellows have been researching." He circled his pipe in Ned's direction. "In fact, this young man has kept himself quite informed about their developments. If the next few years' growth continues as predicted, your Ned could find himself saving a whole lot of money. The farmers who practice this 'new-fangled theory' may get greater returns as well." He tapped the bowl of the pipe into his empty hand and kept talking, almost to himself. "I wonder if it would work with corn, too . . ." His unblinking gaze was locked on the far corner of the room, where no one stood.

Lilly shook her head before she turned to her date. "Sorry, Ned. Are you ready to go?"

"Just a minute, young lady!" Her mother's voice interrupted their exit. "Where are you off to?" Her penciled-in brows rose toward her neat hair-line at the end of her question.

"We were thinking of going to the Frinkmans' barn to listen to a dance band, Mrs. Bradstreet." Ned adjusted the cuffs of his long-sleeved shirt. He had removed his usual dark jacket, but his tie was, as ever, firmly in place at the throat of his starched collar. "We shouldn't be too late."

"No, Mother, I'll be home early. I'm helping Elaine tomorrow at church. It's her mother's turn to serve coffee after Mass." Lilly tucked her sweater into the crook of her elbow so she could steer Ned toward the door with her free hand. "You and Daddy have a nice night."

"Good night, Mr. Bradstreet," Ned called before allowing Lilly to pull him out into the balmy summer evening. "You too, Mrs. Bradstreet, have a pleasant evening." He began to tip his hat before realizing that he'd left it in the car.

Lilly's mother closed the paneled door and switched on the electric porch lights, reminding her daughter to check in when she arrived back home.

Ned escorted Lilly down the flagstone path to the roadside where his new Plymouth sat waiting. He opened the door for her and gently shut it after she'd swung her legs inside. Lilly hoped he hadn't noticed that she wasn't wearing stockings—she could barely abide their pressure encasing and slipping down her legs. Ned could become incensed at things she wouldn't have given a second thought to, like being late for dinner dates or forgetting where she'd placed her sweater. She'd taken the chance that something as trivial as whether or not she wore stockings would escape his notice.

They passed the city limits and continued south on County Road 8. While he drove, both hands on the steering wheel, Ned shared some of the news he'd learned during the week from the customers and clients who patronized First National. "Can you imagine?" he asked. "I don't know where he gets the gall, but I wouldn't put up with that."

Lilly hadn't been following his point that closely. She murmured what she hoped sounded like support and let him continue.

Her window, rolled down to allow her arm to rest along the top of the door, blew a warm, fresh breeze onto her face. Carefully arranged at home, her hair began to loosen in the wind. Sun-kissed tresses danced across her cheek and played with the mandarin collar of the sleeveless shirtwaist she wore. Her eyes closed, her lashes blanketing the tops of her pink cheeks.

Ned took his right hand from the wheel to clasp her left, resting on the blue seat between them. Her eyes popped open and she sat straight up. "What's the matter? Ned, are we—" When she saw no danger, she took a deep breath. "You spooked me! You need both hands to drive, don't you?"

"You look so perfect, just now." He put both hands back on the wheel and looked forward at the road ahead, but his freshly shaven cheeks blushed. "I'm sorry to startle you."

"It's okay," she replied, corralling a loose strand of hair behind her ear. "I wonder what they'll be playing tonight at the Frinkmans'? How did you hear about the band, anyways?"

"Frinkman's man, O'Leary, came by the bank this noon and passed on the news. They've hired a group out of Minnesota, some band that's been traveling here and there all summer." He began slowing the coupe at least a good hundred yards before the stop sign ahead. "I thought you'd like to do something new."

When she replied this time, the enthusiasm in her voice was real. "It sounds like fun. Not that I mind going to the show, you know. That's fun, too." It did take a lot of effort for Lilly to keep herself quiet in her seat for as long as a movie lasted, though. Even if the film was a good one, she'd feel her patience leaking out by the end of the first hour. She wasn't designed to sit still for that long.

The dark was split by a shining halo of light from around the Frinkmans' barn. Close to the property, Lilly began hearing laughter and music over the engines of cars and trucks waiting to park in the field. A neighbor's dog barked, expressing his opinion about the clamor that swirled around him.

Vehicles parked in loose lines next to the barn. The yard light above the big sliding door shone on couples who hurried underneath it. Lilly didn't wait for Ned to come around, but got out of the car and shut her door on her own. "Turkey in the Straw," sawed out by a fiddle, was paired with a guitar that kept the beat. Lilly's heart swelled with the deliciousness of what lay ahead. A pull from deep inside enticed her to become part of the music herself, to allow its pulse to crawl up through the barn's floor and echo her own internal rhythm.

From behind, Ned called for her to wait. Lilly pretended not to hear him and stepped up to the brightly lit building. Lanterns hung from the top of each loft post, and electric lights had been strung along one of the short sides of the barn's headers. Couples swirled together over the sawdust on the floor, the women in bright colors, the men scrubbed clean in denims and pressed shirts. Chairs stood along the length of the barn to catch the breezes through the aisle, but they remained empty. The band commandeered one short side of the structure, the fiddle player, two guitars, a banjo, and an accordion perched atop a parked hay wagon. Mrs. Frinkman stood at a table to their left, overseeing the lemonade and cookies to be sure that nothing illegal would be added to her cut crystal punchbowl. Lilly recognized many of the farmers and neighbors who were dancing nearest the band, but she wasn't familiar with any faces from the dark section in the back.

Ned caught up to Lilly, placing his hand possessively around her waist and bending down to her ear. "Do you want to dance right away, or should we get some refreshments first?"

She turned back to her date, genuine joy radiating from her smile. "Ned, this is wonderful! Thank you for bringing me here." It didn't matter a hill of beans if the band wasn't the same caliber as the musicians she heard over the radio. It was exciting to be here, in person, surrounded by others who seemed as glad as she was to be doing something out of the ordinary for the evening.

The band began playing "Four Leaf Clover." Lilly flung her purse and sweater onto the nearest chair and grabbed Ned's hand. "Let's dance!"

Ned didn't seem as excited as she was to enter the fray. He held back and started to say something about waiting for a slower tempo, but Lilly laughed and pulled him to the front of the floor. "You can't get away from me. After all, you're the one who decided to bring me here tonight."

Her smile was infectious. Ned held her hand, pulled her close, and hesitantly listened for the beat, watching the band as if they would flash him a sign to begin.

She snorted and started off on her own, dragging him along. "Move your feet, clodhopper! You don't have to look good, just have fun!"

They danced together, finally finding their rhythm through the last verse and chorus, and while it didn't look graceful or pretty, Lilly was having the time of her life. Her natural exuberance gave an extra spring to her step. She snapped her hips when Ned circled her, causing her skirt to flare. She appeared as a wild creature in his arms, one who didn't want to be tamed. He tried to tighten his hold right as the band's "Shave and a Haircut" announced the end of the piece, but Lilly disentangled herself from his grip and clapped loudly, facing the band. Ned clapped too, facing Lilly.

The next song was "Goodnight, Irene," a waltz that the boys decided to jazz up a little. Ned didn't give Lilly another moment before clasping her tightly against him again. "Lilly," he began, "I don't want things to change between us when you go to Ames next month."

She used her answer as an excuse to pull away from his tight embrace. Looking up at him, she pushed out a reply. "Why would they, Ned?" She considered sharing her real thoughts, the ones that kept her awake in the quiet at night, but couldn't find the courage to get started. "Why not talk about this after I've been there for a while? I haven't even left yet."

His expression, one of dissatisfaction and frustration, smoothed back into a grin, and he tried again to gather Lilly in. She slipped beneath his arm and pretended he was sending her off for a twirl, then felt herself swung back into his embrace. His arm along the back of her waist felt like an iron bar. "I want you to see new things, Lil, I do, but—"

She didn't want to embarrass him by stepping away, but his comments were making her feel strange, off-balance. "I'll be back for Christmas, Ned. And Ames isn't all that far away."

The song's ending came and went. It seemed the band had decided to tack on another verse. The other couples didn't act perturbed by the extended coda, swaying in harmonious unity. Lilly couldn't wait for the song to be over. She imagined herself like a wooden marionette, being tilted and stretched all the wrong ways.

"Let's get some lemonade, shall we?" Lilly proposed as the music finally concluded. She didn't stop to clap or to wait for Ned but made a quick beeline for Mrs. Frinkman's table. She didn't even look behind her to see if Ned followed.

Intent on the sudden sorrow his words had riled up inside her, she repeated the question that kept her awake at night: Why was she going off to college, anyway? She'd earnestly repeated to her parents and friends that she wanted to extend her learning, but this sudden pang brought a more genuine awareness: she wanted to leave to be something new, to be someone other than a cheerful daughter or a decorous girlfriend.

Standing in line with the others by the punch bowl, she felt off balance, like she was looking down at the dance from the rafters high above. The view was hard to take in: she saw her outside self in bright color, an upbeat smile on her face and her hand tapping along with the band. What couldn't be seen, but could not be unfelt, was the uncertainty in the place nearest the young woman's heart. The double image made Lilly's head spin.

Ned had located her. He was maneuvering closer, squeezing between chatting couples. Lilly excused herself and turned to head outside, into the cool breezes and away from the shining lights. For once, Ned did not follow her.

It took her a few minutes of gulping in fresh air to recognize that she was alone. Making the most of this unexpected gift of solitude, Lilly veered away from the parked vehicles and strode through the shadows toward the tall grasses she heard whispering from the pasture ahead.

The footing in this field was uneven, no doubt due to the deep hoof prints left by the large draft horses the Frinkmans used to have. Now the Frinkmans were as up-to-date as everyone else in Howard County. The horses, "hay burners" to most, had been sold to an Amish family, Lilly heard.

She slowed as the darkness increased, feeling for the steps ahead so she wouldn't tumble and end up a dirty disgrace. Which, of course, she did: one foot navigated a particularly large divot gracelessly, causing her to be thrown off balance. She tried to catch herself but instead collapsed like a sack of rocks into a patch of grass that had yet to be mowed.

For gosh sakes! she thought, grateful that no one had seen her. Sending a silent prayer of thanks above, she rose to her hands and knees and began maneuvering back to a standing position.

"Miss, are you hurt?"

The quiet query came from behind her. It didn't sound like Ned's cultured voice—this man used a more natural manner of speech. "Can I help?"

Lilly stumbled to her feet and wheeled around. She did not like to be caught off guard, not even by Ned or Elaine, but especially not by someone she didn't know. She didn't like feeling vulnerable; she didn't mind the embarrassment so much, but being pinned into a dark corner of a rough field made her start scanning for the best possible ways to escape.

"No!" Her voice came out louder than she intended. She ran her hands down the skirt of her dress to smooth it. "I'm fine, really." She took several quick steps toward the barn.

As she threw a glance over her shoulder, the voice's owner was revealed. He kept himself at a distance, but would obviously be able to reach her before she could get back to the lighted and populated safety of the dance.

He declined to do so. Instead, he removed his hat and stepped backward, away from her, before continuing to speak. "I don't mean you any harm."

She stopped and turned to better see his face. It was the man from Susie's Café.

"I want to be sure that you are not injured," the man finished. Then, he waited.

Lilly saw the light eyes in the stranger's dark face even through the twilight. Handsome, wiry, he looked at her with concern, but then raised his eyes to rest on something beyond her. His expression changed from mild regard to a tight, controlled shuttering of his features: eyes narrowed, lips together and thinned, he placed his hat back onto his dark hair and moved forward past Lilly toward the barn.

"Hold it right there, mister." Lilly had heard Ned using this authoritative tone with one of his "baser customers," as he'd called him, when she'd come upon the two of them handling a delicate issue at Ned's bank. This time, the way that Ned spat out the words, sharpening the word "mister," sounded like darts flung forward by a thug. This time, hearing Ned's voice, Lilly felt ashamed.

"Ned, I'm fine," she called, making herself hurry to his side. He pulled her toward himself protectively, all the while glaring at the man who observed them silently from the lawn's edge.

"Did this man hurt you?" he asked. He spoke in a whisper, but Lilly was certain it was pitched so the other man could hear.

She tried to pull away but was held fast to his side. "Ned. I was getting some air and I fell," she explained. "This . . . gentleman came to help me."

The gentleman in question resumed his route to the barn. "I will leave you now," he said, adding, "if you're sure you're fine?" He looked directly into Lilly's face, moving past her as smoothly as a stream of clear water surrounds and releases the round pebbles in its path. She was taken aback by the directness of his scrutiny. His intensity pierced her all the way through.

"Thank you," Lilly managed. "H-have a nice evening."

The shadows on the side of the barn enveloped his exit.

"Why are you speaking to someone like him?" Ned asked.

She finally worked her way out of his grip and fanned her hot cheeks with her hands. "Ned, he's just a nice man who came along and wanted to help," Lilly asserted with more confidence than she felt. "I thought I was alone. I was only—"

"You're always 'only doing this' or 'only thinking that,'" he interrupted, his anger pulsing the outer corner of one eye. "Dammit, Lilly, you don't think, and that's the problem. I can't trust you not to get yourself into trouble. What's going to become of you if you find yourself in a situation you can't get out of? Then what?" At some point, Ned had rolled up the sleeves of his white shirt and loosened his tie; his closed fists now punctuated each side of his crossed arms.

Lilly recognized the feeling of being judged for something she'd done wrong, again.

"That 'nice man,' Lilly? He's not one of us. God knows where he's from, or what he's capable of doing." He made himself take a breath and rearranged his face into a pleasant, businesslike smile, but his eye kept twitching. "I care about you, Lillian Bradstreet. I don't ever want anyone to harm you." He reached forward to caress her shoulder.

Without thinking, instinct took over and Lilly stepped away from his touch. Hurt showed through Ned's narrowing eyes. His smile faltered.

"I know. I'm sorry," she replied. "I know you want what's best for me."

Lilly felt herself responding in the detached way she'd experienced earlier that night, but in this scenario, the young woman she gazed at from above was not as concerned about Ned's reaction as she used to be.

Dani

———

7

THE MORNING DAWNED bright, calm, and dry, unusual summer weather for this part of the country. You could go from Hades-hot, windy, and 90 percent humidity without a drop of rain to cold, still, and gray as an old sock in less than a few hours. It all depended on which way the air decided to travel: the direction from which it came brought either throaty heat or bracing, pine-scented clarity. Today's wind brought cool, cleansing air from the north.

Dani decided it'd be a good day to spray. As long as the wind held off, she could do all 160 acres herself before the end of the morning. She didn't have the spiderlike sprayer with the long, knee-bobbed rollers her larger neighbors owned, the one that could spray four rows on either side in a single pass, an acre a minute. Dani used a jerry-rigged, two-row sprayer that she powered with an old boat battery. It did the job.

Behind the tractor, the slender stalks winked and sparkled up into the clear sunlight. A fine mist gently shushed out to settle like little prayers on the newly opened green shoots. A male cardinal defended his territory from the windbreak to Dani's east. Ahead, some sort of hawk was chased by a persistent swallow or a little bluebird; it was hard to tell, as flying next to the sun made their bodies into dark shadows.

Dani had figured out a way to stop the jets from spraying as she made her turns at the ends of her field. The system would probably make the men at the café laugh, but it suited her just fine. She was good now about timing the shut-off to avoid double-exposing the crops. If she eventually decided to go organic, she needed to keep herself mindful of which chemicals would need extra time to be eradicated naturally, or she'd never pass certification. Dani knew that a lot of the local farmers scoffed at the whole idea of organic production, but she had studied popular news articles and financials and thought she could make a go of it someday. The problem was that she didn't at have enough acreage to allow the land to lay fallow to revitalize itself while providing for her current standard of living.

Her "standard" of living had changed dramatically. A year ago, she'd been eating most of her meals out, buying coffee and liquor as a daily necessity rather than a weekly purchase, and maintaining the requirements and activities of one Geoff Carlson. The man she was supposed to marry. The man who was supposed to share her dreams, to help her raise two children, to be her equal partner in love, intellect, and activity. Except Geoff had a thing for staying out late, changing "jobs" often, and spending more on chemical enhancements for the party than he remembered to spend on his own welfare.

Dani flipped the silver toggle off, eased up on the gas pedal, and turned her tractor to finish the remaining two rows. Looking out past her plot, she noticed a strand of wispy cotton edging up over the horizon. She congratulated herself on her good timing and decided to reward her judicious farm intelligence with lunch at the café, rather than choking down her usual bologna-and-mayo sandwich and three Oreos from the kitchen at home. It would be another way to check in with Donna, if she could manage to catch her alone—another way to find out more about that mysterious phone call.

DANI WASN'T THE only farmer taking advantage of the weather this fine, windless morning. Two sections to the east, Jacob had also risen early to fire up his new green John Deere. He'd gotten the slightly used sprayer from a guy who'd foreclosed. Crestview Bank gave him a good rate on the

$30K note he'd taken out, and with the time it would save, the deal seemed a good one to Jacob. Proud of his independence, he bragged that he could manage his nearly 3,000 acres just fine on his own. True, he might need a little assistance once and again if he needed to beat the weather during harvest, but his was mostly a solo operation.

The huge wingspan of the sprayer's retractable arms made for a slow exit from Jacob's metal shed. Even tucked in, the machine was wide enough to nearly scrape the aluminum edging on each side of the sliding door. The early sun shone a cheerful greeting onto the vehicle's tinted windshield. Jacob huffed and firmly closed himself into the cab before switching on the air conditioning for comfort and the satellite radio for company.

Heading down the gravel road to his first field, Jacob had to drive by Bud's ramshackle lot with its collection of rusted machinery and castoffs, the former feedlot now a jungle of broken-down metal skeletons in different states of decay. Bud's boys were outside when Jacob passed, the taller boy wrestling with an ancient weed whacker he wielded ineffectively against a maze of grasses at the front of their tilting, white house. Jacob raised two fingers from the steering wheel in the traditional rural wave. He got nothing in return. The darn kid didn't so much as nod in response.

He slowed as he approached the crossroads by the Lutheran cemetery. Stop signs aside, there was no telltale dust from either direction, so he turned expertly to his left and paralleled the overgrown shoulder to his field's egress. The grooves left from dragging out that overgrown tree stung the soil like fresh scars. Slender green cornstalks in the rows immediately next to the path were bent awkwardly and broken into sharp angles. The space where the proud tree had scraped the sky practically screamed now in its gaping emptiness, save for the scabby stump left below. Now, instead of her two palms reaching upward to the heavens, stretching for the edges of the sky, a void loomed—large, barren, endless, and uncontained.

Jacob's father would have taken no time for idle contemplation like this: Jesse would've barked for his son to get his head out of the clouds and get his feet moving. So that's what Jacob did. He slipped the transmission back into low, held the clutch, and flipped the switches to spread open the sprayer's skeletal wings. He busied himself with lowering the air temperature in the cab while the sprayer's arms descended smoothly over the four rows of corn on his right and the four rows to his left.

Then he turned on the jets. This machine was so efficient, a man could cover all his holdings and still make a late lunch at the café. Chemicals sprayed onto the plants in a fine mist. Slippery rainbows danced between the extended metal arms and the flapping green foliage below. The sprayer, automatically anticipating the end of the rows by satellite adjudication, shut off as Jacob arced the machine around for the next portion.

Not that those satellites did Jacob's job for him. He liked to boast to those who would listen that he didn't rely too much on the in-dash GPS screen designed to guide the sprayer's track. He claimed to be more "old school," keeping his eye on the trees planted along the dividing lines to keep his rows straight. The returns were successful, in his opinion, because he kept himself in control of how the big machine moved and functioned.

The sprayer crested a small rill and headed toward the spot where the big tree used to stand. Next to the dark tracks leading away from her, the only remains of the majestic oak were a circle of ruffled dirt and her abandoned stump, jutting up dark and raspy from the field's surface.

Jacob settled himself more firmly in the Deere's ergonomic driver's seat and aimed to edge near the stump as close as he was able to steer.

Right as he passed, the right side of his sprayer bounced once like he'd driven over a large rock. The satellite radio sputtered out and the computer screen on the dashboard went dark. Jacob looked down over his right shoulder to be sure that he'd missed the stump. His tracks showed no contact. There wasn't even a rock. Instead, the long tentacle on that side dipped dangerously low, clipping the ground at its very tip. The jets on that side quit spraying. An alarm shrilled from the cab.

Jacob slammed the flow to the "stop" position and eased the engine to an idle. The machine halted, and he flew down the ladder to inspect the damage. The sprayer gasped one last time. The remaining chemicals dripped out into a dark puddle underneath.

Lilly

8

IF YOU COULD fly like a bird and observe the fertile land stretching out in waves below, you'd see mostly squares of verdant green spread out from horizon to horizon like the hand-worked squares of a bumpy tablecloth. Little puffs of dust would mark the gravel roads that made the edges sharp and crisp. One dark, asphalt artery, running straight north, connected the sections like little charms on a lady's bracelet. In other places, the river would push the lines into luxurious arcs and twists, often hedged by darker globes of cottonwood and oak and rough-barked elder along the bottom lands. Man-made structures would be tidy and careful intrusions, looking embarrassed to be squatting in a place so obviously designed for life and cultivation and growth.

Nearing her father's leased plot, Lilly thought about the look on Ned's face the night before, when she'd stumbled behind the barn and that foreign man had offered to help her. What was it that had crossed his face— disgust? Anger? Fear? Whatever it was, Lilly wasn't used to seeing it directed at her, and it made her uncomfortable. Perhaps there were other things Ned kept hidden from her view.

She wheeled the family's Buick into the half-crescent drive next to her father's workshop and machine shed, tucked her handbag under the driver's seat (her mother said one couldn't be too careful, with the transient workers around), and left the car. Her father liked to spend his summers out here with the workers, reporting the measurements and growth yields of his sample plots back to a colleague at a neighboring university. He was a professor with a desk and an office too, though he often said his best work happened in the fields and shed. Lilly was determined to seek his advice in a place away from her mother's unsolicited opinions.

The interior of the shed was dim and cool. Lilly's voice echoed as she called out her father's name, moving toward the small space he'd enclosed in one corner as an office. There were voices inside, only one of which she recognized. She put her hand to the knob, ready to open the door.

The knob turned for her, and she was suddenly face-to-face with the man who'd tried to help her the night before. She must have gasped as she pulled away, for he was gentle in his address: "Good morning, miss. I trust you are recovered from your fall?"

His eyes were a deeper blue this morning, sparkling as he smiled from inside the doorway. He wasn't a big man, but his shoulders roped together muscle and grit. Not one ounce of softness was evident, save for the look that he directed at her. She blushed and realized that she must have been standing speechless for a while, at least long enough to have scanned his being and completed a checklist of his physical attributes.

"Yes, good morning," Lilly reciprocated. She reached up to smooth her hair back from her face. Perhaps he'd think she was merely warm, not affected by running into him again so soon. "I'm fine, thank you for asking." She looked away—they were the same height—and excused herself to pass through the door he held open.

Her father, unlit pipe in place, was oblivious to the whole exchange; he was bent over a large paper map that spread out across a waist-high drafter's table. Various sections had been shaded different colors. He was adding more yellow to a section toward the south when Lilly addressed him.

"Dad, do you know that man?"

"Hmm?" he mumbled, consumed by the diagram on his desk.

"Daddy," she began again, "can you please look at me?"

He turned from his work, surprised to see her standing there. "Lilly!

Hello! To what do I owe this pleasure?" He removed the pipe from his mouth, looked down at the unpacked bowl, and took his tobacco pouch from his pocket. He concentrated on lighting the pipe as Lilly adjusted herself onto a high, gray stool next to the drafting table.

"Weren't you and your mother going shopping today, Rabbit?" Silvery wisps of tobacco smoke spilled out with his words.

"We may, this afternoon. If it's not too hot." She twirled a bit on the swiveling stool. "Do you have a minute to visit?"

"Of course I do. What would you like to visit about?" He turned his attention to his daughter, puffing to get his pipe going, one hand resting on the table next to her.

She looked away. "I'm all sorts of, I don't know—confused, I guess, about going away."

He waited for her to continue.

"Elaine's decided to stay home and help her dad instead of coming with me to Ames, so now it's only me leaving, and, well, I don't know if I want to go through with it by myself." Lilly held still for her father's reply.

A tendril of cherry-scented smoke floated upward. This was a comforting scent; it made her shoulders release their tension. Her pulse slowed.

"What is your reason for wanting to go to college?" her father asked, stressing the word "your."

Mulling it over, her foot started tapping of its own accord on the metal rung beneath her. "I want to . . . I want to see more of the world, more of the people and places I've read about," Lilly began. "I want to know more than what I've been able to learn in a school where most of my classmates just want to pick up where their parents leave off." She paused, rocking back and forth on the stool. "I don't know what I want to 'do' or what I want to 'be.' I only know that I want to go away for a while, to see what the world outside of Crestview, Iowa looks like." She returned to stillness again. "Is that. . ." she struggled for the right word, ". . . acceptable?"

Lilly searched her father's eyes intensely. She held her breath, then sighed. "It's a lot of money for not being able to say what degree I want to pursue."

Throughout her speech he had remained silent, the thin plume wafting up from his pipe. Seeing that his daughter had finished, he removed his pipe to speak. "You don't need to decide right away, Lilly. We talked about this last fall, when you first brought up the idea of going to Ames." He awkwardly patted her shoulder. "You don't need to be afraid to go by yourself. You're a smart girl, you know how to stay out of trouble—and isn't that the reason you want to go in the first place? To meet these new people? To learn what makes them different?" He started to turn back to his work. The place where his hand had rested on her shoulder now felt chilled. "And don't worry about the money. I've been talking to a good friend of yours, and he's offered to help. Seems he's got some plans ahead"—he looked away—"and he wants to make sure you've 'sown your wild oats,' so to speak, before you settle down." His measured speech complete, he put both elbows onto the table and directed his attention back to the colored map.

Lilly's throat tightened. Ned must have spoken about this to her father, without consulting with her first. *What nerve!* she thought, gathering herself up to step off the stool. A mixture of anger and disappointment surged through her. She hadn't expected her father, her champion and solid support, to so casually transfer her welfare and future to a man she'd never acknowledged that she wanted to marry. "See you tonight, Daddy," she said, turning for the door. "Remember, Mother and I might be shopping and not home for dinner. You may have to 'bach' it on your own."

"Um-hmm," came his muffled reply. He was using a scarlet pencil to shade in a new section.

She hurried to exit the shed, her short heels quickly thumping across the wooden floor in an annoying echo of her mother's own footsteps. At this point, however, upset and scattered as she was about what her father had unintentionally let slip, the staccato similarity escaped her awareness completely.

She pushed through the outside door as if escaping from a fire. Eyes down, she nearly bumped into someone standing there. "Oh! Excuse me, I didn't see you; I was . . ."

Lilly froze for a short second, surprised to see the same man once again.

Recovering her quick pace, she headed for her car.

The man removed his wide-brimmed hat and matched his steps to hers. "Miss Bradstreet?" he began. "I was wondering if I could ask of you a favor."

She looked over to him, the vehicle now between them. She wondered how he knew her name, but then he'd just seen her with her father. Or perhaps he'd learned it from someone in town. She was pretty well known, after all, as the population in this part of the county was small and static. Except, of course, for the workers who showed up at harvest time.

"Yes?" Lilly opened the door on her side of the Buick.

"It may be presumptuous of me to ask, but would you drop me off at the edge of the field?" he asked. "It seems that my partner has gone and left me here to find my own way back to work." He hesitated, adding when Lilly did not respond right away, "Though I don't want to take you away from your plans." He placed his hat back on his head and touched the brim with one hand in dismissal. "I can walk, it's no problem." He turned to go. "Thank you, all the same."

"Wait, please." Lilly heard her voice but didn't recognize the force from within that set it into motion. Despite the caution that her mother had tried to cultivate within her, she became conscious of her own instinct springing forth, the possibility of a different path for her to follow. "I'm going by there now. It'd be no trouble." She settled herself into the driver's seat and fished underneath it for her handbag. Drawing out her sunshades, she heard a chuckle from outside the passenger's window.

"Do you feel comfortable taking a person such as myself in your car with you?"

She didn't answer.

He gestured to the handbag, now located on the dashboard. "Do you feel unsafe with us here?"

Another blush suffused her cheeks. "Certainly not," she replied, hearing her mother's haughty tone in her response. She tamed it. "Please, get in." Lilly placed her sunglasses over her eyes and started the engine. With easy grace, the stranger slid into the passenger's seat and closed the car door.

"Thank you," he said. Nothing more.

Lilly turned the car onto the gravel road which led back into town. In the silence, she worked on formulating the explanation she'd have to give her mother if she ever found out through the town grapevine that Lilly was chauffeuring a migrant worker around.

He seemed comfortable with the quiet. She was not. "Where is your home?"

"I am from Texicali, in Mexico," he replied. "Near Texas."

"And how did you decide to come all the way to Iowa, of all places?" Lilly turned to the right. From the corner of her eye, she could see that the man was looking out his own window to the green fields and clear blue sky above.

"I wanted to see something new," he responded after a while. "Where I am from, the colors are brown and gold. The people in my town, so far from the ocean and away from the river, are not accustomed to such . . ." He waited a beat before continuing. ". . . lushness, such ripeness, as you have growing here."

His description of the land seemed a bit profane, almost seductive, to Lilly's ears, much too abundant compared to the salt and dirt in the words she was used to hearing. He seemed personally acquainted with the warmth and growth and possibility of the fertile land. To her memory, those who'd farmed here their whole lives had never spoken of the earth in such intimate, loving terms.

"Your father, he has asked me to stay, to see to the other workers as they come through."

She slowed to stop near the corner of the field. "And will you? Stay?"

"This is good land." He got out of the car but looked back through the open window. "I thank you for your kindness, Lillian. You are a good woman, a credit to your father." He touched the brim of his hat, turned, and strode down through the ditch toward the makeshift resting area the workers had erected: a few two-by-fours covered with a tarp against the bright sunlight, their bags and belongings in the shade underneath.

"Yo, Cisco!" another worker called out from an old red tractor turning at the end of one row. So that was the man's name. Without skipping a beat, Cisco grabbed hold of a metal bar as the tractor completed the turn and swung himself into place beside the driver. They began chatting in Spanish as the machine's metal discs churned the hardened dirt into pliable softness below.

Dani

9

THERE WAS NO traffic when Dani left her land for Susie's Café. Other than an Amish wagon along the side of County Road 8, she passed exactly one other truck coming her direction during the entire seven-mile drive. Dani tried to calculate the amount of time it would take the three Amish workers, clad in their traditional long-sleeved garb and head coverings, to not only transfer the loose ditch grass to their wagon, but to drive that full wagon home, unload it, and somehow stack it in such a way to keep it usable until the long winter months when it would be needed. She respected their values and their practices, but were she in their position she'd have to toss off the floppy bonnet, strip off the long plain-colored dress, and hitch that damn wagon to the back of a baler (pulled by a John Deere; no one in these parts drove anything else) to get it done.

She stopped at the only light in Crestview and waited for the green. She lifted two fingers in the customary wave to some guy in a dented Ford, wearing a cap so low she couldn't see his face. Again, she pondered the call she'd gotten from Donna, when she'd tried to warn Dani about getting involved with that tree. Dani hoped she could catch the woman away from the other diners, so she could get some clarity about the questions that had been floating through her mind ever since.

There were customs and practices in this little corner of the world that she hadn't seen or even considered before coming here to try this thing called farming. What seemed normal to a suburbanite, like watching the news for weather updates, was shunned by these folks, whose daily procedure included studying cloud formations or the compass points they came from. On the other hand, the day-to-day dispensation of a chicken for dinner, say, or staying up for yet another long night to help your neighbor during harvest, was dismissed by the locals as next to nothing in importance. Dani guessed that some of these practices had been continued and supported through decades. She also recognized that she'd probably never learn or understand the locals' traditions and behaviors.

The regulars hardly looked up when Dani stepped into the diner. The first few times this had happened, when she'd first come to the area, she'd felt slighted and wondered what she'd done wrong. She'd come to realize that outsiders, especially women, *especially* single women who farmed alone, would need to prove their permanence before anyone took the effort to get to know them. She might grow old waiting.

Besides, it looked like she'd walked into the middle of a pretty heated conversation. Bud was holding court from the seat that faced the room's entrance, the seat from which Jacob usually presided. Jacob was nowhere in sight. His absence made the most reticent farmers practically holler to share their opinions over the other voices vying to be heard. Dani had definitely chosen a good time to come to town for lunch.

She didn't see Donna on her way in. She poked her head around the corner between the counter and the kitchen window and got a greasy glare from someone's overweight mama, standing idly in front of a large fryer with a spatula dangling from her hand. She looked to be the only one back there. Dani snagged an empty chair from the table next to the large one and, angling it to face the crowd, settled in at the argument's periphery.

Donna appeared at her side and placed an empty mug next to her elbow. Dani opened her mouth to greet her, but the other woman filled the cup and left without saying a word.

"Say what you will," an older guy broke in. The wrinkled creases around his eyes, folded by the outdoor sun, looked white-rimmed in the dim light of the café. Dani couldn't look away from the deep, pale, spiderlike tracings. He spat out, "The man never held to any beliefs but his own. I know, I've known him since we sat next to each other in parochial school." He shook his thin-haired head; his scalp, beneath the wispy strands, was pale and smooth, a contrast to his nut-brown face and neck. "Sister Jean had her hands full with the two of us, I tell ya."

Lloyd interrupted. "We don't need no trip down memory lane, Don."

An uncomfortable laugh barked out, then the men quieted to hear Lloyd's interjection. "We all know Jacob has his own ways of doing things. I say what happened to his sprayer was a coincidence. It ain't related to that business with the tree. I think—"

"But what about the hog fans, Lloyd? How do you answer for that?" This query came from a smaller, darker man who looked to have a sprinkle of Mexican heritage in his family tree. His moustache, neatly trimmed, bounced with his words. "I can see one machine acting up, but two? On the very next day after the tree was cut?" He shook his head. His short-cropped hair was shot through with silver. "I don't like it, is all."

Dani leaned over to a tall, slim guy next to her to find out what had happened. The man shifted toward Dani to answer. "Seems Jacob ran one end of his new sprayer into the ground, out near where that old double-headed tree stood." He didn't look at her when he answered. Dani had the suspicion that she was being evaluated, again, before he finished relaying the news. But he went on. "When he got the thing back to the shed, guess somehow the outflow fan over his hog pen wasn't running." He shifted back to sit up straight once more.

Then Bud turned his attention to her. "Say, Dani, weren't you out there with Jacob and my boys taking down that tree?"

The chatter stopped. Each set of eyes, hooded, questioning, narrowed, curious, turned to rest on Dani.

"I helped Jacob. He's not someone to say 'no' to, I've learned that much," Dani replied, arranging a half-smile for their benefit. Her effort was a waste of time. They appeared more solemn than before, if that was even a possibility. "I didn't think it was that big a deal."

Donna bustled over again. Gauging the temperature at the table, she delicately set down the plastic carafe and backed away. Her appearance did seem to break the tension in the room somewhat.

"Don't you know the story behind that tree?" a male voice asked. Dani couldn't see which man had spoken—someone off to her right.

"I think I do," Dani replied. She reached for the carafe to add more coffee to her cup. For once, a hand from the middle of the table pushed the container closer. She topped off her beverage and leaned back. "He said he thought that Mr. Swenson was the last one who'd been alive at that time. But he also said he didn't believe in any of that 'BS' about the curse."

The man who'd spoken to Dani turned and faced her. He drummed the brown fingers of his right hand on the tabletop. "You know why that curse came about?"

Dani shook her head.

The man stopped drumming to scan the rest of the faces around the table. "My daddy and uncle told me that a town girl was ravished by one of the Mexicans up here working the fields for a season. During the war, when our boys were mostly off defending the country. The hired help, the Mexican workers, pretty much pulled us through, you know." He fell silent and removed his hand from the table to scratch his lean chest. "But once the beaner was found out, they say he hung himself from that tree instead of facing his consequences like a man." His jaw tightened. His words took on hard edges. "You know where those two parts of that tree split, and the one sort of grew forward of the other? He did it there. Supposed to have kicked the ladder outta the way and stayed there a whole night before someone noticed."

Dani absorbed the men's serious attitudes. Clearing her throat, she spoke up, after considering that her question might further separate her from the company of those who had only begun thawing to her presence in their town. "What happened to the girl?"

Bud took this one. His gritty, dirt-lined paws steepled over his large gut. "She went away to college, same as she always planned to do. But she never came back. And the fella she left behind, why, he never was the same."

Other voices started murmuring now, offering bits of news that differ-ent families had gathered over the years. Dani kept herself still, trying to take in and balance the information that flowed.

"He was a banker, wasn't he? Her fiancé?" This from a guy wearing a short-sleeved plaid shirt with fancy snap buttons.

"Her parents moved away, not long after." Chuck, at Lloyd's elbow, add-ed his two cents' worth. He'd been the "new guy" until Dani had come to take his place on the low end of the totem pole. "The section I started with had a shack on it that belonged to that family. The dad was a professor or something, used the land for some ag experiments."

"Could've been," Bud concluded. "Anyhow, by that witness tree, that land's been in Jacob's family since Indian days, and they weren't going to let it go fallow on account of some foreigner dying there. 'Course, they—"

Dani interrupted—she couldn't help herself. "So the man hung himself? Or was he hung by someone else?"

Bud let his stink-eye settle on Dani for an uncomfortable moment. "A neighbor saw the body swingin'. Old Mr. Dorn took it down. That's what my pop told us." He leaned forward and started rummaging through the large bib pocket of his overalls. "Course, that was so long ago, who knows? All's I know is that no one 'round here was willing to mess with the way that situation ended, on account of respect for the girl and her family, you know."

Dani didn't know. As watchful as she was, these people had some code they followed that she had no idea how to decipher.

The others began searching their pockets and wallets to pay Donna. Dani pressed on for one last answer. "I know Jacob owns the land where the guy hung himself," she said, "but what does that have to do with his sprayer and his fan not working?"

The tall fellow next to Dani stood. "See, that's what we were all talking about when you came in," he replied. "We thought that those who were alive to witness that . . . situation . . . were all buried, now that Swenson passed. Evidently not."

Dani stood too, the last one to rise to her feet. They formed a solemn ring around the table, no one breaking away.

Bud tried to tie it up. "The story most of us were told, Dani, is that the tree should remain standing, or trouble would fall on those who took her down before her time."

Lloyd finished: "Those workers put a curse on it, after their brother hung himself, and 'til now, not even Jacob wanted to deal with a mess like that." He slapped his feed cap onto his head. "Somebody's still livin' that shoulda been gone by now, and it looks like Jacob's going to be the one to pay the price."

Dani

10

IN TOWN, THERE was one main place to get your farm incidentals and a bite of the latest gossip. While Susie's did a brisk business for the midday lunch and after-Mass crowds, for serious talk you had to go to Crestview Farm & Feed. The building itself, a proud, red-brick two-story abutting the main drag, was originally designed as a hotel or rooming house of sorts. That's why the bigger pieces of merchandise, like chains, tires, bales of wire, and lumber had their own newer building along the back, where the alley used to be. The inside of the store held bagged feed, vaccines, grease and oil, shorter lengths of rope and fencing—the standard wear-and-tear fixups. Major catastrophes went directly to the John Deere lot in Decorah.

Lloyd Gilbert had his little grandson with him when he stopped by the Farm & Feed for some advice from their small engine repair shop. His lawn tractor had started skipping, and Lloyd didn't know if it was a dirty carburetor or old plugs. He'd placed blond Brandon in the front of a shopping cart and given the little boy a small bag of cheese puffs to keep him busy. The boy had smeared orange powder from one ear to another, down the front of his shirt and, somehow, into the crown of his previously clean hair.

"Marilyn's not going to like that!" Burt called from behind the counter. The lenses in his glasses were so smudged, Lloyd didn't know how he could determine who or what stood before him. His stained uniform shirt, alternating stripes of light blue and navy, had the store logo and Burt's name sewn into its upper left side with red thread. It, too, was smeared in dark oil.

"Ahh, they baby the boy," Lloyd responded. "He won't have a chance unless I let him mess himself up a little. They're going to make a little girly man out of him!" He did, however, remove his clean white hanky and try to mop up some of the powder. The little boy shrugged the opposite way and kept chewing.

Burt hunched over the counter, facing Lloyd and his grandson. "What do you hear about Jacob? Anything definite about what caused that power outage?"

Lloyd shook his head. "Nah, seems like it was a fluke. He had Bernie from the co-op up there before too long, and he was able to get the fans going again."

The little boy dropped his bag onto the floor. He didn't whine or even make a peep, but put his chubby, orange hands on the cart handle and peered over to see where the snack had landed. Then he looked at his grandpa, expecting or hoping that he'd help. Which Lloyd did, his knees cracking as he put one gnarled hand onto the cart edge for support, swooping down to snag the bag. "Here you go, buddy, keep hold of it now." The little boy blinked solemnly and took up where he left off, shoving orange puffs into his mouth and chewing like the pistons in a machine.

Burt was called away to help another customer. When he returned, Lloyd finished passing on what he knew of the situation. "Anyhow, seems there was a fuse or a, I don't know, some computer thing, in the main box that snapped or went bad. Bernie fixed it and the fans came on right away." Burt watched little Brandon consume the cheese puffs. "Good thing, too— supposed to get real hot this weekend. Wouldn't be good to have them hogs getting overheated."

Burt nodded agreement. "What about the sprayer? He get that fixed?"

"Think he had to call the Deere guys to come up and get it. He couldn't fix it himself, and he didn't have a trailer big enough to haul that monster on the road."

Brandon finished eating his snack and solemnly held out the empty bag to his grandfather. Lloyd handed it over to Burt, who dropped it into the trash behind the counter and wiped the remaining orange powder on top of his greasy shirt.

"Anyhow," said Lloyd, "I came in for some plugs. That lawn tractor won't run smooth."

The men debated the merits of different brands while little Brandon watched the other shoppers.

As THE TWO men turned from Jacob's troubles to tractor plugs, Dani ducked her head back into the side aisle she'd been eavesdropping from. She hefted a four-pack of winter-weight oil from a shelf before retreating to the front of the store.

A young cashier, blonde and confident in pink lip gloss and sassy, plastic press-on nails, gave Dani incorrect change. Dani noticed the mistake but let it go; she didn't want to break her train of thought. Perhaps the destruction of the witness tree *did* set something in motion. If it was true that there had been a curse attached to the tree, then Dani too might be snagged in its web. A solid, dead weight attached itself to the inside of her chest and pulled her breath down toward her feet.

She left the feed store through the front door, her heart thudding against the concrete with every heavy footstep she took. The plausible explanations Dani tried talking herself into for Jacob's misfortune had no chance to take hold, crowded out by the stronger voices of her fears.

As she toted her purchase down the sidewalk, she counseled herself against giving in. But she couldn't stop wondering if the range of this curse, if it were real, would affect all who were helping that day or just the one who'd made the final decision to take the old tree down.

She crossed the street to her vehicle, slid the oil case into the truck bed, and shut the tailgate. Jacob had shrugged off the existence of the curse when in the larger company of men, but would he be so bold if it were only Dani who confronted him? She had to do something to quiet her insistent dread.

She turned the old Ford onto Main Street. Up ahead sat the squat, white building that housed Susie's Café. It looked like an updated version of the boxy, aluminum drive-in restaurants that had been popular in the sixties. Old tires lived a second life as pots for several bright red geraniums. The front window was steamy, either from the hot food or the heated conversations inside. The lot, as Dani pulled in, was mostly empty.

She hurried into the café, but the farmers' round table was abandoned, crumpled napkins and egg-swiped plates still littering its surface.

"Morning, Donna." She sat at the counter.

"Morning yourself." Donna set down a blue-and-white Land O'Lakes mug and filled it with coffee. She didn't seem surprised to see Dani. "What's dragged you in here this fine day?" She held the carafe in one hand and waited for an answer.

"I was in town and thought I'd stop by to hear what happened with Jacob Dorn's sprayer. And something about his barn, too?"

Donna snapped her gum.

"Have you heard anything?" Dani pressed.

"Waiting on an order." The waitress threw a look over her shoulder at the rear door. "No one needs coffee, so I figure I got time for a cigarette out back. Want to join me?"

Dani nodded and stood up to follow.

Donna set the coffee pot back onto its warming plate and started into the kitchen. "Ginny!" she yelled over the noisy exhaust fan at the stout, sweating woman by the fry pad. "I'll be out back for a smoke. Yell when you need me!" The woman waved her spatula in response.

The rear door led to an unpaved section of the parking lot. A dilapidated wooden picnic table crouched there, one side leaning against the café's siding. Donna sat on the table, rested her feet on its bench, and lit up. She looked at Dani with squinty eyes through the smoke that wreathed her. "Guess you got more questions, huh?"

Dani settled herself next to Donna and wished that she'd chosen the other side instead, the one away from the smoke.

"You said there was something I should know."

Donna stayed quiet, her eyes narrowing to slits. The slim cylinder between her lips twitched.

"What else did you want to tell me, that night you called?" Dani asked.

The waitress tapped her ashes into a chipped dish next to her. Other crushed butts rested there. Soot rimmed the edges like a soiled cloud. "It's too late, darlin'," she answered. "What's done is done." She leaned her crossed arms on her knees. "But it got me to thinking on something my aunty told me, though I only remember bits and pieces to that." She scratched one nylon-covered knee, then continued. "My aunt's momma did some work for a rich family in town, long time ago. Seems they had a daughter, a girl who got messed up in some business she shouldn't have."

"When was this?" Dani asked. She let her mug dangle, the coffee inside almost spilling out.

"Quite a while back." The other woman looked sideways at Dani. "Before me and you were born, anyhow."

Dani waited for Donna to go on. She took a sip of the lukewarm liquid in her cup and decided to let the rest stream out onto the ground after all.

"What I remember hearing is that this girl, a nice girl—I mean, she didn't let the money make her proud, you know? She was natural, liked to visit with my aunt, when she was over there working. Anyhow, she set off to college, somewhere not so far. And it was strange, 'cause she never came back." She stubbed the butt out on the table and left it in the cracked saucer with the others.

Loud clanging started up from the kitchen, but Donna continued. "My aunty told me that the stories started then, about the migrant and her boss's daughter." Donna began to rise from the picnic table. "She said the momma, a real pretty lady with fancy clothes—she wore gloves and hats into town, every time she went?" Her voice invited Dani to create the picture for herself. "Well, she didn't care so much about anything after her daughter left, and she sort of let herself go." Donna stood up and stretched, readying herself to get back to work.

"So what's the connection, then?"

Donna answered but didn't look back as she strode toward the door. "Somehow, that tree on Jacob Dorn's land, and that guy who died there, have to be connected to that girl and why she never came back." She reapplied a line of rose-colored lipstick and waited for Dani to catch up. She put the tube into her apron pocket and nodded for the younger woman to open the screen door.

The waitress headed for the warming table, her voice almost indiscernible through the noises of the fryer and the cook in front of it. "I heard the other day on TV that the Mexicans have a calendar, and it's running out of days. They say that means the end of the world is coming." She gave Dani a smile and arranged the sandwich platters to balance on both arms. "Guess old Jacob'll be finding out for sure, one way or the other!"

Donna winked and sailed out of the kitchen, a mixed aroma of BLTs, cigarettes, and Avon perfume trailing her like a scented jet stream.

Lilly

II

THE NEXT WEEK brought humidity again, and the high temperatures made everything feel sticky. When she was younger, on days like these Lilly and her friends would swim in a wide eddy of the river, a languorous, swirling pool of cool water shaded by leafy branches that formed a canopy overhead. Now, Lilly spent the hottest parts of the days indoors, fanning herself and drinking cool lemonade or tea.

The last few days, she hadn't been able to concentrate on her book. Her head lolling back over the arm of a chair, she thought more about Ned and what her father had hinted about. She knew they were talking about marriage. *Her* marriage.

She thought about the women and girls she knew, comparing their behaviors and clothing and ways of talking. She tried to remember when one of them would allow her carefree, inner personality out for an airing. Her mother was as tightly cosseted as the girdle she wore, even to bed. Her female teacher, Elaine, and her sisters and mother . . . Lilly was hard-pressed to recall *any* instance or expression of personal freedom, especially once each one reached maturity. Every woman in her circle appeared groomed and programmed to serve her family. Lilly shuddered, unable to see herself attached to that unending chain.

Once, she had dreamed that her true love would show up like a character in a book come to life, someone to immediately recognize and grasp onto with both hands and a full heart. Wasn't love supposed to sink into your soul and leave you gasping? The real lives she examined through the hours didn't really resemble the lives she loved to read about. Maybe that type of love could only be found in black and white, on paper pages.

She heard a rhythmic cadence of footsteps near the darkened parlor. "Lillian, I wish you wouldn't lay about with your legs on the chair arms," her mother declared, setting down a slightly wilted arrangement of pink peonies on a console table. Lilly swung her legs back to the floor. "And where are your stockings? Honestly, I just don't know," her mother sighed. She pursed her lips and marched off to continue her battle in the next room.

Ugly despair bloomed in Lilly's chest. She was almost overcome by the sadness that swarmed through her body, making it hard for her to swallow. She tried to give herself a talking-to, listing the friendships, family, home, and provisions she often took for granted. There was no reason to be sad, she told herself. No reason she couldn't make an adjustment here or there to let her soul have the sunshine and space she craved. She pushed her book aside and stood on the sticky wooden floor to slip her bare feet into thin loafers.

Lilly found her mother in the back of the kitchen. The windows there looked out from the back of their home to the tidy yard and her father's home garden beyond. Warm, clear waves of heat wafted up from the greenery like naughty dancing girls. Not a leaf or a flower moved, though; the thick air was still.

She saw her mother looking out the center window, drying her petite hands with an embroidered dish towel. She turned, welcomed her daughter, and offered to pour her a glass of iced tea. Lilly politely declined. She positioned herself next to her mother and looked out the same window. Her elbow brushed against her mother's cool, sleeveless skin.

"Did you ever wonder if you were doing the right thing?" Lilly ventured. "When you were my age, I mean. Did you worry about what was ahead, or if your decisions now would mean the rest of your life would be changed forever?" The heavy weight in her chest seemed to be trying to find its way out of her with the words she'd let escape, their pressure pushing the air from her lungs.

Her mother's face relaxed slightly. She resumed rummaging through the dish cabinet for some glasses. "Things were different when I was your age," Mrs. Bradstreet replied. "Families didn't know then if there would be food enough or heat for the winters . . ." Her voice trailed off. "I guess we did learn, though, to live each day as its own. We couldn't predict what our futures would be, so we did the best we could and tried to find a little happiness wherever we could get it."

She placed the glasses on the counter in front of Lilly. "But things are different for you. You have stability. You don't have to worry about what you'll eat or how to get it. Why, you're soon to embark on your own adventure!" Her little laugh trilled like silver bells. It sounded forced to Lilly's ear and grated on her nerves. "What do you have to be worried about?"

Lilly withdrew to sit at the kitchen table. Her mother reached into the icebox for the aluminum pitcher and poured two teas, which she garnished with lemons. She brought these with her to sit by her daughter. "Tell me what's bothering you, Lillian."

Lilly managed to sip a little tea. Its coolness trickled past the large lump in her throat. She held the sweating glass to her forehead. "I thought things would be different, I guess," she began. "From when I was little, I mean." She set the glass down; her mother moved it from the tabletop onto a coaster. "I used to think that I would be certain about my life's plan by now, that I would be confident, I guess, about my future." She sighed.

"Hmm." Her mother focused on the bird feeder outside their window. Her penciled brows drew together.

"I don't really know what's ahead for me, and I guess not knowing is what scares me most."

Mrs. Bradstreet smiled then. "You're not a little girl anymore, Lillian. Your little-girl dreams have had to grow up, that's all. You have a wonderful future ahead: a chance to go to college, a man who is willing to wait for your return, and a life that will be easy and comfortable." She stood up quickly, like a darting hummingbird, and brought their glasses back to the sink. The conversation, from her end, was over. "Many young women would trade places with you in an instant."

Lilly's thoughts cataloged the unsuccessful attempts she'd made to express how unsettled she was. She'd tried to share her feelings with Elaine, with her parents, even with Ned, without success or clarification. Maybe the separation she felt was natural for a person who was determined to go her own way. If so, Lilly wondered if she'd always feel so alone.

She stood and kissed her mother gently on her cool, powdered cheek; even in the heat, the other woman was controlled and implacable. "Thank you, Momma," Lilly used the nursery name she hadn't uttered in years. She walked away from her mother toward the front of the house.

Passing the telephone in the hallway, Lilly paused to ring Elaine. Elaine had one thing going for her that Lilly lacked: serenity. Because her decisions had mostly been made for her, there was no dithering back and forth about what might or might not be her best option. Even Elaine's future family seemed solid—she and Lonny had been a couple for so long that they could finish one another's sentences. Each one's dream was a mirror of the other's: a farm, a family, another generation of the Swenson family in the same town, finding rest in the same cemetery section when their turn around the wheel ceased to spin.

The party line was open, so Lilly was able to ring Elaine's home without having to wait for someone else down the line to finish their conversation first. Elaine's little brother answered. "Hello?"

"Stevie, is that you?" Lilly asked, smiling. "Aren't you supposed to answer with your family name, like your parents asked you to do?" she teased.

"Hi, Lilly," the boy responded, ignoring her first question and anticipating the next one. "Lainey's not here. She's buying fabric with Momma." His voice pulled away for a moment, as if to answer someone in the background. He came back. "I'll tell her you called. Bye!"

"Stevie, wait!" Lilly tried to interrupt, but the boy hung up first. Such a little man, she thought. Thinks he knows the answers and doesn't lack confidence.

She replaced the phone handle on its cradle and dragged herself up the steps to the second floor. Her new idea was to gather her library books and take a trip downtown to the Crestview Public Library. It was cool and quiet there, and Lilly could lose herself in the stacks for hours.

"Mother," she called as she descended the staircase a moment later, three novels in one arm and her purse on the other. "Do you have anything for me to return to the library?"

Mrs. Bradstreet had not yet finished her own book, but asked her daughter to pick up another title that had been placed on hold for her. "When do you think you'll be back?" she asked as Lilly went out the front door.

"I'll be home for dinner." She paused. "And thanks for talking with me, earlier."

Her mother, silent, looked at her daughter for a long moment. Her eyes bored into Lilly's. "It will all turn out right as rain, you'll see. Now, have a nice afternoon. And be careful driving! You know how those men are." She turned back toward the kitchen again. "No one bothers to signal. They all think they know where the other is off to, anyway." Her words trailed her clacking feet down the hall.

Lilly drove toward town. She thought back on the previous twenty-four hours and the differences between the ways Ned and the stranger, Cisco, had spoken with her. Ned treated her as a commodity that was movable, tradeable, exchangeable; a "thing" that required manipulation, rather than a being with separate thoughts and desires. Take the way he'd steered her on the dance floor, or the way he'd practically stepped over her in order to stake his claim behind the barn after she'd fallen. On the other hand, Cisco had openly shared his thoughts about his summer work as they drove together. He seemed focused on what was happening in front of him instead of always pushing ahead the way Ned did. Lilly wondered how two men could be so different.

She recognized another feeling, too: a twinge of guilt that she was taking time to actually compare the man she thought she knew to a man she'd probably never see again.

Entering the library, she made a concerted effort to keep her loafers quiet as she crossed over the cool marble floor to the fiction section. Miss

Barnard smiled to see her, gesturing her over to the information desk. She handed Lilly a book which she'd kept out of sight underneath the large counter.

"I've been saving this for you," she whispered, slyly sliding the novel in her direction. The book was bound in yellow with blue lettering: *Kitty Foyle*. "I know you like to keep up with what's popular." But then she looked away, like she was second-guessing herself. "This might be a little risqué for your taste, but it's been on the best-seller list all year."

"Oh, I read about this!" Lilly opened the dust cover and began paging through the first chapter. "Ginger Rogers is going to be in a movie about this book."

"I thought you'd like it." She stamped the circulation card and filed it. "But be sure to keep it in your lower desk drawer with the others you've hidden from your mother." She winked at Lilly, who smiled and settled herself into a heavy armchair in a cool corner to start reading.

LATER THAT NIGHT, Lilly planned to go with Ned, Elaine, and Lonny to see a new dance band in Mason City. They were leaving early in order to have a picnic supper along the way. Elaine packed the food; she told Lilly that, if Lilly were to do it, they'd end up with two jars of pickles, bread, and no napkins. Lilly was instead tasked with bringing one thermos of coffee, another of iced tea, and a blanket for them to sit on.

Ned was a few minutes ahead of schedule, as usual. Lilly heard her mother's excited exclamations as she made her way to the staircase. Stepping down, slower now, she saw her father pumping Ned's arm, holding the boy's hand with two of his own while her mother patted him on his broad shoulder.

"Here she is now!" Mrs. Bradstreet twittered in a voice at least an octave above her usual range.

Mr. Bradstreet grinned broadly, pipe clenched in the corner of his smile. "Enjoy your evening, now, and don't worry about getting back early. We know you have miles to go tonight."

Lilly looked at the trio. Ned's chest was puffed out; his dimples seemed extra deep. She knew that they'd been consorting behind her back. She would have to be stupid not to figure out that he had designs on proposing to her, perhaps even tonight.

She didn't feel the excitement one would think would come with this news. She didn't feel happy, or nervous, or even embarrassed. Lilly didn't feel anything. There was only that same void in her chest, the one she'd hoped, one day, a partner would fit into just perfectly. As far as she could tell, standing alone, trying to smile at her parents and Ned, that was all. Nothing but empty space.

"We'd better get a move on, Ned." It was best, she guessed, to keep playing the game. She finished descending the stairs and turned toward the kitchen. "Would you please take the picnic blanket for me? I'll get the drinks, and then we're off." She didn't bother to look back.

A short time later, they were on their way to Elaine's home. Ned had donned a pair of black sunglasses. He looked handsome this way, his hair slicked back, singing along with the radio. Lilly felt queasy.

He slowed to park in front of Elaine's house. Lilly didn't wait for him, slipping out before he could turn off the car. "I'll get them! You can wait here."

She sped up the pavement that led to the front door. She didn't have to knock; Stevie was playing marbles with a friend on the step and told her to go in.

"Lainey! We're here!"

"Coming!" Lilly heard Elaine laughing. She and her Prince Charming were each carrying a picnic basket.

"How long are we staying?" Lilly opened the door for them to pass outside. "You've got enough food for weeks."

Elaine giggled again. "We're feeding two hungry men, Lilly. It would be awful to run out." Ned had opened the trunk and was inspecting something inside. "Besides, we can have a light snack after the dance, if we have enough left over."

Lonny opened the back door for Elaine, but Lilly hopped in. Looking at her strangely, Elaine also took a back seat. Lonny didn't say anything but he looked a little disappointed as he adjusted himself next to Ned.

It was seventy or so miles to Mason City. That meant they'd have a good hour to ride before eating, and then another near-hour before arriving at the dance. Lilly waited for a chance to share her news with Elaine sometime before their first stop, but the boys kept including them in their discussions.

"What do you think, Lillian?" Lonny asked her now. "You think the war will reach our shores?"

Lilly gulped. "I hope not. I hope we never have to see one here, ever."

Ned broke in. "That's naïve thinking, Lil. You know that the world looks to us for protection and leadership." He glanced over his shoulder, continuing the lecture. "We're the number-one country on the map, and if it comes to us, we'll be expected to show ourselves in the heat of that battle, too."

"I agree with Lilly," Elaine ventured. "And I think it's a shame to ask our boys to head out to defend places they haven't seen or know. But I don't think the war's bound to come here. That would be different."

"You can't sit back and wait. I think we need to act before they reach our shores. Get the first shot in, so they know they should stay away." Ned was adamant on this point.

The young men continued the discussion in the front seat. It was a perfect opportunity to try to tell Elaine what she thought was going to happen. "Lainey." Lilly looked straight ahead. "Lainey."

Her friend got it then, and whispered back from the corner of her mouth, keeping her eyes on the windshield. "What?"

"I think Ned's going to propose. He—"

Elaine broke the rules and turned to her friend. "Lilly! That's wonderful. Aren't you—" She stopped when she encountered her friend's cool, closed demeanor. Lilly's eyes were fixed straight ahead, her face immobile without a hint of a smile.

Elaine fell back into ranks. "How do you know?"

Leaning over to point at absolutely nothing out of Elaine's window, Lilly hissed, "I saw him talking to my parents. They were ecstatic. Then they all hushed up when I came down the steps."

Elaine waited a moment. She drew up her purse from the floor, removed her compact, and leaned toward Lilly with the mirror opened. "Aren't you thrilled? Why, I'd be . . ."

She stopped whispering and patted some powder over her nose—she'd observed Ned's eyes watching them from the mirror in front. In her normal voice, she redirected their conversation, sitting up and snapping the compact shut. "It's not really your color, Lilly." Elaine gave her friend a direct stare, eyes wide, when the conversation up front picked up again.

Lilly turned to look out her own window. She thought about the years behind her, filled with birthday parties and skating parties and football games against other small towns. Every occasion she could remember, from the time she was small, was filled with the faces and voices of the same people. Not that they were bad—these friends and neighbors were the backbone of her life. They were the bookends of her memories. But that was the problem, she decided, looking at the moving grasses and bright wildflowers sprouting from the ditches they sped past. The bookends crowded her in. The rules and customs dictated by her small town seemed designed to keep her in Crestview forever. Lilly decided, at that moment, that she needed to find a way to free herself. She wanted to push against the far ends, to move the edges of her own boundaries, to see where a different sort of road would lead. She said a silent goodbye to the girl Crestview wanted Lilly to become. She smiled, her hair blowing free in the breeze.

Soon after, Ned pulled the Plymouth onto a side road bordered by a thin forest of scrub trees. A grassy spot under one of them had been flattened by frequent use; he parked there. The four climbed out and hauled their picnic items to the shaded spot. Lonny flapped open the picnic blanket, but part of it was in the sun. He rearranged it twice before Elaine was satisfied. She directed Ned to place both baskets in the middle, and the four sat themselves around the edges. Ned settled himself close to Lilly, which caused her to suddenly take interest in handing out sandwiches and cups.

The picnic took less time to consume than it had to plan. They decided that they should get back on the road again, to get to the dance before it got so crowded that they were turned away. Lonny shook out the blanket while Elaine piled the baskets into Ned's arms. She told the boys to get the car packed while she and Lilly took care of "girl business." Taking Lilly's arm, Elaine led her around the back of a large tree where they wouldn't be observed.

"What has gotten into you, Lillian Jane?" she asked. Elaine's fists were pressed against her hips. Her words, though quiet, sliced through the air like broken glass. "Tell me what's going on, right now."

Lilly looked away. Her shoulders slumped. When she finally met her friend's eyes, Elaine could see the misery that filled them.

Elaine softened and put her arms around her friend's shoulders, drawing her close.

Lilly took a deep breath and shuddered. "Lainey? I think I'm about to mess things up again."

"Don't be silly." Elaine released Lilly from the embrace but kept her hands firmly planted on her friend's shoulders. "You have your whole life ahead of you," she said. "And Ned—"

Lilly pulled back. When she saw that Elaine was hurt by her quick retreat, she reached back out to take her friend's hands. "That's what I'm about to mess up. Ned."

They stared at each other. Neither spoke.

Elaine broke the silence when they heard the car's engine start. One of the boys gave a smart *beep-beep* to get them moving. "Why?"

"It's not right," Lilly began, trying to keep her eyes on Elaine's. "*He's* not right. I mean, he's not right for *me*." She kept hold of Elaine's hands but looked down. "I know he's a catch, and my parents want me to marry him, I can see, but . . ."

Elaine stepped forward then and gave her friend a quick squeeze. "C'mon then," she said, and turned back toward the waiting car. "We'll get you through this."

THERE WERE TRUCKS and cars parked in a dusty row along the edge of the field as far as they could see when they pulled into the supper club outside of Mason City. This establishment was rumored to have been on John Dillinger's route as he dallied through the Midwest during the Depression. Some said he'd had a girl or guns or liquor stashed onsite. Rumors like this were enough to keep the business humming during Dillinger's time and long afterward—the notoriety was a big part of the draw, as the building itself had seen better days. Gray boulders framed its entrance. A section of the old roof was mossy green, under the shade of a towering cottonwood.

Both couples joined the stream of people moving toward the entrance, the smell of fried onions, cigarettes, and ladies' perfume greeting them at the door. Almost immediately they were pushed along by newer arrivals from behind and flocked together to one of the remaining small tables near the back of the room, away from the band stage.

Ned pulled out Lilly's chair and settled himself closely next to her. He pulled a paper-wrapped bottle from his jacket. After seating Elaine, Lonny went up to the bar area to purchase four ginger ales. The large room was warm and a bit stuffy, though all of the windows were pushed open. More and more cars filed past, their headlights and taillights twinkling like fireflies through the window panes.

Lonny returned to their table with four glass bottles and four drinking glasses. "Ice's extra, can you believe it?" he said, settling himself into the empty chair next to Elaine. "They can keep it, for Pete's sake." He thumped the glasses gracelessly into the table's center. He used his penknife to open two of the ginger ales, and after Ned poured two healthy draughts and two dainty ones from his bottle, added the fizzing soda to their glasses. "Here's mud in yer eyes!" he chortled, raising his glass up high.

"Cheers!" Elaine echoed. She clinked her glass against Lilly's and winked at her.

The concoction settled the dust in Lilly's throat and spread a glow through her chest. She didn't want to cough, but the beverage tasted strongly of alcohol. Lilly liked to take a nip now and again (for research purposes, she told herself), but this drink was enough to bring tears to her eyes.

They settled back amidst the excited talk and laughter around them and watched the crowd. Most were people their own age, but there were a few older couples as well. One set near the bandstand was dressed more splendidly than the rest. They had a bottle of champagne in a bucket of ice on their table. The women wore sparkling earrings and shiny dresses;

all three men at the table had thin neckties and dark suit coats. One had a thin black moustache balanced on his upper lip. They looked expensive and sophisticated. They also looked bored.

Lilly continued to watch as other couples made their way indoors to form a loose ring around the tables, which by this time were all taken. The dance floor remained empty, but she assumed it would fill quickly once the music began. Which it did, a moment later.

First, a very good-looking blond man in a white dinner jacket and bow tie came onstage and strode to the microphone. As the applause died down, he introduced himself as Garret Dahlman and welcomed the audience to the show. A slight woman with curly, dark hair and big, brown eyes settled herself on the piano stool at the back of the stage. Two more men, one with buck teeth and the other with a looping moustache, brought their banjo and accordion to either side of the microphone. Garret went to the back of the stage to pick up a trumpet as the last man seated himself behind a trio of drums set to the rear.

The band started a popular swing tune called "In the Mood," which was on the radio so often that the first few chords had couples up and out of their chairs. The dance floor was immediately overtaken; some couples returned to their tables or back against the walls again to wait for a turn.

After the band finished that number, a beautiful brunette with a silver dress and big, bright red lips sashayed to the mic. She thanked the audience for clapping as the band began "Moonglow." Her voice was sultry, but she didn't over-sing like so many locals seemed to do; she was seasoned on the stage and the band was tight behind her. The banjo player had exchanged his instrument for a saxophone, which played a beautiful duo with the trumpet. It sounded as good as what was heard on the radio, and Lilly was entranced.

"Let's dance, Ned!" She wanted to join the swaying pulse of the music. She plucked his sleeve from the table and encouraged him again. Ned picked up his glass and downed the rest of the golden liquid before joining her on the cramped floor.

They weren't able to move much, but being so close to that sound was like being enveloped in a honeyed cloud. The swell of the saxophone's golden tones lifted Lilly's soul up out of the close room and allowed her a taste of freedom. She sighed and leaned into Ned, completely taken by the music.

Ned bent down then, and said in a low voice, "Lilly, there's something I want to ask you."

She stiffened and pulled away.

He held her closer, pulled her in by the force of his arm behind her. "Lilly, are you scared of me?" he chuckled. His warm breath smelled like whiskey so close to her face. Lilly felt like she was drowning.

"Don't you think we make a smart couple?" he asked, attempting a twirl. He bumped her into another couple, causing the male half to look peeved at the intrusion. Ned must have had more to drink than she had seen. He grinned even wider and pulled her in for a tight embrace. "Lillian, Lillian, you are enough to make a man go crazy!"

The breath she'd fought for before was completely squeezed from her body. She began to panic. She wished she was brave enough to scream or to faint, anything to get away, when she saw Elaine's concerned face over Ned's shoulder.

Elaine tapped Ned smartly from behind. "C'mon, you two, let's switch partners."

Lilly had never been so grateful to her friend. Ned had no choice but to acquiesce. Before he let her go, though, he moved in to kiss her mouth. Lilly turned slightly so that his wet lips landed next to her own. She made herself laugh. "Ned, there are others watching."

"What do I care?" he managed. "If others want to watch, they might see it again." He seemed a bit off-balance as he turned to embrace Elaine. She made a face of her own, over his shoulder, at Lilly.

The tension seeped out of her as Lonny stepped her away from the others.

"Elaine said that you might be looking for a diversion," he said, trying to avoid the couple next to them. He was as clumsy and sweet as a brother, and Lilly was thankful for his down-to-earth manners and lack of pretension.

"Thanks, Lonny. You're always such a good sport." She was light on her feet again and began to concentrate on the music once more.

The couples sat down at their table after the song ended. Ned poured himself another beverage—this time, his glass was dark amber from the amount of liquor he added. Lonny declined his friend's offer to "top it off" and kept his own glass away from Ned's reach. The next number, "All the Things You Are," brought Lilly out of her chair before she had time to remember to hold herself back.

Right behind her, Ned pushed her to the edge of the floor. He was soused. His pupils had taken over the rest of his eyes. He swayed before grabbing onto Lilly for support.

"Ned!" she hissed, "Have you had too much?"

"Not enough, not yet!" he crowed, and promptly bumped backwards into a stalwart farmer and his wife. She was pushed into her husband's broad chest and gave a shriek of surprise. Lilly drew away from Ned, apologized to the red-faced man and his calicoed wife, and pulled her date by his clammy hand off the floor.

"Wha . . . where we goin'?" His language skills were not as far gone as his balance was. He lurched sideways and fell into another gentleman's lap, a man who'd been sitting at the table to their immediate right.

"Watch it, buddy!" the man snarled. He forcibly pushed Ned off. Ned bounced into Lilly and she tipped onto Elaine, who'd just been rising to help.

Lilly had never been so embarrassed. Elaine managed to regain her balance and helped Lilly to get Ned settled into a chair. He had a big smile on his face with evidently no reason to believe that this evening was not a total success.

When the band took a break twenty minutes later, Ned seemed to have sobered up a bit and was talking to a fellow at the next table about the war. They got up and took their drinks outside. Lonny shrugged and got up to join them, after Elaine gave him a pointed look and nodded her head toward the door.

"What's gotten into him?" Lilly asked as Lonny pushed his way through the crowd to keep an eye on their intoxicated driver. "I've never seen him drink like this."

"Maybe he's nervous," Elaine responded, "and doesn't realize what a fool he's acting. Why, I thought that farmer was about to slug him earlier!" She gestured to the large man and his wife. Happily, they looked cheerful now, having a good time sharing something from a brown bottle.

Elaine turned back to Lilly again. "Do you think you ought to confront him, and tip your hand a bit? You could say—"

"No! I don't want to have that conversation at all tonight, least of all when Ned's not himself. I'd rather avoid the whole thing altogether, if you want to know the truth." Lilly looked around the room, trying to capture the appropriate words to tell her best friend how awkward it was, wanting not to be proposed to. In doing so, she completely missed Elaine's desperate signal to be quiet and her admonitions to *Shh!*

"What?" Lilly demanded. Elaine wasn't paying attention to what she was saying, not at all.

"You don't need to say anything more." Ned's voice silenced her. He'd evidently come back to the dance floor before Lilly had time to see him—at least, time to see him quickly enough to curb what she'd been sharing with Elaine.

The wooden chair next to her shot back under the table as if driven by the force of a violent machine. Ned continued, "I think it's time to head home, don't you?"

"C'mon, Ned," Elaine cut in. "Let's have a good time and enjoy ourselves, okay?" She and Lilly both got to their feet. Lonny was back at the table too. "Who knows what's in store for any of us? Let's enjoy ourselves while we can!" She grabbed Lonny and turned to the dance floor. She gestured for the other two to join them.

Lilly and Ned remained where they stood. They stared at one another. For once, Lilly did not want to look away from Ned's piercing scrutiny. His eyes were full of accusation, but she did not want to assuage him by taking his bait.

After another moment he leaned forward, grabbed the liquor bottle from the table, and stalked out of the dance hall.

Lilly pulled out the chair Ned had so forcibly thrust away and settled herself into it, content to watch the couples turn and sway on the wooden floor in front of her.

Dani

12

As she worked through her chores over the next three days, Dani's thoughts constantly returned to Donna's story. Her mind delved backward to a different decade while she changed the oil in the old Deere tractor. She knew the basic history of World War II and the Depression, but her own personal interests in high school had run more along the lines of what to wear and weekend plans. She wished she would've thought to ask Donna the name of the girl who went away, or whether she knew the name of the man who had met his death at the witness tree. She'd stopped by Susie's twice, but Donna hadn't been on duty either time. When she tried Donna's number on her phone's redial, she got the answering machine.

Returning to the house from the shed, she kicked stray stones back onto the driveway from the edge of her browning lawn. The poplars' leaves were in full splendor, the sunlight that shone through them causing a deep green glow. Off in the distance, Dani heard an engine slip into a lower gear, probably to make the upward climb around the bend that led out of Crestview a few miles off. Out here you could hear forever. Except by the river, the terrain was mostly flat, or had been made so through years of tilling and wind, and sounds carried for miles. The normal clamor of animals and machinery rang out regularly in scheduled, daily concerts. When Dani heard something different, it stuck out.

She took a rinse more than a proper shower, then tied up her wet hair before heading out. It was difficult to get a reliable internet connection through many parts of Howard County. The library in town had the most reliable web service, and Dani wanted to spend some time doing a little research online. At the last moment, she grabbed her cell phone from the hall table before leaving. She didn't lock the front door, didn't even shut it; almost nobody did, she'd come to learn, and besides, the breeze felt nice as it slid in through the front screen.

The library was one of the oldest buildings in Crestview. It was square and squat and solemn. Dani parked in front and left her window rolled down. Climbing the stone steps, she wondered what prankster had caused the parallel scrapes down each step leading into the building: perhaps a skateboarder, or someone moving a piano, had left their permanent inscriptions. The gouges were sharp and new and out of place compared to the other edges and corners, worn smooth and gentle by many-thousand footsteps.

She yanked open the heavy wooden door. The cool air of the dim interior smelled of musty books and wet carpet. Right inside the entryway were two more half-flights of steps—the lower leading to the children's section and the archive, the upper leading to the current collection. There were public computers upstairs for registered patron use, as well as two meeting rooms. When Dani was new in town, trying to figure out the best way to get going on her new venture, she'd used one of those rooms as a place to spread out her papers and books. The librarian had frowned upon this practice, however, and gently suggested that she use the large table in the common area instead. She preferred to leave the enclosed rooms reserved for group meetings.

Dani had been to the library since then, but she'd never seen a meeting room in use. Passing the first one on her way to the computers, though, she noticed the lights were on, a small group of teenagers arranged around the table inside. They had notebooks open and serious expressions on their faces. Dani smiled and sat down at the first computer station.

She removed her plastic library card from her wallet and typed in her patron ID and password, then waited for the connection to the server to go through. She decided to start with the Crestview *American* weekly newspaper, and entered this name into the search engine. A fly buzzed around overhead, darting from monitor to monitor every ten seconds or so, just often enough for Dani to forget and then be startled into annoyance again.

The *American*'s site came up and Dani clicked over to it, entering a date range of "1935–1945" in the section labeled "back issues." She'd settled on this date range after speculating on Jacob Dorn's age, then extrapolating an approximate time frame back to his father.

No luck. The paper's scanned issues appeared to have been entered from the early '70s on, much too late to be useful.

She moved on to the public records section of the Howard County government site. Here, Dani's search was a bit more fruitful. She found a listing of births, deaths, marriages, and marriage dissolutions stretching back to the nineteenth century. While this site could be useful, until she had a name or names she was stuck. She wondered if the records would note whether death certificates were issued for suicides or murders.

Again, Dani went with the date range she'd tried on the newspaper site. In those ten years, she learned, between fourteen and thirty-two children were born annually, around ten people died each year, and the marriage applications held steady at about twenty per year until 1942, when they dropped to the single digits. She spent the most time in the deaths records searching for anyone who'd died under unusual circumstances, but found nothing that stuck out. She also looked for men between the ages of twenty and forty, which she thought might be the age range for the type of man who'd be most likely to migrate from farm to farm looking for seasonal work. She found nothing relevant.

She slumped back into her chair. The kids down the hall had finished their meeting and were cheerfully, noisily heading back outdoors. Dani remembered that Donna had said the family her aunt had worked for was rich: was there a way to search for local taxpayers from that time period?

Opening the browser again, she was rewarded with a hit on a site that listed principal landowners and their assessments in Howard County. She confirmed a connection when she cross-checked the names against property sales and found a small number of men listed in both places.

Comparing the sites, Dani discovered some interesting information. First of all, a single name topped the tax list for highest assessments each of the ten years in this sample: Jesse Dorn. He had to be Jacob's father. Secondly, a man named Borlaug was second on the list, but only for five years. She searched both names, but only Borlaug's scored a hit: he was a scientist who'd developed some seeds and was evidently pretty famous in the area. A third name, Bradstreet, came up right under the first two for the second part of the sample. She couldn't find any other name as consistently recorded during this time as these three.

Dani then went back to the county birth records and searched again, starting at the beginning of the 1900s, until she found some related names: a Gerhardt Dorn had been registered as a citizen in 1912, buying a section of land near Saude. A year later, a Jesse Dorn bought a section near Crestview in Howard County; his son, Jacob, was born in 1933. The Bradstreet name provided the best clues. A Eugene Bradstreet was listed as purchasing a section near the Beaver Creek in 1924. Census records showed the birth of a daughter, Lillian, in 1922. Her mother, named Mary Margaret, died in 1946. Their land was sold at an auction in 1951 after foreclosure.

Dani got up and crossed over to the information desk to ask where the copies of the Crestview *American* newspapers prior to 1970 were located. The woman seated there told her that many of the copies were available on microfiche film and bustled around the desk to lead Dani down the granite staircase. She didn't talk as they went down the wide steps. She limped and used the handrail.

As they neared an industrial, gray file cabinet, the librarian asked which years Dani was most interested in. Dani thought she'd expand the range a bit more and requested the years between 1930 and 1950. The librarian opened the second drawer and pulled out three spools of microfiche, then bustled over to the projector to get Dani started. "Here's what we have," she said, threading the edge of the first film into the machine and flipping its magnification light on. "Do you know how to use this dinosaur?" Her eyes twinkled. Dani was momentarily taken by surprise; she hadn't expected any spark or vivacity from the quiet woman.

"I think I remember," Dani replied, turning the knob and looking through the viewfinder. "I used a machine like this in college."

"You can print out copies if you want," the librarian said, turning to leave. "Keep track of the number, and you can pay me when you're finished." She stepped away.

Dani spent the next few hours learning about the difficult lives the area's people had endured. The early papers covered a history of how citizens fared during the Dust Bowl years. While hardships were noted, it seemed that the editor was a bit of a cheerleader and wanted to convey a positive message to his readers. He encouraged them to stay put and show the tough stuff they were made of, promising that better days were certain to come. The most interesting article from this time for Dani was about a man who had been hired by an "anonymous donor" to create rain for the thirsty crops. Evidently this huckster would set off huge explosions in an attempt to send debris soaring into the clouds—this, he said, would produce an imbalance that would cause rain to fall below. It didn't work. The man was encouraged to pack up and ply his trade elsewhere.

The news seemed to improve as the decade turned; folks were able to experience a few years of good harvests. Dani noted that the man named Borlaug brought some recognition to the area when his ideas for wheat production began to be adopted and yielded great results. Unfortunately, the Depression lurked around the corner, and these times of prosperity were to be short-lived. Dani swallowed her dread, knowing what was ahead for the hardworking, decent people around Crestview.

She took a break, getting up to find the drinking fountains in the back hallway. She realized that she'd missed eating lunch but felt compelled to finish her search of the microfiche, as long as no one else was waiting for the machine, before grabbing a bite.

Straightening up from the fountain, Dani put her hands to her waist and bent backward to stretch. She noticed, above each drinking fountain, two small plaques that had been painted over. She wondered what the signs had said before they were obliterated—why hadn't someone just taken them down instead? Seemed a little lazy for this industrious group of people, she thought. Shrugging, she turned to get back to her task.

The librarian was hovering over the microfiche reader when Dani returned. She seemed a bit surprised, and then guilty, at being caught looking at what Dani was studying. "I came to see if you needed any help," she stuttered, backing away from the microfiche machine.

"No, it's going fine," Dani replied. She watched the older woman turn to retreat. "I'm learning more about the social habits of the Crestview folks than I ever cared to know," she joked. "Especially who invited guests for dinner."

"How far have you gotten, then?" the librarian asked. She'd stopped at a low children's table to straighten the picture books on display there.

"I'm into the early forties. I don't know exactly what I'm looking for, so I've been trolling through pretty much everything." Dani paused to consider her next question. "Please don't be offended by my asking, but . . . have you lived here long? I mean," she hastened to add, starting to feel awkward, "not to imply that you're old . . ." She gave up the attempt to salvage herself gracefully and shut her mouth.

The older lady's eyes regained some of their twinkle. "I was born in this small town. I became librarian here in the early sixties," she said. "Even so, I try not to get involved in the politics here." She paused and turned back to Dani. "I prefer my drama in fiction form." She passed under the transom doorway. "Let me know if you need any help. We close this afternoon at five." Her gait beat an uneven tempo up the steps and out of Dani's hearing.

Dani figured that she'd made no great strides in cultivating a friendship with her last question. She was becoming all too aware of the politics the librarian had mentioned—there were certain questions here that were safe to ask, and others that one did not talk about. Dani still didn't know what line divided the two.

She sat down to the reader and put her eyes back to the glass. The paper below her, dated Wednesday, May 15 of 1943, bore as its centerpiece a short article about the sixteen graduates of Crestview High and their plans for their immediate futures. Dani had not left off here when she'd taken a break—the librarian must have been looking at the film herself while Dani was away.

She began to read the article. Her heart skipped as the reporter shared a quote from one of the female graduates. A Miss Lillian Bradstreet had said, "I'm excited to be heading to Iowa State College in the fall, and I'm looking forward to seeing more of the world!" Dani twisted the scanning knob to find anything else Miss Bradstreet may have said, but there was only the one comment. At the bottom of that page, though, she was rewarded with a picture of the girl and her friend.

Dani stopped here for a long moment. The one identified as Lillian Bradstreet was dressed in a pleated blouse that was buttoned to the top, though her light-colored hair was loose and her smile was light. Her arm was around the other girl; their heads leaned toward one another. The other girl was darker in color, a bit more reserved in her smile, and there was something in her face that seemed familiar to Dani. She thought that the other girl, identified as Elaine Thompson, looked vaguely like someone she thought she should know.

Or maybe not. She'd been sitting in the basement for the entire afternoon, looking through hundreds of grainy black-and-white newspaper photos; it was pointless to try to recall the individual faces she'd scanned in the time she'd been sitting there.

Dani decided to stop by the café again on her way home, to see if Donna could remember the name of the family her aunt had worked for during the Depression. First she gave herself another hour to peruse the films for anything else about the three surnames at the top of the property lists. In a June article, she read an editorial reminding the readers that their neighbors of German descent had nothing to do with the disturbances in Europe, and that they should be treated like anyone else. "After all," the editor cautioned, "we're all Americans first." Dani wondered if any reader at that time had been convinced.

A few minutes later, she came across an article by a different writer who reported on the increasing possibility of the US joining the war overseas. This writer attempted to come across as a neutral voice, but his last line gave him away: he wrote about "taking the fight to them, rather than wait-ing for the fight to come home to us." The next week's paper stated that a voluntary military enrollment station had been established in Decorah, and that any man eighteen or older in good health could volunteer his services to his country. This notice jogged another puzzle piece loose for Dani: she wondered about the fallout this call-up would have caused for the farmers in Howard County, with their crops still in the ground and their debts awaiting autumn payment.

She was beginning to get a bit heavy-lidded. Her hour up, it was time to call it a day. Her stomach growled, causing some children at the ta-ble behind her to giggle. Shutting down the microfiche reader, she ran through the mostly empty calendar in her head and decided to come back again sometime in the next week. She'd look for anything more about the Bradstreets, if indeed that was the rich family's name, and see if there were any records or news about a hanging death around that time. So far, the only deaths she'd uncovered were of the natural variety.

Dani climbed the double staircase and made her way back to the in-formation desk for the last time that day. Waiting for the librarian to fin-ish checking out books for a harried young mother and her three active kids, Dani glimpsed the nameplate on the desk behind the front counter: *Eleanor Swenson*, it read.

After the noisy family had departed, Dani thanked the librarian again for her help and said that she hadn't printed any copies that afternoon. She told her that she'd left the microfiche next to the cabinet they'd been taken from. Before she departed, Dani asked, "Are you Ms. Swenson?"

"I am," she said, and looked at Dani directly.

"Are you related to the gentleman who passed away last week?"

Her thin eyebrows drew together a bit, but her smile remained. "He was my brother-in-law. My late husband's brother. My sister Elaine and I married the Swenson brothers."

"I'm sorry for your loss."

Mrs. Swenson dipped her head slightly to acknowledge Dani's words, but remained silent.

"You must know something about that rumor, then," the younger woman put forth, "about the hanging at the tree?"

Mrs. Swenson's face closed up as quickly as shades being drawn tight. She picked up the magazines the little ones had ruffled through and turned away from the counter, away from Dani. "I'm sorry. I don't know much about that," she replied from underneath the desk.

Dani heard the magazines being slapped onto a shelf below.

"And it's time for me to shut down for the evening," Mrs. Swenson continued. She stood back up. Her face was pale but for two red splotches on her cheeks. She didn't look at Dani. "I'll see you again, I'm sure. Have a nice night."

She went to the wall behind her desk; the lights overhead began snapping off one by one.

Dani knew she had insulted or hurt the librarian but didn't know how or in what way. Perhaps she was upset about her brother-in-law, and Dani's question caught her off guard. It could also be something completely different, she reminded herself as she jogged down the outside steps. As Mrs. Swenson herself had said earlier, people in Crestview had their own ways that outsiders didn't have a chance of understanding.

The late afternoon sun slanted sideways into the pickup's cab. Dust motes inside swirled lazily through the beams; when Dani opened the driver's door, they twisted away like tiny funnel clouds. The steering wheel was hot to the touch. Dani slid over the baking seat and was about to insert the key into the ignition when she heard a beep from her phone, which she'd placed in the truck's glovebox before going into the library.

Dani opened the box and saw that she'd missed four calls and had two voicemails—that was unusual. The only people she cared about knew she didn't usually take the time to listen to her messages. She punched in her code and started the truck.

The messages were from her mother, who sounded worried and distraught. "Dani, you must call as soon as you can," her voice pleaded. "Geoff—Geoff's had an accident, and . . ."

Silence. Then: "Please call me as soon as you can. I love you, honey."

Lilly

13

LILLY'S IMAGINATION KEPT looping through two scenes from the last night: how intoxicated Ned had become, and how rude and closed-off he'd acted when he'd overheard her talking to Elaine. These images, along with his dark stare and the way he'd ignored her before upping his alcohol intake again, sped through her imagination over and over like a deranged slide-show, each snapshot slightly altered so that she began to wonder which version was most correct.

At least the morning had brought a fresh change in the weather. Lilly slipped on some old slacks and a sleeveless blouse and escaped through the kitchen door soon after she woke. She hoped that the cooler temperature and some exercise outside would ease her mind and spirit.

The air was bracing, but the early morning sunshine was warm. She smiled to herself, enjoying the breeze on her bare skin. It was almost cool enough to turn back for a sweater, but Lilly didn't want to risk waking her parents or having to answer their excited questions, so she continued, step-ping carefully on dew-covered tufts of grass to escape as quietly as possible.

Ned. What was she going to do about him, anyway?

When he'd finally come back to the dance, he'd apologized for his "bad manners," as he'd called them. He'd put his arm clumsily around her and said that it was her fault—that she'd made him so nervous because she knew what he was about to do. His whole being reeked of whiskey. She noticed that the bottle he'd taken with him on his departure had not returned.

Then, on their drive home, he started fumbling for something in his pocket. Lilly sat up and pushed him off, whispering forcefully that he was in no position to be serious at a time like this. Elaine and Lonny, silent and stoic in the front seat, shared a look; Elaine turned up the volume on the car radio.

"How could you, Ned?" Lilly had continued. "I've never been asked to leave a place before, and in front of all those people, too?" Her whisper grew louder than she'd anticipated. Ned's face arranged itself into a queasy frown. "What has gotten into you?" She backed as far away from him as was possible in the back seat of the car. His long legs took up most of the space anyway, so she turned and looked out her window.

No one spoke during the drive back to Crestview. They didn't stop for their evening picnic. Lonny drove straight to Lilly's house to let her off first. For quite a while, Ned had been fast asleep, his dark head against the backrest, his mouth open and arms thrown wide. He was handsome, even in his incapacitated state, but Lilly was so infuriated she couldn't find space or time for any tender thoughts. Since she couldn't argue with him, she argued with herself: she wasn't just angry at Ned's behavior, but also at herself, for letting their time together progress past the point of a comfortable truce.

He awoke briefly as Lilly got out to say good night and offer another apology, but evidently a headache had begun to plague him. He returned quite quickly to his prone position, this time with tight eyes and an injured scowl on his pale face.

Elaine got out to help Lilly pull herself out of the back seat. She held her friend back for a moment with a quick hug. "Try not to be too mad, Lilly," she said. "He was really nervous, after all."

Lilly broke away and scrutinized her oldest friend, her disgust obvious.

"Well, who knows how these things can affect people!" Elaine continued. "Get some sleep, Lil. I'll call you in the morning." And Lonny drove the trio away, presumably to drop off Ned's inebriated body while he still had Elaine along for assistance.

Lilly tried to put away these images as she found her stride. She walked steadily toward her father's shed along the river road. Darting birds dipped in front of her, crisscrossing from the tree line on her left to the grass-edged fields on her right. The air smelled fresh and free of dust. Passing a wild rose bush blooming with tinges of pink and cream, Lilly was rewarded with its robust scent.

No vehicles were out this early in the day, and she enjoyed the freedom of not having to look out for anyone but herself. She grew warm and, surprisingly, happy. Happy and light. She swung her arms confidently, heading toward the last bend before her father's section of land began. Thinking about the year ahead, she no longer felt the pang of emptiness that had been there since she'd learned that Elaine wouldn't be coming with her. Everything would be all right—the upcoming months would be an adventure. She only had to get through the rest of the summer, and then she'd be alone in Ames, able to determine all her next steps by herself.

These thoughts kept Lilly occupied so fully that a spray of gravel from behind startled her. An old pickup truck was slowly approaching. Lilly wasn't exactly afraid, but inconvenienced—she'd finally found some distance for herself, away from the pressures of her family and Ned, and now someone dared to encroach her privacy. She turned to look, but sharp rays from the rising sun glared across the truck's windshield, obscuring the driver.

She moved into the grass that edged the ditch, but the truck didn't seem to be in any hurry to pass, maintaining its infuriating pace behind her. Lilly decided she'd had enough and whirled around to face the driver again. She stiffened her shoulders, trying to make her body look strong and immobile.

The truck rolled to a stop. The driver's door opened and a man stepped out, his dark features wreathed in the early light. It was the man who worked for her father. His name jumped like heat lightning to the front of her brain. *Cisco.*

"I don't mean to alarm you, miss," he called, keeping one hand on the open truck door. "Can I give you a ride somewhere?"

She relaxed and smiled then, moving toward him a bit so she wouldn't have to shout. "Good morning," she said. "No, thank you. I'm out for some exercise, is all." She gave a little wave and began to turn away. "Have a good day!"

"Miss?" he called out again.

"Yes?"

He stepped completely away from the truck and looked directly into her face. Her breath came faster. "There will be more workers along shortly, Miss Lillian. Some of them are not, well, of the most friendly character." He pulled off his hat and continued. "I would feel better if you would allow me to drive you somewhere else, perhaps back to town? Some of the fellows are a bit . . ." Cisco paused, then added, "unpolished, in their behaviors." He waited for her response. He seemed to be in no hurry. His blue eyes matched the cloudless sky above them.

Lilly was surprised by what he said. That he would confess the others might approach her for their own entertainment, or worse—well, she hadn't even considered the possibility, certainly not here in Crestview, Iowa. She'd read enough (her immediate thought was of that novel the young librarian had shared with her) to know that there were those in the world who might take advantage of a young woman, but she'd grown up in this place and felt secure here. The idea that someone would try to misuse her here, in her hometown, caused her world to tilt a bit. The happiness she'd enjoyed flew away; a chill tiptoed up her arms and neck.

Another thought occurred then: perhaps she shouldn't trust this man in front of her, either. He seemed well-spoken and polite enough, but Lilly didn't know him.

There would be no rescuing, she decided—she had to learn to follow her own instincts and take care of herself. "I'll be fine," she called out, turning to enlarge the space between them. "I was about to head back, anyway." She didn't want to tell him where she planned to go. She wanted him to be off and on his way so that she could get to her father's office safely, before these other men—these *dangerous* men, as she now thought of them— came upon her, alone on the road.

"Miss Lillian," he put forth. It was like he could read her thoughts. "You will be safe with me, I promise you. Nothing would harm you in my care."

He didn't come toward her but held her with his gaze.

"Thank you, but I know a place up ahead to get off the road and rest awhile," Lilly answered. She turned around and kept walking, determined to regain the independence and freedom she'd enjoyed just moments before. How could she expect to live on her own in the big city of Ames if she couldn't do so in this tiny little town?

She heard the truck door close behind her. The engine slipped into gear. The tires resumed parting the gravel and stones as Cisco carefully maneuvered past her. He nodded and waved his free hand through the passenger window in a sort of salute.

Lilly was proud of herself. She had shown strength when she stood up to a man, and he'd respected her decision.

Just ahead, over a slight rise, she saw the tree she was aiming for. It grew at the center of a section farmed in halves. The trunk had somehow split itself as it grew so that the two upper arms were equally balanced atop its juncture—they were as large around as the singular trunk which supported them. The canopy threw a large oblong of shade around its base, ringed by tall grasses.

She left the weeds and milkpods by the roadside and stepped carefully onto the earth between two rows. On either side of her chosen path, the rows followed the dips and rises of the land in perfectly parallel lines, moving closer together as they stretched farther away. Lilly continued ahead until she reached the hidden spot under the arms of the oak. It was its own little world, encircled by verdant, prolific greenery. Once the grasses and fallen leaves underneath had been smashed down to Lilly's liking, it was a cozy little den, separate from the rest of the world.

Lilly sat for quite a while, back against the rough bark, knees pulled up so her arms could rest upon them. She felt safe. At ease. She realized that she was really looking forward to getting away from the prying eyes and whispered secrets of her small town. Resting her chin on her forearm, she smiled. Maybe she could get a summer job next year—she wouldn't have to return at all.

As she schemed, she became aware of a buzz of voices coming her way.

She rolled up to her knees and peered out through the stalks. Workers were coming toward her on the paths between the towering rows. They wore long sleeves despite the warming weather and strange leather straps wrapped around their hands. They were removing the tassels from the ears of corn, stripping the spiky tops off the stalks and dropping them onto the ground as they walked. Their musical voices tossed their sentences back and forth, frequently interrupted by laughter.

They moved quickly. Because they were all wearing wide-brimmed hats, Lilly couldn't tell if the workers were men or women. Their voices were all higher pitched and more quickly articulated than the slow, low growls of the farmers her father knew.

Her moment of peace and solitude was shattered. She didn't know whether to stay hidden like a squirrel beneath the tree's shelter or to start her exit right now, before they got any closer. Her heart raced like a caged animal's. Her eyes darted between the encroaching workers and the gravel road a few hundred feet away.

The cornstalks nearest Lilly bent. A man pushed his way through to her sanctuary. Before she could do or say anything, Lilly recognized him as Cisco. He winked at her, turned back around so that she was behind him, and called out something to the rest of the workers. They continued past him, appearing not to notice Lilly.

She sat on her heels, knees to the cool ground, waiting for her pulse to stop pounding. Cisco removed the tassels himself from the stalks around her on both sides, then touched the brim of his hat before leaving to catch up with his company.

Dani

14

"How bad is he?" Dani asked. She'd stayed in her truck, parked in front of the Crestview library. She heard the words tumbling forth from her mom, but they penetrated no further. She was immobile, inanimate.

"Not so good, Dani. The doctors don't think he'll regain consciousness again." She was crying when she added, "I'm sorry, honey."

The news itself didn't take Dani by surprise: she'd expected, sooner or later, that she'd be faced with the fact that Geoff's life had come to a dangerous end, either by his own hand or someone else's. "How did it happen?"

She heard her dad's voice in the background, but her mom ignored him and continued explaining. "His parents got a phone call from St. Luke's. He'd been dropped off outside the emergency room, already unconscious. No one stayed with him, so the doctors don't know what happened exactly, but they did determine that he had a number of drugs in his system, and that . . ." she stopped, taking a moment to compose herself, but could no longer hold back her tears. "I'm afraid there's no brain activity."

Dani didn't blink, didn't breathe, looking through the dust that had collected on her windshield. Her eyes remained dry. "When's the last time anyone saw him? Spoke to him?"

"He didn't come home for Christmas this year." Her dad had taken the phone. "Hello, honey." He cleared his throat. "He usually tries to make it home then—sorry, you know that—but this year was different." An old Chevy whooshed past, radio blaring.

He pushed on. "Diane said that she and Angie had driven downtown right after the first of the year, to where Angie thought he'd been staying." Angie was Geoff's younger sister; Diane was their mom. Angie worshiped her older brother—she had been more upset at the breakup with Dani than Geoff had been. She was a good student, conscientious in her school duties and club responsibilities, striving to make up for the heartbreak and disappointment her brother had brought to their family. "The people living there said he'd taken off. They didn't know where he went."

Dani didn't have anything to say. Her thoughts trailed back through the years to Geoff at their high school prom, eyes dancing as he showed her the slim flask concealed in his tux pocket; his laughter as they rode one night around the dark cul-de-sac, trying to stay unnoticed on their neighbor's "borrowed" motorcycle; the way he competed with her, whether biking or running or trying to be the first to open a door, always wanting to be a step or a stride or a length ahead of her. She missed that Geoff.

She didn't miss the Geoff he'd become, after they graduated high school and he began to find the excitement they'd had a little too tame for his growing tastes. He'd taken a semester off during their sophomore year at the University of Minnesota and never come back. At first, he'd claimed it was a financial thing and got himself a job as a bartender in the Warehouse District, but Dani didn't care for the people he'd begun hanging out with. They'd started communicating solely through answering machine messages. They rarely saw each other anymore.

Her dad's gentle voice broke through her thoughts. "Dani. Are you there?"

Blinking, Dani became aware of the pressing heat closing in on her and the warm trickle of sweat down between her shoulder blades. She switched the phone to her right side and rolled down the truck's window. "Yup." The warm breeze outside didn't cool her. "How is his family?"

"Well . . ." her dad said, hesitating, ". . . his parents got another call last night, from a policeman."

Dani waited for a few moments of silence before reassuring him. "It's okay, Dad. I know that things got bad after we split up. It was part of the reason I couldn't stay. I couldn't just watch him . . ."

He cleared his throat. "I wish there was something we could have done to help you, or him, or something."

"There was nothing for us to do," Dani replied. She stressed the word *us*. "You know that, Dad. He was the only one who could help himself." She realized she had a lump in her throat. "He had to be the one to decide it was time to quit. All we could do was wait." She was suspended between anger on one side and a chasm of sharp hurt on the other. She fought to keep herself on the tightrope between the two.

Her dad promised to call again when he learned about the funeral arrangements. "You'll let me know if you need anything, won't you?" he added.

"Yup," was all Dani could manage. *I love you, Dad*, she added silently, afraid to trust herself to speak out loud.

She didn't sleep, didn't even try to make it upstairs to her bedroom during the long night. Instead she curled up on the plaid sofa and thought back to the times when Geoff was healthy and happy and whole. She didn't feel guilty about mourning her loss a second time as she sifted through these memories; she'd already mourned Geoff's passing once, minute by late minute, every time he didn't show up, didn't come home, wouldn't return her calls. She'd felt her loss most acutely when she'd packed up and moved herself away and into a new life. A life without Geoff.

It wasn't that hard. It was as if she'd given him permission to do what she knew or expected he would eventually do anyway. That it was hastened or in some way propelled by her own growing distaste for her own profession was neither good nor bad, to her thinking—it just was. For herself, Dani had never belonged in that concrete and steel structure on the corner of South Sixth and Second Avenue, downtown Minneapolis. As for being a legal assistant to two cocky young attorneys, she remembered thinking that the results of the billing reports she filed and the money awards she sent out seemed to profit the lawyers more than their clients. Geoff's role in her decision to leave, like it or not, had probably only sped things up by a few months.

And then, 9/11. The world had stopped as they watched, over and over on the TV, the souls of those whose lives had been violated by the events of that day. Dani had ached for the losses of the nameless people whose loved ones she couldn't help but grieve with. And she'd taken the country's sudden standstill as a reason to propel herself into changing a life that didn't seem too worthwhile anymore. She'd slipped away from the sorrow and indecision and backwards glances and plunged herself into the Iowa countryside as easily as a fish returning back to its pond.

And yet. And yet she ached for the man he never became. Dani forced herself to close her mind to the possibilities of his final days, his final hours. Once, after he'd disappeared on a week-long binge, she'd tried to force Geoff back into reality by comparing his path to the track his "friend" Ellie had taken. This dirty, tattooed girl, beyond thin, was a user Geoff would shack up with, sharing heroin and needles and who knows what else, until she'd died one night of an overdose. Dani would never forget Geoff's flatlined response: "So? It wasn't me," he'd said with a shrug. Geoff's indifference, his disregard, had shocked her. He refused to acknowledge that another person was no longer living because she couldn't or wouldn't open herself up to the reality that her drug use was going to kill her.

This time, that reality showed up for Geoff.

Her eyes closed, Dani searched for that moment of peace which usually came right before sleep. A solitary cricket called out from her porch, insistently; he got no reply. Instead, the witness tree groaned and shuddered, over and over, in her memory.

Lilly

15

WHEN LILLY ARRIVED back home from her morning walk, Ned's coupe was parked in the driveway. Her courage evaporated. She took a big breath and firmly straightened her spine before opening the kitchen door. If he or her mother were anywhere in the front of the house, they would have seen her pass by on her way to the back door; she wasn't surprised, then, when she turned the knob and stepped inside to hear her mother's voice calling.

"Lilly, dear?" The staccato heels approached. "Ned's here to see you, Lilly." Her mother frowned as she came near to help Lilly close the door. She whispered, "He seems upset. Is everything all right?"

Lilly wanted to answer this question about as much as she wanted to walk out and face Ned. "He—he wasn't himself last night. I think he wants to talk to me about that," she told her mother, and made her way down the hall to the front room where he waited.

Ned stood to meet her. He took her forearms and bent to kiss her. Lilly lowered her chin; his kiss grazed the crown of her hair.

"Lilly." He released her and returned to one of her mother's side chairs. He leaned forward toward her. "Forgive me for acting so foolishly last night." He straightened his tie. "I'm sorry for embarrassing you and your friends."

"They're your friends too, aren't they, Ned?" she returned. She sat across

92

the room from him, on a small sofa her mother called a "settee." She crossed one ankle behind the other. Her back felt sticky and warm from her morning's exertion.

He held still, staring at her until she met his gaze. "It's no secret that I care for you, Lillian. While my actions last night leave a lot to be desired"—he reached into his coat pocket as he talked—"I hope this token of my affection does not."

He pulled out a small, black box and stood to open it in front of Lilly. "I've asked your father's approval, and now I'm asking for yours." The silver band nestled in the blue, velvet box was set with a large, marquis-cut diamond that shot brilliant light prisms throughout the room. "Will you have me?"

"Oh, Ned," she began. "I don't know what to say." She kept her eyes on him, avoiding the box.

"Say you will." Before she could protest, he sat down next to her on the settee. He put one arm around her and held the ring out to her with the other. "We're meant to be together," he coaxed. "There's no one else here for me."

And that, to Lilly, was the problem. If she stayed in Crestview, there would be no one else for her either. No one else in town or in the surrounding countryside might come as close as Ned, but "close" was a relative term. This realization gave her strength to try to speak her thoughts aloud. "I thank you, Ned, I really do," she began, "but I'm not ready to be married. I'm not ready—"

He interrupted. "We don't need to be married right away," he said. "You can wear my ring as long as you like, through your year at college, even, before we have our ceremony." He wasn't listening to her. "We could have it next summer. That would give me enough time to find a house, and—"

This time, Lilly intervened. "Ned. You're not listening." His eyes suddenly focused on hers. "I don't want to be married to you, to anyone, until I've finished college."

His eyes narrowed and he sat up straight, pulling his arm away from her. "What do you mean? This college lark—you don't even know what you're going to study, for cat's sake!" He stood. "How can you say you're 'not ready'?" Visibly refocusing himself, he closed his eyes and took a breath. "Don't you think a year away would be more than enough time to get this, this *lark* out of your system?"

Lilly stood. She faced him. "I want to see more of the world than what's kept inside Howard County." Her voice became as strident as his had been moments before. "I don't want to settle down until I know more of what's out there, what others think and do, and the places they live and work, and . . ."

She trailed off as Ned stood and snapped the jewelry box shut and pushed it deep into his coat pocket.

"I see," he said. His bearing was as immobile as a stone wall, his eyes two glittering coals. "I'm not enough for you, is that it?" His right hand swept the circumference of the front room's ceiling to make a point. "This town, these people, we're not good enough for you, huh?" He shoved both hands into his jacket pockets. "I get it. Miss Lillian Bradstreet has designs on the big ol' world. She's too important to stay home and be content with those who love her."

She put her hand out to touch his arm, but he pulled away. "I'll see myself out, if you don't mind."

"Wait, Ned, let me explain this to you," Lilly started, but Ned had already passed through the doorway in his rush to be gone. He didn't turn back. He didn't even slow down.

She listened to his steps as he strode through the front door. In a blink, his car engine turned over—he revved the motor once before peeling out of their driveway. Lilly heard her mother's approach from the kitchen.

"Honey, what happened? Where's Ned?" Bustling past her daughter, who stood like a statue, she pulled back the white sheers covering the front window and peered out after Ned's car. "What's going on here?"

Lilly collapsed back onto the settee, pulling her knees up and resting her heels on its edge. She hid her eyes under the shelter of her crossed arms. "He wants to get married," she replied softly.

Her mother snapped the curtains down and spun toward her daughter.

"Did you refuse him?"

"Yes." Lilly took a breath. "I don't want to be married. Not to Ned, not to anyone." She tried to continue. "What's so hard to understand? I'm only eighteen years old!" She sat up and looked at her mother.

Mrs. Bradstreet's face was cold. She ran an appraising look over her daughter, as if she didn't know her.

"I don't know how to explain myself, Mother. I only know that I need to be away from here, to go places and see things I haven't seen before."

"You could do that with Ned," her mother shot back.

"No, I couldn't." Lilly was calm in her reply. "Don't you see? I'd be looking through the eyes of a married woman, through the eyes of a compromise." She thought for a moment. "I want to see things for *me*, not as a daughter or a wife or someone's tagalong."

"You're being selfish!" her mother interrupted. She pointed one manicured finger at Lilly. "You are making a big mistake!" Her finger lowered, but not her tone of voice. "You'll see. You'll regret this day, when you're back from your big adventures. Ned isn't the kind to wait, you know. Some other girl will snap him up and then she'll have the life you threw away!"

She paused dramatically, waiting for Lilly's response. When her daughter stayed silent, Mrs. Bradstreet threw up both hands and went upstairs to the comfort of her own bedroom.

After her mother was gone, Lilly answered. "You may be right, Mother. You may be right." And she too left the room, grabbing her shoes from the back door and heading out into the sunlight.

AN HOUR OR so later, Lilly was at Elaine's house explaining the drama to her best friend. The two sat on a wooden swing that hung from the front-porch ceiling.

"He doesn't understand," Lilly continued. "He thinks that my going off to college is a one-time thing." She took a sip of lemonade and put the sweating glass onto the floor beneath her. "Mother, too. She can't accept that I have my own ideas, my own plans, even though they're not very specific. She thinks she knows what I need better than I do."

Elaine didn't say very much through this outburst. She'd learned that it was best to let Lilly get out all of her details and musings first, and then, like an emptied pitcher or vase, she'd be ready to be filled up again. "What did your father say?"

"I don't know." Lilly pushed against the floor with her toe, setting the swing back into its gentle, soothing rhythm. "I'm sure Mother has called him. I don't know if he'll pick up, you know how he is." She was silent for a moment and then added, "He's different. He goes along with whatever Mother thinks is best, usually. He doesn't want anyone to be angry, least of all her, so he'll probably stay away until the dust blows over." She laughed, but it wasn't because she was feeling light-hearted. "He's never really lived 'with' us, do you know what I mean? Even when I was little, his mind was always somewhere else. I don't know how the two of them ever found anything in common."

Elaine's mom came to the door, her features distorted through the screen. "Lilly, your mother just called, looking for you. I told her that you and Elaine were visiting. She said to tell you to be home for dinner, that there will be company to get ready for." Music swelled somewhere inside the house, indicating the return of a radio program. Before Elaine's mother turned away, she added, "When do you leave for Ames, dear?"

"I'm planning to go the Friday after next. I want to get there early and see a little of the city before orientation begins."

Elaine's mother chuckled. "It's not that big a city, Lilly, but you'll find the nooks and crannies, I'm sure. Stop by and say goodbye before you go, won't you?" And with that she was off, back to her schedule and duties.

"Your mother is so much more . . ." Lilly struggled for the right word. ". . . approachable, isn't she?"

Elaine nodded.

"You could tell her about anything." Lilly picked at the fabric of her slacks, trying to re-crease the ridge the warm day and her exercise had worn away.

"Don't be so sure," Elaine said. "She's pretty nosy. I think she's read my diary, too." She lowered her voice. "That's why I keep two now: one for her

in the same spot under my bed, and the 'real' one in a box in my closet."
She sat up and used her normal voice again. "I think it's time we're treated
like grownups, don't you?"

"Lainey, let's not lose touch!" Lilly's sudden movement made the swing
bob from side to side. "Let's write each other every week, and meet for
lunch, or, I don't know, a movie, at least once a month."

Elaine hugged Lilly's shoulders, feeling her bones through the fabric of
her blouse. "I promise. We'll stay friends, right?"

"Right." Lilly stood up and brushed the seat of her trousers. "Lainey, can
I use your bike?"

"Sure, you know where it is." Elaine gathered the empty lemonade glasses. "Are you heading home?"

"You know, Lainey, I don't think that I am," she answered. She skipped
down the porch steps and added, "I'm tired of being the girl everyone wants
me to be. I think I'll ride around a little and think about the girl *I* want to
be." Lilly blew her friend a kiss and disappeared around the corner of the
house to the garage in back.

She rode toward the sunset, which took her past the town and into the
area favored by some of the newer farmers, Amish people who dressed,
planted, and cared for their animals in the simplest ways possible. They
kept to themselves and didn't seem to mind the rockier soil, or the way
the land here started to roil and bubble into hillocks and mounds; they
preferred farmland next to like-minded neighbors. Lilly passed a couple
of younger children along the road and called out a greeting in advance so
they wouldn't be surprised. The littlest one gaped and became still, but her
older sister smiled at Lilly and bade her a good evening.

She continued toward the riverbank. The shadows had fallen here already, casting triangular wedges between clumps of trees. Birds called to
one another from their nighttime perches. The river sang quietly to itself
under an old plank bridge.

Across the river, Lilly let the Schwinn coast to a stop and hopped off.
She hid the bike behind a tree near the road and followed a deer path
toward the river bank. A few hundred feet ahead, she found a dry spot

beneath an old elm tree and settled in to watch the river and its light flow past. Little glimmers of fading sun cast flashing gemstones onto the water's rippling surface.

She considered the events of the last few days and resolved to leave those negative memories behind. She told herself it was time to look forward now, to plan for her future and what was ahead.

Concentrating on her thoughts, it took Lilly a while to notice that she wasn't alone. A constant whir and catch, whir and catch, punctuated by a sliver of silence between each episode, sounded like a fisherman trying his luck somewhere down the line. She got up to look for the cause of the sound but saw no one nearby. The noise continued.

She remembered reading that Indians could walk through the densest forests without making a sound. She tried to move silently, transferring her weight carefully from one foot to the next, hoping she'd be able to determine the cause of the activity without bringing attention to herself.

She'd successfully climbed over a fallen tree trunk and was sidling toward the edge of the river, crouching low to the earth behind some raspberry canes, when the man who stood thirty-some feet ahead called out to her. He didn't even turn to face her, but said from over his shoulder, "If you are trying to be sneaky, you have failed."

It was Cisco. Lilly felt like a fool. She stood and brushed the dirt from her knees with her messy hands, making big smudges on each pant leg. "Hello," she called, attempting to sound confident. Alone on a riverbank at night with a man she didn't know—her mother would have a fit if she could see her daughter navigating her way through this situation.

"Are you fishing tonight as well?" he asked. He continued casting and reeling in the silvery line, attached to a long pole by a knob at its end.

"No," she replied. "I was out for a ride and thought I'd visit the river." She hadn't planned on having to explain her spying mission and scrambled for a likely excuse. There was absolutely nothing logical to say. "Anyhow, I'll leave you to it."

He turned to look at her, smiling with hooded eyes and a hint of a grin on his lips. "It's a beautiful night, is it not?" He waited for her reply.

"Yes, just beautiful," Lilly said, moving her eyes from him to the far shallows, bathed in the sunset's deep purples and grays. She stood still for a moment longer, then added, "Thank you, you know, for earlier today. For hiding me when the . . . when the others were around." She looked back to him again. He remained still, his eyes easily resting on her own.

"You seem to like this 'hiding' more than others do, I notice," he remarked. Turning back to the river, he cast the line forth again with a flick of his wrist. A shiny, silver spoon at the end flew like a bullet to rest momentarily in the same shallows Lilly had admired a moment before. "It makes me wonder, what does a young woman like yourself think she needs to be hiding from?"

Lilly was dumbfounded by this stranger's simple observation—how he so precisely defined the nebulous, watery-edged feelings that had lately flooded her consciousness. How was it that this man she had only spoken with twice, and very briefly at that, could find the exact words to define the restlessness that hung over her so unpredictably? She took a step nearer.

"I—I . . ." She didn't know how to respond. In addition to presuming to understand her, he shunned the difference between their positions: this man did not act like he was supposed to, as her inferior. He was a worker, not part of her town. He was a person she'd most likely never socialize with, dance with, nor claim as a friend. And yet, he'd eased her insistent uncertainties by simply putting words to the clouds and mists in her mind and heart, by naming things for what they truly were. Lilly preferred hiding. Her first instincts were to hide from the future and its uncertainties, afraid that the unformed decisions she felt pressured to make now might somehow irrevocably ruin her life.

Lilly took another deep breath and another step forward. "How can you say these things?" she asked. "You don't know me. How can you tell me what you think is true?"

He reeled in the line and clipped the spoon to the bottom edge of the pole. Placing it on the ground, he sat down facing the river. His legs stretched out before him; he leaned back onto his elbows. His hat drew a shadow over his eyes, but a grass stem twitched from under its brim.

Lilly drew closer, seating herself an arm's length away. The two of them remained so for moments that stretched out with the sun's final rays, grasping brilliantly at the edges of the leaves, the crags of limestone that rimmed the river bank, the bottoms of the tufted clouds arrayed like majestic pillows across the horizon.

At last, the sun sank, leaving behind an echo of warmth, swallows swooping to their nests, and the leaves' quiet whispers to the river below.

The twilight deepened. The birds became quiet, though the river burbled on.

Reclaiming thought and awareness, Lilly remembered where she was. Who she was with. This awareness brought her to her feet—her parents would be worried about her return. Cisco stood as well. He gathered up his pole and knapsack with one hand and with the other gestured toward the trail that led back to the road, nodding that he would follow.

Lilly was barely able to see the trail in the dusk and hoped she'd be able to avoid stumbling. Twinkling bugs flitted like lit darts through the darkened tree line as they hiked to the road.

Finally, Lilly located her bike. She hauled it upright and straddled it.

"Would you like a ride into town?" Cisco asked, pausing next to her on his way to his truck parked ahead. Lilly hadn't seen it earlier when she'd decided to stop here; if she had, she would've continued on in order to find herself more privacy.

"I'm okay, I think." She sat on the bike's seat and put a foot onto the pedal. "I like riding at night."

"I will say good night, then," he replied. He laid his pole and knapsack into the bed of his truck.

Lilly heard the truck's engine struggle once before it caught. She had pedaled to the top of the first rise already, where the sunset on the horizon threw a few feeble curtsies to the far smears of purple that were desperate to finish encasing the sky. She coasted down the hill toward town with the bike's headlight off, enjoying the naked thrill of choosing the unexpected.

Dani

16

Dani sat at a table by herself next to the group of men. She'd been looking out the window, listening to them, when she saw Jacob drive up and park in the gravel lot next to Susie's. He strode in through the screen door with his signature flair, aiming for the round table of men in the back.

Seven pairs of eyes looked at him as he took the single step down into the eating area. His usual place, under the TV near the corner, was taken. Lloyd sat there.

As Jacob approached, the various conversations died. Dani didn't know which side to watch, drawn in by the drama but aware of her relegation to the side.

"Fellas, how're we doing today?" Jacob asked.

Lloyd picked up his coffee cup and took a sip.

"Say Lloyd, ain't you sitting in my chair? Is it 'switch day' today?" Jacob joked.

No one laughed.

Jacob seated himself at the only empty place, nearest the step where the waitresses had to move back and forth in their duties—the worst chair to have. The men on either side barely moved to give him space as he pulled up.

Having never shown any particular form of situational insight before, even he could tell that the universe was off-balance this morning. "Fellas, what gives?"

"There's been an accident," Burt answered. "Bud's boys." He paused, looking around the table for someone else to continue, but the other men were intent on finishing their own coffees and didn't speak up. "It's not good."

"What happened?" Jacob asked.

Donna butted in and slammed a mug of coffee in front of him. It wasn't his regular mug, the one with his name, but a chipped one. Liquid sloshed over the side and left a thin brown puddle. The waitress stormed away.

Lloyd plunged into the details. It was like his was the only voice in the building. "Bud's boys, you know how they ride them four-wheelers every-where." The rest of the men were still. Someone in the kitchen snapped off the radio. "They cross that road twenty, thirty times a day, delivering parts, fishing, who knows what." He tapped his empty cup on the tabletop, connecting rings in the spills there. "Bud says he tells them all the time, pay attention to the road, you know, people come speeding along there, not looking or paying attention."

He had a hard time regaining his composure before he could finish. "They got hit last night, coming back from somewheres. Big trailer, hauling hogs for the Kleinschmidts. Hit them broadside. Tater's holding on; he had to be airlifted to Rochester. But Tot . . ."

Burt shifted his gaze to rest on Jacob. Lloyd concentrated on his coffee cup. The rest of the men kept statue-still. Diners at surrounding tables were also paused, observing.

"Hell!" Jacob spat. "Those boys! They ain't got sense enough between the two of them—"

"Hold on just a goddam minute!" Lloyd got up and out of his chair and leaned over the table toward Jacob. He shook his finger at the smaller man. His eyes shot fire. Spit flew out somehow from between his tightened lips. "That ain't their situation!"

Dani sat up, her eyes flicking between Jacob and Lloyd. Lloyd contin-ued, punctuating each word with a jab of his meaty forefinger. "Those boys ain't never done nothing but what they're told. They work hard and they stay outta everybody's way. No, Jacob, this one's on you." Burt, next to him, stood up in case the other man launched himself across the table toward Jacob.

"How the Sam hell you putting this on me?" Jacob answered, also standing. He used both hands to gesture as he returned the volley. "I wasn't driving that truck. I didn't tell those lame brains to drive into the side of a semi."

One farmer got up, threw his money onto the table, and stalked out. Burt had a hand on Lloyd's shoulder, trying to get him to sit back down. Donna stood behind Jacob with her tray, waiting to see how things would settle.

The tension fizzled and settled a bit, murmurs from behind and alongside the table growing. It sounded like everyone in the café had an opinion on the matter. Lloyd sat with a grunt but never took his eyes off Jacob. Burt turned to his right to talk with two other regulars, who were rehashing the accident details. Jacob reseated himself and arranged his spine as tall and straight as he could, then looked in a circle around the table. When he spoke, his words were clipped and measured. "I didn't have anything to do with those boys' accident. Blaming me ain't right. I told you, I—"

This time, Dani interrupted. Her face was pale; her cheeks looked sunken. Her usually bright eyes were dull and rimmed with red. "You know, the talk this morning is about how these things, these bad things, started happening since we helped you cut down that tree." The men turned their stone faces to her like they were seeing her for the first time. "First your sprayer broke, then that hog shed next to your property blew its electricals. I got . . ." Dani's eyes filled. She took a deep breath, then continued. "I got some bad news from home. And now? Now, Bud's sons have this accident."

Burt jumped in to continue the litany. "We ain't had so much misfortune all at a time for ages. Only reason I can see, Jacob, is because you had to chop down that tree." Others nodded or echoed their agreement.

"That's a bunch of bullshit, and you all know it!" Jacob spat back. "There ain't no truth to that story, no matter how you tell it. You can't think all this is because that devil-headed tree came down? Why, I never thought we here believed in witch hunts or magic." He stood up. "I ain't got time for this foolishness. Unlike some of you, I got work to do." He slammed his chair under the table and finished: "And while I'm sorry about those boys, that ain't no one's fault but their own." He turned and marched out of the café.

Diners leaned in to rehash what had transpired. Donna, her thick mascara running down her rouged cheeks, backed away and stumbled toward the kitchen. The men at the center table, friends since their beginnings or the times of their fathers before them, sat and looked at each other. They didn't have the protocol to deal with this situation, hadn't ever encountered anything like this before. Sure, they'd heard about the hanging and the curse, but that was long before they'd been born. It'd been nothing but a story for them. Until now.

Dani stood behind the chair Jacob had cast aside. "How much longer is this going to go on?" A few of the men shifted; no one answered. She tried one more time. "What do you guys know about the man who died there, really?"

Burt looked at the faces around his table, but when no one else spoke up, he tried to put the pieces together. "We've known the story since we were little; everyone had his own version." He waited for someone else to contribute, but none of the others was ready to jump in. "The one thing I know is that Jacob's daddy, Jesse, was part of that original brouhaha. Jacob probably knows more than the rest of us; more than what he lets on, anyway."

Dani sat. "How exactly was Jacob's dad involved?"

Lloyd took this one. "Seems old Jesse didn't have the money he made out he did."

"Yeah, he had the most land, but times were tough and he wasn't making enough to keep it all," Chuck added. He didn't come into town but once a week—he had one of the last dairy farms in the county and lived the farthest out of all the men at the table. "My dad told me prices were so low that grain was left to rot in the silos. They couldn't get a decent price, and it cost more to buy the seed than to sell the crop."

"Lots of families went bust then," continued Sonny Gilbert, Lloyd's nephew. "At first, Jesse bought them out; gave them a nickel on the dollar. That's how he got so much acreage." He took a sip of his coffee. "He reckoned on prices climbing up again sooner than they did."

Dani didn't see the connection. "So how did Jacob's dad get involved in a hanging?"

Lloyd took another turn. "Well, there was a young banker in town then. Fred? Ned? Can't remember his name, but he had a, a *less-than-proper* way to do business." He looked around the café, saw Donna, and gestured for her to bring more coffee. "My pop said this banker could arrange for, what'd he call it? 'Creative financing'? Anyhow, old Jesse took advantage of that. And when times continued to fail, Jesse was under the banker's thumb. They say he took some of that financing, in order to keep himself afloat."

Burt broke in. "I wondered about that, myself. See, I remember my dad and my uncles trying to work together to save their land by pooling whatever they had. They talked once about going to see the banker, but my dad said he'd rather lose it all than be beholden to that kind of man."

Donna came back and placed a full carafe on the table. The black streaks had been scrubbed from her cheeks. She waited around to listen in on the rest of the conversation.

"What did this finance business have to do with a hanging?" Dani asked.

Chuck told her the man was found hanging from the double-headed tree that grew on Jesse's property. "The dead guy wasn't one of his workers, though. Old Jesse had his local guys for his hired help, said he didn't trust no migrant to do things the right way."

Burt asked, "Didn't the bank close up for a while, a few years after?" Some nodded; the rest looked on. "Got bought out by some bigger outfit out of Des Moines or some place around that same time, I think." He rearranged his cap more firmly over his thinning hair. "I dunno; I can't remember half of nothing anymore, seems like."

The conversation dragged to a standstill. Men left their bills and coins and prepared to return to their fields and farms. Dani looked up to try to determine what Donna made of this, but she'd left their area and was taking another table's order. Dani hesitated a moment, then followed the men outside.

Lloyd kept talking as they ambled through the gravel parking lot to their trucks. "Who's going to the auction on Friday?"

"What auction?" Dani asked him.

"Swenson's place. Ain't no one left to farm it but his sister-in-law, the librarian. She don't want it." Burt removed his wallet from the back of his jeans, getting ready to place it above the driver's sunshade. All the farmers kept their wallets there, Dani noticed. "Thing is, the land ain't all that good. It's up on a rise, you know, out by the highway. Most of that topsoil's been gone for years." He heaved himself up onto the running board of his diesel truck. "Good view, though."

Dani said goodbye and watched the dust whirl behind the departing vehicles. Turning to her own truck at the back of the café, she noted that the tilting picnic table was empty. She hoisted herself into the cab and looked past the kitchen door to see if Donna was inside, but saw only the breezy-headed counter girl and that guy they'd hired as a second cook. Perhaps she should plan to go to the auction, she thought. Maybe it would be a good place for a new farmer to stake her claim.

Lilly

———

17

NED CRUISED SILENTLY a few blocks behind Lilly, trailing her as she pedaled slowly back to her home. She didn't seem to be in much of a hurry, and sometimes had to check herself from steering absent-mindedly into the middle of the street. Not that it mattered; it was almost ten thirty and dark, no vehicles moving on the roads save for his own.

He'd picked up her trail by accident as she'd biked up into town from the river bluff. Mrs. Bradstreet had called the bank after the dinner hour and asked Ned if he'd seen Lilly. When he'd replied that he hadn't, she'd confessed that she and Lilly's father were quite worried. They hadn't seen her since lunch, and it wasn't like her to stay out without letting her parents know her whereabouts. Even Elaine, who'd visited with Lilly that after-noon, was at a loss about where her friend might have ventured. She'd said that Lilly had borrowed her bicycle—maybe she'd gone on a ride and got-ten lost, or perhaps had some mechanical issues. Ned assured Lilly's mom that it would be no trouble to drive around town with his eyes open, as he was on his way home anyway and would be happy to help. He welcomed the opportunity to try to catch Lilly alone, though he didn't share this part of his thinking with her mother.

And so he'd been out for a few hours, driving up and down the gravel roads that corralled the endless land into squares and rectangles. In a few spots where the land heaved up enough to provide a view, he got out and tried to scan the horizon, but his search was fruitless. The various tree lines were just thick enough to hide many of the roads from sight. Ned became frustrated, imagining that she was probably only yards away. He doubled back over some of the main lanes, thinking he could catch her riding out from behind their leafy coverage. That plan didn't work either.

About ten o'clock, after the languid summer sun had finally gone to rest, he found himself on a dirt road past the river, near the camp area the migrant workers used during their visits. Several campfires burned through the sultry air; guitar music and children's laughter bracketed the evening sounds of insects and night-prowling animals. Ned shook his head, disgusted with the frankness, the vivacity these people dared to exhibit in *his* town. Whenever Ned ran into them on the street or, rarely, in the bank, each encounter was a slap of sharp recognition that they did not, at any time, belong here, with their loud colors and dark skin, their suspicious accents, the way they let their children play and behave. They had no urgency, no responsibility, moving as they did in big groups from one place to the next. Their children were illiterate and looked half-asleep during the daytime hours. In Ned's mind, Mexicans belonged in Mexico, or, at worst, down South somewhere with more of their kind.

Ned ruminated on these thoughts as he killed the lights and drove slowly past the camp. He was curious about what they did around their fires at night: did they practice voodoo, as Mrs. Dorn swore they did? They came to Mass every Sunday, sat in the back two rows, but everyone knew they weren't following the rites the way the church required. Mrs. Dorn claimed it was because they mixed their sacraments with their own native religion; that's what her sister, who'd moved down to Dallas, told her.

Ned observed the adults sitting in a loose ring around the biggest fire. They weren't dancing or cavorting about, as he'd been led to believe; they seemed to be relaxing, listening to a man who sang and strummed a guitar. Childish voices suddenly shot out from the scrub on the side of the road. Ned decided he was risking discovery, and pulled the car into a turn back toward the protection of the town.

He flicked on his lights when he saw the bridge ahead. In the nick of time, too—another vehicle was approaching from the opposite side, but slowed to allow his car to pass over first. Ned eased across the wooden planks and, drawing near the old pickup, saw that the driver was the beaner that Lilly's father had employed as his foreman for the season. The man touched the brim of his hat, like a regular guy would do, and dropped his truck into gear to take his turn across the river.

"Just another example of the audacity of these people," Ned mumbled, speeding up the hill to return to Crestview proper. They thought they could address you as equals. He wondered how this upstart got to feeling so high and mighty, when his way of living depended on so many different bosses.

Ned eventually came upon his intended, wending her way home through the dark night. She had no idea he was tailing her, he was sure, because her speed (such as it was) didn't waver from its dreamy pace. Her shoulders were back as she looked up at the night, the stars, the trees above her. Frankly, he thought she looked a bit touched. He was glad that he was the only witness to this childlike, rather bizarre behavior.

He parked in front of a home three doors down before Lilly arrived at her own driveway. She looked at her home as if its appearance there suddenly surprised her: she almost missed her turn, she was so lost in her reveries. Adjusting at the last moment, she turned up the drive and pedaled her way silently past the sleeping house toward the garage. Only the light on the porch and the lights in the front room were shining.

Ned closed his car door with a gentle click before following her on foot, crossing the yards between them to intercept her before she went inside. She climbed off the bicycle and leaned it up against the corner of the garage. For a moment he watched her as she stood, still facing the bike, absently stroking the seat, her mind obviously somewhere far, far away.

"Where have you been?" His harsh words twirled her around faster than his hands could have. "Your parents have been frantic."

Lilly backed into the bike. Her hands were at her throat, her eyes wide. "Ned!" she gasped. "You—you scared me!" She stood up straighter. The wistfulness was wiped from her face, replaced now by annoyance. "What are you doing here?"

"I've been searching for you." He stepped closer. "Your mother called me, worried that you hadn't returned for dinner. I've been looking ever since."

His explanation did not impress her. "It's not your business," she stated firmly. Her mind, however, started cataloguing the evening's prior events, checking off possible places where she could have been observed by Ned during his sojourn to save her. "Thank you for your help, but I'd better go in and find my parents." She lowered her eyes and started past him. "Good ni—"

He grabbed her roughly by the upper arms. "Hold on a minute, Lilly. You owe me an explanation. Where have you been for the last six hours?"

She tried to shrug him off, but his jarring speech continued. "Elaine said you left her house this afternoon. It's almost eleven o'clock. Don't tell me you've been 'exploring' on that bike the whole time?" His anger singed her face.

"Let me be!" Lilly cried, raising her arms to break away. The light over the door flashed on at that moment, causing Ned to abruptly let go.

She'd been so intent on pulling away that his sudden release caused her to whirl away from him as if she'd been pushed. She caught herself before she fell, using the momentum to carry herself toward her home and away from his anger.

The double-sectioned kitchen door opened. White café curtains at the top swished in a froth. The lighting within framed her mother's silhouette, just inside. "Lillian, is that you?" she called. Her tone sounded anxious. "Are you all right?"

Ned hastened forward. "Everything's fine, Mrs. Bradstreet. She's safe and sound."

Lilly leapt up the concrete steps and brushed past her mother.

"Lillian! What on earth!" Mrs. Bradstreet turned to observe her daughter's retreating figure catapult itself further into their house. Ned moved to reassure her, but she gave scant thanks for his help. She closed the kitchen door, clicked off the outside light, and followed after her daughter.

Ned was left in darkness. He strode back to his coupe, cursing at his inability to wrestle out the answers he thought he deserved to hear. He'd get to the bottom of it, he muttered to himself; there'd be no more nonsense like this once they were engaged and married.

A FEW MORNINGS later, heavy clouds swept down to rest above the treetops. Silver sheets of rain drew runny lines between furrows in the fields. Fog nestled in low areas. In town, folks drove with their headlights on. Most around these parts welcomed the moisture, but others gauged and calculated it obsessively, anxious about too much or not enough or all at the wrong time.

Ned didn't pay too much attention to things like weather. His concerns lay in black, penciled columns, bound in journals kept neatly behind his desk. He dealt in drawing up amortization charts and calculating interest. He thought a lot about making the most of what he'd been given, and recognized that his vigilance and sense of duty had kept this bank afloat during times that, as anyone with a brain could have predicted, had caused neighboring institutions to go belly-up during the Dust Bowl years.

Jesse Dorn stopped by about mid-morning. His boots tracked a muddy trail as he strode through the bank's lobby to Ned's private office. The secretary's desk outside his door was abandoned, but that wouldn't have mattered: Jesse helped himself through the door to settle into the chair across from Ned's desk. "Need to visit with you a bit about my note. You know it's due in three weeks, but this rain's going to mess with my schedule." He leaned back, waiting for Ned to pay him the attention he deserved.

Ned closed his black ledger and allowed the farmer to continue.

Jesse cleared his throat and looked at the young banker directly. "You reckon we could work something out, maybe delay that payment for a while?"

At first, Ned didn't respond; he simply leaned back and steepled his long fingers, holding the other man's gaze. He lifted one side of his mouth in a slight smile, as though he savored the power and ability he had to determine the future course of this small town and its inhabitants. Leaning forward, he dropped his clasped hands to his desk blotter. "What did you have in mind, Jesse?"

"Well, I reckon you got enough capital with Frederick's payment to keep yourself going, and I could sure use that time to be sure my corn's ready." He paused to find a more comfortable position. "I'd consider it a personal favor if you'd be willing to extend that note a bit longer." The words were out. Jesse leaned back to see how they'd land.

Ned took more time than was generally considered good manners before he responded. "What's in it for the bank? What return do we get on this little extension?"

Jesse pretended that the question caught him off guard, but both men knew his act was just that, an act. Negotiations had begun. "Why, what do you mean? I'm good for it! Ain't my business here reward enough for you?"

"Here's how it stands, Jesse," Ned's face was implacable, his words as perfectly creased and sharp as his suit. "I can't give out favors to everyone, or I'll lose that capital I've been entrusted by the bank's board to maintain. To grow. This is a business here, same as yours. What I do for you, I'll have to do for Johnson and Blumberg and Frederick, because I know they'll hear about it or figure it out. And that can't happen." He paused for effect. "I won't let it happen."

"But you know how much I got invested," Jesse protested, leaning forward and placing his burly forearm atop Ned's clean desk. "You're the one who told me to take advantage of the farms that weren't making it, to buy them up and increase my own worth. What good's that going to do me, if I can't get a few extra weeks to get your cash back to you?" His tone dropped to the verge of pleading for this extra consideration, this little bit of grace, to help him maintain his place in this world. "Hell, you know I ain't going to tell no one, and you know I'm good for it."

Ned's hooded eyes did not blink.

Jesse gave it one last try. "I'd be willing to meet you halfway, if that's what it takes. I got a cousin in Saude, he drives down South every now and then; I could get some of those fine cigars you like, or that bourbon—"

"Please. Enough," Ned interrupted. "Don't debase yourself, Jesse." He stood and buttoned his coat as he moved around to the front of his desk. "You're a businessman, as I am. I'm sure we can come to some sort of agreement."

He nodded to the office door behind Jesse. "Why don't you close that, so we can continue our conversation in private."

Dani

18

Trucks and cars were parked in neat rows all across the field next to Swenson's barn; both sides of his drive were bracketed by vehicles. The auction looked to be a fair sight more popular than Dani had expected. Then again, there wasn't a lot by way of entertainment around Crestview, she thought, nosing her pickup between an old Ford half-ton and a sensible Buick. She hoped she didn't know the driver of the sedan—she had to squeeze her truck right next to the driver's side. She reminded herself to be one of the first to leave.

She met up with Burt at the line leading to the registration table. "Morning, Burt. What's going on?"

"Aw, I almost forgot; you're still a newcomer, ain't you?" Burt joked, his eyes crinkling behind his dirty lenses. He wasn't wearing a Farm & Feed shirt today, though the one he did have on was equally as greasy as his work duds. "We got to register before we get the number." He gestured to a card table set up in the barnyard. "You show the gal your driver's license and your proof of funds, and she gives you a number so's you can place your bid." He tongued a hunk of chaw to his other cheek. "That way it's all legal." He rubbed his chins with his free hand and smiled at her.

"I didn't know you had to have your money set ahead of time." Dani didn't have any money to purchase a piece of land, anyway; after she'd driven by the property, she'd sat down and gone over her dismal finances. Even if she did manage to make a profit on her crop this first year, the money would be used for buying seed and tuning up the tractor next spring. If she had any left over, she wanted to see about investing in a new cultivator, as the one that had come with the property she rented was on its last legs. There was virtually no way a newcomer could find his or her way into owning their own land until they'd built up enough collateral for a loan, and as any such "extra" would go first into the care and keeping of that land, Dani was not likely to be a property owner in her lifetime. She told herself that it was enough for her to be able to live on the small piece she now called home, even if it involved paying the real owner for the privilege.

"I'm here to see how it's done," she finally responded. "Are you interested in the property yourself?"

"Naw, just helping Llo—just helpin' out a friend," he caught himself. "Going to help the bidding, if needs be." The line moved forward. Burt was next up, a rather large woman finishing her check-in ahead of him. Dani hoped this wasn't the driver of the car she'd blocked in the field.

Burt stepped up for his number. Dani wished him good luck and left, making her way across the yard toward the flatbed the auctioneer had commandeered. Neighbors formed a semi-circle at its front. The auctioneer, wearing the requisite checkered shirt tucked into pressed jeans, had a belt buckle the size of a small plate just barely peeking out from under the round expanse of his belly. It looked uncomfortable, pressing into the man's flesh when he bent down to untangle a microphone cord. He straightened himself and barked at his assistant, or perhaps a son—his dress mirrored the older man's down to the gigantic buckle. The young guy made the adjustment and the microphone screeched to life.

The auctioneer's velvety voice contrasted the country look of his get-up: "Five minutes, folks. We're gonna get this started on time. Find your places, please, and let's get this show on the road." He sounded more like a high school principal or a prison warden than a salesman. He clicked off the sound and wiped his broad, sweating forehead with a kerchief he'd plucked from somewhere. Dani was thoroughly entertained and would have continued to stand and watch if Bud hadn't come up behind her.

"Looking to buy, then?" he asked, bushy white eyebrows raising themselves up like arching caterpillars.

"Hi there, Bud. How's Tater doing?" Dani asked in response.

His voice grew gruff. "Things're looking better, thanks." He looked down at his worn work boots.

"I'm sorry about your loss," Dani continued. She didn't want to say too much, especially out here in the open with everyone in the county around, but she thought she should acknowledge the boys and their misfortune regardless. "I'm sad to hear about it."

"Thanks. 'Preciate it." Bud cleared his throat and shifted to a safer topic. "How many people you reckon are here today?"

"Quite a crowd. I haven't been to one of these before. I'm looking forward to seeing how the whole thing works."

"Well, you're in for a treat!" the older man said, his face suddenly lighting up. He leaned in to share a bit of information he'd gleaned on the way in. "Seems we'll be witnessing a wrasslin' match between two strong opponents," he continued. "Jacob wants to add on to his hog operation, and that parcel would be perfect for another lot." He scratched behind his ear. "But that couple that came down a few years back out of Minnesota, can't recall their name, they want the piece because it's right across the road from their home place." Bud actually washed his hands together in the air as he gleefully finished, "Yup, it's gonna get messy!" It looked like he was genuinely looking forward to watching the fight play out.

They turned to face the auctioneer, who was welcoming a woman Dani recognized as the town librarian up to the microphone. She looked grave and serious. The respectful crowd grew quiet, save for some young boys way in the back who were teasing and having a game of tag.

"I'd like to thank you all for coming today," she started. Her face looked sad, but her voice was strong. "Many of you knew Lonny and my sister, and I know he'd be happy today, seeing you here to make sure their land and property are well taken care of." Some of the ladies in the front started a gentle clapping but stopped when no one else joined in. "I hope whoever emerges as the new owner will have a life of prosperity and good fortune." She looked around the group. Many nodded; all eyes were on her. "Good luck, then, and thanks for coming out today." She handed the mic back to the auctioneer. The clapping started again, strong but reserved out of respect for the lady and the land her sister and brother-in-law had loved through their last days.

"Thank you, Mrs. Swenson!" the auctioneer barked, startling the crowd back to its purpose. "Let's get the rules down now, and we'll begin! Here's how it'll go." And with that, he explained the protocol and introduced the spotters who would help him track the bidding process. He added that he'd be starting with the property itself, because a person wouldn't want to bid on the machinery and all until he knew if he'd have the property to use it on. His rationale was met with polite chuckles.

"So here we go then!" he began. "Who'll give me four, see me four, who has four . . ." The words spewed faster and faster, flowing so seamlessly together that Dani lost track of the actual words being shouted. The auctioneer kept track of the bids by noting the numbers the spotters shouted back, prodding his patter to an even more frenzied momentum.

Bud had sidled up to Dani during the intros and stood watching with her, his big arms crossed in front of his bibbed overalls. He chewed on a patch of snoose quietly and didn't say anything until he noticed Burt raising his bid paddle, a few feet ahead and off to the right.

"Fool," he muttered, more to himself than to Dani. "Should'a waited. That ain't going to help." Dani had no idea what misstep Burt had taken, other than to cause the auctioneer to take a breath before taking off on another animated gust.

The paddles' motions became less frequent as the price increased. The auction had become a ping pong volley between two players. Spotters on one side focused on a man Dani didn't recognize, wearing what would pass as "farm appropriate" garb in the suburbs but what the local color in Crestview would label a "city slicker" outfit. He was grim-faced, flipping the paddle up like a sword every time his bid was overtaken. Jacob Dorn was the other bidder. He was surrounded by guys from the café and seemed to be enjoying the parlay, joking with the others while raising his paddle with the lassitude of a fancy Southern woman and her fan. The rest of the crowd bent their heads back and forth between the two bidders in rhythm. Dani was so wholly absorbed that she didn't notice the woman who'd come up next to her elbow until the gavel came down and the men around Jacob clapped him on the shoulder in congratulation.

The woman spoke to Dani a second time. "I said, is this your first auction?"

Dani whipped around to see the librarian standing at her side. "I'm sorry! I didn't hear you at first." One corner of her mouth crooked upward in a self-deprecating smile. "That obvious, huh?"

The librarian smiled back. "You do seem entranced. I think it would be more entertaining to me if it wasn't my sister's home that's being disposed of." She looked away, sadness behind her smile. "It's meant to be. It's time." She shook her gray curls, then set her shoulders back. The blue eyes behind her dated frames refocused on Dani again. "I want to ask you something," she started. "I don't want to be presumptuous, but if you have free time now, before harvesting starts, could I hire you to help me clean out and dispose of the furnishings and boxes from the house? I imagine Jacob Dorn will be pulling down the buildings before too long, and I'd like to make sure my sister Elaine's things are taken care of properly before he begins." She waited a moment, then said, "I couldn't pay you much, but I'd be happy to let you take your pick of her furniture or kitchen items. Whatever you'd want. I imagine a single lady like you might be able to use a few more household things."

Dani reached out to her before thinking. Her touch on the older woman's shoulder seemed to pull her back into reality again, back to the noise and the auctioneer's raucous voice and the smell of diesel fuel as another farm machine started up to be demonstrated. "Sorry, I didn't mean to scare you." Dani's voice was quiet. "I'd be glad to help. Just tell me when."

Truth be told, she didn't really need to be looking at the clock each day at three to open the bottle of Jack she kept out on the kitchen counter. She'd thought a bit about getting a dog, but hadn't gotten the momentum up to actually go out to find one. She slept late most mornings; she ate what could be heated in a pan on the stovetop. This auction was the second time she'd ventured out into society since she'd heard the news about Geoff. The confrontation with Jacob she'd witnessed at Susie's earlier in the week hadn't helped her mood much, either. Mrs. Swenson's invitation actually sounded appealing to Dani. She said she'd be ready to get to work whenever Mrs. Swenson was prepared to start.

Lilly

19

THE MORNING SUNRISE boasted brilliant colors through Lilly's open window. The birds trilled each other messages from their lofty branches. Lilly had slept well and woke with her sights set on what was ahead. She'd stopped looking inward; she didn't feel anxious or uncertain anymore.

Lilly's mother believed in a hot breakfast every morning, even in summer. The family of three met at the table daily and gathered once again in the evening for dinner in the dining room. "Good morning, Papa," Lilly called as she made her way into the dining room, kissing her father on his gray temple and flouncing into her breakfast chair. For the first time in a long time, he brought his gaze to her own right away, returning her greeting (perhaps not as cheerfully) before resuming the studied dissection of his sausage meat. Mrs. Bradstreet brought a covered plate to rest in front of her daughter, careful not to miss a single detail of her demeanor. Her eyes had been moving, her brain furiously knitting, since she'd observed Lilly being so roughly handled by Ned the evening before. She'd anticipated that her daughter would be trailing the remains of that indignity behind her well through the next day, and her careful plan for the morning review of the situation was a bit dashed by Lilly's unexpected buoyancy. "Well, good morning to you, Lillian! You're certainly bright and bushy-tailed today!"

"I was thinking that we should take that shopping trip soon," Lilly replied. "There are only a few weeks left before I leave, and I have a few more things on my list that I'd like to have with me." She helped herself to a piece of toast and began chewing, focused on something other than what was in front of her.

Her father continued to cut the items on his plate into equal, bite-sized squares. For once, his attention wasn't captivated by hybridizing grain. His wife had woken him late last night and apprised him of what he'd missed, sharing her concerns about the mistake their daughter was making. *Sidestepping a husband who could keep her comfortable and established for the lark of a college adventure?* Now he watched his daughter like a new project, his laser-like focus monitoring her actions, moods, and words. Lilly was oblivious to his redirected attentions.

"You've decided on your coursework, then?" he asked after carefully wiping his lips with a linen napkin.

Lilly seemed surprised but pleased by his unexpected attention. "Yes. I've chosen two of the courses the college recommends, Freshman Composition and World History, but for my third class, I—"

"To whom are these courses recommended?" he interrupted.

Lilly thought for a moment. "They're part of the general freshman program. I think the credits can be applied to another degree, though, when the student decides on her major."

Mr. Bradstreet grew quiet. His wife, who never stopped her frenetic activities around the kitchen most mornings, was also still and silent. Lilly felt the weight of their unusual attention and unspoken questions. They were upset about Ned and her refusal of his proposal. Their dissatisfaction showed through the words they did not say.

Lilly's father put his napkin next to his plate, leaving the rest of his breakfast uneaten. Kissing his wife on the cheek, another unusual behavior, he left the kitchen. The charged atmosphere unnerved Lilly, but she was determined to push through the layers of judgment and control she perceived.

"Are you free to drive to Decorah with me today?" Lilly asked her mother.

"That sounds nice. We could shop this morning and eat lunch at the Winneshiek before we return." Mrs. Bradstreet loved to visit the hotel, made famous by a recent visit by Norway's king and queen. She removed her husband's plate and utensils from the table. "Would you like to invite Elaine to accompany us?"

"Elaine's not going to Iowa State after all."

"Hmm." Mrs. Bradstreet grew still. "What changed?"

Lilly got up and brought her own dishes and uneaten breakfast to the sink. "She's decided to work for her father, instead." She set her dishes into the soapy water. "I think her family's financial situation caused her to make new plans."

"Ah." Her mother seemed strangely satisfied with Lilly's answer. "Just us then." The two were out the door and on the road in forty minutes.

THE DAY PASSED quickly, and, to Lilly's mind, the interactions with her mother were smooth and uncomplicated. They seemed to agree on appropriate clothing; they purchased a lovely bed linen set; Mrs. Bradstreet insisted that Lilly choose a handsome leather satchel to carry her books and papers. They ate at the Winneshiek Hotel and were served by an ancient gentleman in white gloves. Even the drive to and from the city was lovely: the air was clean and bright, and the two chatted about classes, Lilly's move-in date, and living in a dormitory. Ned's name did not come up. Cisco's name never left her thoughts.

They arrived back in Crestview late in the afternoon, and Mrs. Bradstreet urged Lilly to drive to her father's shed to pick him up for dinner while she put their meal together. Lilly welcomed the chance to drive alone, the windows all fully open, warm August air blowing in. The sun on her forearm made her whole body glow.

She drove slowly around the corner by the Lutheran cemetery, treacherous if a truck or tractor was hugging the curve from the opposite lane. Dust spirals danced in her wake. It was a beautiful summer afternoon, the kind a person would like to keep forever, especially when the cold winds blew snow from every angle and one could feel her body withdraw into itself to stay warm.

The crops in the field next to her father's shed had grown since her visit last week. Great green stalks towered upward, thrusting majestically toward the sun. The slightest gusts set their long-fingered leaves to pointing and waving at one another. Lilly watched the soldierly rows march by, precise and shady cool, and was tempted to run through their leafy tunnels again as she had when she was younger. She was so intent on her observations that she started to drive past the entrance to the shed and had to stop and reverse the car before turning in. She was embarrassed to see a blue truck drawing near as she did so.

The truck followed her as she coasted to the shed's entrance, pulling to a stop on the other side. She slammed her door shut and moved quickly toward the shed's steel door, hoping to avoid the driver and his sure-to-follow comments about "women drivers."

"Good afternoon, Miss Lillian." The smooth, deep voice made her pause. She turned, her heart two steps ahead of her.

"Hello, Cisco," she said, a smile working its way up her face. He stepped out of the truck, his hat shading his blue eyes. His smile sent warm sunshine directly through her veins. "I was hoping no one had seen my mistake on the road," she continued. "It must have looked like an idiot was driving back there."

"Or someone who was simply enjoying the beauty of the day," he answered. His hand rested on the hood of the truck. She stepped away from the building, moving closer to the worker to continue their conversation.

"It *is* beautiful. I love days like these! If I could, I'd—"

The shed door opened behind them. Lilly turned to see her father standing there, watching the two of them.

"Hello!" Guilt about being caught caused her face to redden. "Mother sent me to bring you home. She's making dinner tonight, so you won't have to eat cold cuts." Lilly chastised herself for sounding so, well, school-girlish. She'd thought she was so grown up riding through the moonlight after coming upon Cisco, and now—now she felt about fourteen years old.

"I'll be home soon, then," her father replied. "I need to stop at the post office first." He nodded to Cisco and then shifted his gaze back to his daughter. "Will you be coming along?"

"Of course," Lilly answered. She didn't feel brave enough to try to meet Cisco's eyes. She hurried back to her own vehicle, thinking furiously all the while about being independent and bold and away on her own.

Cisco's low voice broke in. "Mr. Bradstreet, I'd be glad to drop off your mail for you. I'm heading through town myself."

Lilly heard her father's response as she settled herself in the driver's seat of her own car—he thanked Cisco but said he'd rather do it himself, as there was some question about postage and he needed to be sure he'd added enough to get the material safely to the university. She noted that his voice didn't have its usual warmth. Lilly's face grew warm yet again, embarrassed to have been seen talking so cordially with a foreigner, then embarrassed at herself for caring so deeply about her father's silent censure.

She snuck a peek out her window to see Cisco's reaction as she turned the ignition key. Looking openly at her, he touched the brim of his hat, dipped his chin in her direction, then bade both her and her father a good evening. His step toward his truck was confident and bold. He moved like a man who knew who he was. Lilly envied how easy things were with Cisco. His confidence buoyed her.

She sat herself upright and prepared to return to her home for dinner.

She didn't notice that her father continued to watch her, as she'd watched Cisco. She didn't see that Mr. Bradstreet remained, still, at the side of the shed with his clutched envelopes in one hand, watching the dust settle after she and the Mexican foreman had both driven away.

Dani

20

IT WAS ALREADY humid when Dani parked her truck under a large cottonwood at Mrs. Swenson's sister's place. The meager shade the tree provided did nothing to cut through the moist, still air that clamped down with the subtlety of a large, wet blanket. It was early, too—Dani imagined that they'd get a few hours in at most before it grew too hot to finish. That was all right with her. She was waiting for harvest, same as the other farmers, but where they had machines to tune and fences to fix, a renter like Dani found herself with more free time than she knew what to do with. She was tired of being in a funk but didn't know what to do to escape it.

Mrs. Swenson must have heard the truck door slam, because she opened the screen door and met Dani as she trotted up the porch steps. The house was in disrepair: the porch floor sagged and was missing a board in the corner, where it looked as though rain had flowed unimpeded for years. The paint was practically gone, faded or flaked off, but Dani could see signs of careful attention in the way the white siding met the dull green of the window frames. It was sad that the house had fallen into such a sorry condition, and Dani wished once again that she had the means to fix this treasure before it was toppled into a heap of scraps to be hauled away and burned.

Mrs. Swenson didn't seem to have any romantic ideas at all about the house. She stepped over a gaping hole where another porch board was missing as if it were nothing. She and Dani met under a snaky black wire that probably used to connect to a porch light. Mrs. Swenson greeted her young assistant, all businesslike and energized to begin.

Returning inside and glancing down at the paper list she held, she warned Dani that there was another flooring issue at the back of the kitchen. "We won't have to worry much about that room, though," she continued. "It seems Lonny gave away many of their kitchen items already. Perhaps he wasn't a cook?" Her voice trailed off. Her off-kilter step remained brisk and firm.

The interior of the entryway was dark. Dingy wallpaper flopped in strips down the walls like faded, sagging soldiers. An old coat tree, missing a limb, stood dejectedly next to a small bench with faded, gold velveteen fabric. The main living area, more modern, was on the left: a brown corduroy sofa along the wall faced an old TV cabinet, a low table covered in stacks of papers and books standing between them. A saggy recliner was hunched against the far wall, in front of a floor-to-ceiling bookcase filled with any number of books, empty flower pots, pictures, and other doodads too smashed together to determine individually. To their right, they passed a dining table covered in newspapers and magazines; cardboard boxes ringed the table and sat atop all of the dining chairs but one. A dusty brass chandelier hung over the mess. It was turned on, but only one lightbulb of the five was working.

"As you can see," Mrs. Swenson continued, "we have our work cut out for us." She stopped suddenly, toward the back of the dark hall, and turned to Dani. "You don't have to stay until the bitter end, you know; your help with a few things I can't manage would be great."

"I don't mind," Dani said and smiled. "I've got as much time as you need."

Mrs. Swenson returned Dani's smile, then resumed her disjointed march to the back of the house. They entered a yellow kitchen, bright in the morning sun. A round dinette had been cleared of paper. Dani saw brown shopping bags, full, near that low spot she'd been warned about. Two chairs were pulled out and a red thermos sat on the table between two mugs. "I brought coffee. I didn't have any cream, though; I hope you'll be all right with that."

"No problem," she replied. "What's the plan?" She held out her hand to receive a mug of strong, black coffee and waited for direction.

"Well," the librarian said, pouring a half-cup for herself, "I've taken a quick inventory and have determined that we have four areas to 'conquer' before the wrecking ball comes."

"Is that what Jacob said, then?" Dani asked, her free hand resting on the ladderback chair nearest to her. "He's taking it down?"

"He told me after Mass on Sunday that he'd like to get in here next weekend to tear down what he can. He has a crew coming up from Des Moines the following Monday to shut off the utilities and bury the foundation, and wants to save some money by making the area as flat as he can before they arrive." She took a sip and set her cup down. "I don't know if we can realistically get through it all before then, so I think we should concentrate on what's most important. He paid the money; he can deal with what's left." A gleam entered her countenance then—not of malice, but distrust, or perhaps dislike. Dani expected there was a history between the two of them that was making its way out of Mrs. Swenson's careful demeanor, despite her staid and practical control. She thought about asking for a little clarification, but knew better than to jump right in.

"Sounds good to me. Where do you want me to start?" Dani drained the rest of the strong brew and placed the mug in the kitchen sink. Old spoons and bowls were stacked already in a cardboard box resting on a stained draining board.

"Well, before it gets too warm, I think we should start up in the attic." Dani raised her eyebrows. Mrs. Swenson reassured her, "We, or you, can bring down anything we need to go through. It's cooler here for now, and we can quit when it gets to be too much." She added her mug to the sink and exited the kitchen onto a dark porch in back. "Why don't you head up first, and I'll follow behind on the ladder? I can try to point out what looks important enough to bring down. I can't get all the way up there myself, or I would've done so before." Her voice quieted. "I suppose there's nothing of much value, other than some old pictures and letters." It sounded as though she'd finished the thought more for herself than for Dani.

The older woman began tugging on a string, trying to lower a folding ladder which was obviously warped and squeaky from disuse.

"Here, why don't you let me?" Dani asked. She grasped the clothesline rope and pulled. It disintegrated in her hand. "Shoot!"

"Don't worry; we've a ladder here. Somewhere." Mrs. Swenson retreated to the kitchen. More clanks and murmuring issued when she opened the back door. Dani helped her drag in an old wooden ladder from the back porch. They hefted it back together to rest against the wall under the trapdoor. Dani tested each rung before putting her full weight on it. Eventually, she was able to peel down the front edge of the attic panel with her fingertips. The hinges inside continued squealing as Dani reversed slowly back down the ladder, opening the door wider with each lowered step.

By the time they'd gotten the trap ladder unfolded, they decided it was too risky to use, so Dani placed the wooden ladder up into the ceiling opening instead. She cautiously climbed up once more. Reaching the top, she swept her hand around for a firm surface to place her weight on and almost broke through a sheet of plaster at the top. "Mrs. Swenson?"

She was right there below the attic opening. "Can you see a light or a chain to pull?"

"Nope, I can't see a thing," Dani responded. She should have brought a flashlight. She seemed to be a half-step or more behind lately.

"Not a problem; here." Mrs. Swenson handed up a square, plastic-cased flashlight that must have weighed five pounds, of the same vintage as the old red thermos. "I put in fresh batteries last night." She pronounced the word 'bat-reys', the first time Dani had ever heard the librarian using a word from the local dialect.

Dani spied a metal trunk set off from the entrance, resting atop two joists; that was it. This attic had never had a floor put in, so there wasn't anywhere to place boxes or bags: they'd fall right through the thin ceiling plasterboard. She was able to slide the trunk closer to the attic entrance, but had no idea of how to get the thing through the porthole and safely back to the ground. She shared her concern with Mrs. Swenson, who vanished into the kitchen and came back again with a hank of stout cord. "Goodness knows what they were saving this for," she said, reaching up to hand the coil to Dani.

She climbed all the way through the attic entry with the rope, hoping the joists were solid enough to bear her weight. She shimmied across them to the trunk and tested both handles to see which was most likely to hold; the cord wasn't long enough to loop around both. Tying off one end of the cord and checking the trunk's latch to be sure it was closed, she pushed the box toward the opening. "Mrs. Swenson? Stay away for a moment now, I don't know how well this is going to work."

The woman's muffled reply floated up, indecipherable. Dani wrapped the other end of the cord around her hand, grasped a section with both fists, and tipped the trunk into the opening with her feet in front of her. It teetered for a moment and then, with a clang, slapped heavily onto the rungs of the ancient ladder. The ladder groaned but held. Dani slowly worked the trunk down, using the ladder like a slide. She both heard and felt the shifting of its contents and braced herself for any sudden accident.

There was none. It arrived on the floor at an angle. Mrs. Swenson's delighted voice flew upwards. "It's Elaine's! Oh, I'm so glad you were able to retrieve it!" Dani lowered herself down the ladder and hopped the last few feet over the tilted trunk. Mrs. Swenson had gone to the kitchen for a wet cloth, which she used to wipe off grime and dust after Dani righted the heavy case.

"Where would you like it?"

"Let's see—are you able to get it back into the kitchen? I could sift through it there." She disappeared, assuming Dani had the strength to move or slide the object herself.

Dani clumsily wrangled the trunk to rest at the front of the table. Mrs. Swenson gathered a number of brown grocery bags and held these out to Dani as she settled the case. "Would you start in the front room?" she asked, holding out the bags to the sweating young woman. "I'm sure most of what's out there is ready for the burn can. Put aside anything you question; I'll deal with that later. If it's really important, it will find its way back to me anyway, so don't hesitate about tossing it. I'd like that room and the dining room done today."

Dani had imagined this day would be spent lugging furniture and moving large objects; after the trunk episode, she felt almost let down as she trudged back into the front room. It had grown warmer. A moldy stink hovered under one window on the same wall as that hole in the porch outside. She looked from pile to pile, deciding where to begin. When her knee accidentally nudged a musty recliner, poofs of dust and dirt wafted up to the ceiling. She'd start here, she decided, and work her way to the middle. Maybe after that she could think of an excuse to leave.

It didn't take as long as she'd imagined. Dani began pulling newspapers and old magazines first, loading as many as she could into each brown grocery sack. When that was finished, she fashioned two piles out of the leftover papers: a short stack of what looked like bills from the table next to the recliner, and another, taller tower of receipts and old manuals and county newsletters. These she smashed into grocery bags and, her task completed earlier than she anticipated, began hauling them to the backyard. Each time she passed Mrs. Swenson inside, she saw that the librarian was engrossed in a different world entirely. She appeared to be reading from a stack of letters.

Right before lunch, she finished toting the final bag to the burn pile. She approached the kitchen door from the yard and knocked gently, so as not to startle Mrs. Swenson from her reverie.

It didn't work. "Oh!" the older woman gasped. "There you are. Are you finished already?"

Dani apologized for surprising her and assured her that the two front rooms were now free of the paper that had cluttered each surface there. "Do you want me to start on the furniture, or should I begin boxing up the books?" she asked.

"Let's take a break," Mrs. Swenson responded, folding a thin, flower-edged paper and placing it on top of her square leather purse. "I've brought sandwiches, if that suits you, or you could head back to town, if you'd prefer."

Dani found that she was actually energized from the morning's labor, satisfied about being productive after a long stretch of inactivity. "I'd take a sandwich, if you have enough," she answered. "I'd just as soon get started on your next job before it gets much hotter. I can come back earlier tomorrow to finish."

Her younger eyes caught the older woman's—Dani could see that they were strained and tired behind her dated eyeglasses. "Thank you. I do appreciate your help." She grew quiet; her hands, in the midst of unpacking the food, became still. "I didn't expect to get caught up in . . . never mind, it's not important." She drew herself up and handed Dani a meat-and-cheese combination on a paper napkin. She started eating her own sandwich and, after a few bites, continued. "I didn't expect that my sister would have kept some of the things she did in that trunk. Opening that this morning has been like opening a Pandora's Box of sorts, and I feel a little discombobulated."

Dani hadn't heard that word before, but knew exactly how it felt—it was how she'd been feeling since learning about Geoff. Nothing seemed to fit quite right into the spaces of before. Things had changed their shapes.

They ate quietly and quickly. Dani wiped her hands, drained the rest of the soda Mrs. Swenson had provided, and stood. "I'd like to get some of that furniture out into the pickup and bring it by the church on my way through town. I heard they're having a rummage sale this fall; maybe they'll take it."

Mrs. Swenson nodded. "I wish I could help."

"Don't worry. If the house were going to be saved, I'd worry about scratching the floor or walls, but as it is, well, I think I can wrangle those pieces out fine on my own."

The older lady smiled. "Thank you." She paused. "Thank you for coming out here today."

Dani laid the cushions from the furniture in her truck bed first, thinking they'd stay held down by the bulk of the furniture's frames. Returning to the front of the old farmhouse again, she slid and twisted and pulled the sofa and old recliner out and, with the help of that clothesline rope, up into the bed of her truck. By then she was wet with sweat and about ready to head back to town.

She searched in the back of the house for a hose or spigot to rinse off before saying goodbye to Mrs. Swenson. Finding neither, she settled for mopping up her face with a kitchen towel hanging on the back railing. She opened the screen door and brought the towel inside with her, planning to rinse it out and hang it up again for tomorrow's use.

Mrs. Swenson wasn't at the table. The items from the trunk had been sorted: letters in one pile on the tabletop, old baby clothes and pictures in another, and two scrapbooks, pulling apart at the binding, placed carefully on the seat of the other kitchen chair.

"Mrs. Swenson?" Dani called. She heard a thump from upstairs. A voice threaded its way down, saying she'd be with Dani in another minute.

Dani collapsed into the chair she'd used at the start of the day. Her eyes roamed the tabletop as she thought about the long, cool shower waiting for her at home.

Her attention was suddenly seized by the signature scrawled at the bottom of an old letter on top of the pile: it read, *As ever, Lilly* in an elegant cursive hand.

Lilly. Her mind raced—had this been written by Lilly Bradstreet, the woman she'd uncovered in her library search? Dani heard the plumbing moan from the floor above. She took the time to wipe her hands once again on the towel before pulling the letter off the pile:

. . . and it's been more pleasant than I would have imagined. Just think, I'm helping to put together the ammunition our boys need to fight those awful men! I never thought I'd be able to do it ten hours a day, but the other gals have been swell and we visit during our shifts (when the boss man isn't around!) and it's altogether better than I had hoped.

Lainey, if it hadn't been for you, I don't know if I could've made it here to—

Mrs. Swenson's footsteps sounded down the steps. Dani heard her voice and panicked, hastily putting the letter back on the pile before the older lady entered the room and caught her snooping.

"What was that?" Dani managed to say, moving to position herself by the back door.

Mrs. Swenson entered the room, her words preceding her. "I said, I'm so glad that you . . ."

Her voice faded away, her eyes scanning the distance between the table, the letter, and Dani, red-faced, standing a short step away.

Lilly

21

LILLY MET ELAINE at their usual table at the café the next morning after breakfast. The girls ordered iced tea and shared a brownie: Elaine was conscious of gaining weight, she said, and Lilly was too wound up to feel like eating.

"Lainey, you have to swear that you won't tell anyone, even Lonny, about this," she began in a hushed voice. Elaine was more than used to these admonitions, having repeated such promises since childhood. She vowed to maintain Lilly's latest secret and took a corner of the frosted chocolate, settling herself in to absorb the latest development in the drama that was Lilly.

"I've had the most eye-opening experience!" she began. Her bubbly personality was having a difficult time staying seated. "Do you know that man my father hired as foreman this season, that dark man with the blue truck?"

"The Mexican?" Elaine stopped chewing. She didn't even bother to cover her lips as she responded.

"Well yes, I guess so," Lilly answered. "He's not just 'a Mexican,' Lainey, for Pete's sake." She frowned for a second, but couldn't wait any longer to go on. "I've been talking with him, you know, here and there, and—"

"What do you mean, you've been talking with a Mexican?" Elaine's face was a stone, her neat eyebrows drawn so tightly together they looked like one straight serious line. "You know better than to talk to them, Lilly. They're not trustworthy. My dad says they're dirty and lazy." She dropped both hands to her lap but continued to aim her displeasure across the table. "If it wasn't for this call-up taking our own boys, we wouldn't even have them in this town anymore. My dad says——"

Her speech was cut off by Lilly's fevered reply. "Elaine. You don't know. You haven't talked to any, or spent time with any, to know for yourself." She pushed on. "You're only repeating what your dad told you." As the last words left her lips, though, Lilly wondered if this comment might have been a little too much.

When Elaine did reply, her voice was chilly. "I will agree with you, Lilly. I have repeated what I've heard, but I haven't had any experience with any of them, myself." Her tone warmed only slightly as she leaned in closer. "But that doesn't mean it's not the truth. You don't know, either, Lilly. You shouldn't be talking to people we don't know, especially the kind who aren't from around here." She reorganized the cutlery at the side of her paper placemat. "And what happened with Ned? Have you seen him, since the dance?"

"No." Lilly sat back. "And I'm not going to."

"But why not?"

The other tables in the café were empty—it was an hour past coffee and not yet lunchtime. Neither girl had noticed that both the cook from the back and Carole, the waitress, were watching their argument from behind the serving counter. The latter couldn't endure the standoff any longer. She grabbed a pitcher and hustled out to their table as if nothing were amiss. "Would either of you like a refill?" she trilled. She looked from frozen face to frozen face. A slight thaw grudgingly began at the waitress's presence.

"No, thank you," began Elaine, as Lilly simultaneously asked for a half-glass. Carole poured. The two girls looked at one another, ready to challenge the impasse as soon as the waitress left the table. Carole took her time.

Lilly began. "Elaine." She paused, attempting to gather the right words into a true reflection of what had sprung up inside her. "I don't know how to explain this to you." Her words, to her ears, sounded naive and unformed.

Fumbling with the paper napkin, pressing it into the drips on the table, Lilly stumbled on. She summarized the awkward rejection of Ned's proposal, her mother's fretful response, and her escape to the river. She glossed over the time spent with Cisco, but added enough spice to Ned's nighttime confrontation to earn a satisfying gasp from Elaine.

"It's that I finally feel, well, sure about things for the first time in, I don't know, a long time," Lilly finished. "I don't have to be who they want me to be."

Elaine knew she had a tough job ahead if she wanted to break through Lilly's stubbornness. Her concern about her friend's refusal of Ned was second now to her fear that Lilly saw no reason to ignore the attentions of this stranger. Lilly didn't think she had anything to be ashamed of, but Elaine was determined to persuade her friend of the danger of consorting with that type of person who was here one day and suddenly gone the next.

Dani

22

MRS. SWENSON RETRIEVED a dark bottle of whiskey from under the sink and added some to their coffees. They sat outside on the back steps, the afternoon shade drawing long lines across the neglected lawn, as she unfolded the story of her sister's best friend, Lillian Bradstreet.

"Lilly moved to Minneapolis after she learned she was pregnant, sometime during that first year at Iowa State," Mrs. Swenson said. "She didn't want people to know. In fact, I think the first time they thought something was odd was when she didn't come home for Thanksgiving. That Christmas, when she did arrive, she didn't stay but for a few days."

She looked off into the haze that had slowly settled over the heated fields. Her cup, limp in her right hand, dangled from the end of her wrist. Dani didn't want to disrupt her, but found herself anticipating the moment the tepid liquid inside would spill out over its lip.

After several moments, the silence had continued past the point of Dani's patience—she finally had to cut in. "Did they ever see her again?"

"I don't know about the Bradstreets, but I remember that my sister was upset by Lilly's last visit, later that year or the following, I can't recall." She blinked, looking past the dried brown grass in the yard as if she were describing a scene unfolding in front of her, not the one she'd been a third-party witness to so many years ago. "Elaine was married by then. Her husband was away in the service. After Lilly left that last time, she ran up to her old room and didn't come down for days." She smiled, but without warmth. "Of course, I was much younger, so it might not have been quite as dramatic as that."

Dani gently tried again. "So how did you come to learn all the details?"

Now that the conversation had widened in scope to include her, Mrs. Swenson was able to collect herself. She sat up straight. "My sister, Elaine, was Lilly's best friend since the time the two were little girls."

"Did you know Lilly very well?" Dani asked.

A great vee of Canadian geese flew over, steadfast in their noisy flight to the southwest side of the city, where a body of water offered a night's lodging to them and a few hundred more of their honking relatives. Their ragtag formation needed work: four fellows straggled behind the flying arrowhead, unable to gain the momentum needed to slip into their powerful jet stream. No matter; after a few hours' rest, they'd be strong enough to try again the next day, their journey resuming before the crack of dawn.

"My oldest sister, Susan, and Elaine were born after my parents were married." Eleanor Swenson took a sip of her cold coffee cocktail, then threw the rest out into the dead grass. "I came ten years later—a bit of a surprise, I gather." She smiled a little. "People didn't talk then about their private lives as they do now, you know. I had a little brother, too, Stevie. He was the end of our parents' line."

Dani wanted to sketch out a list of the names and ages of these people and how they were related; they were all becoming a bit muddled in her brain. That, or the late afternoon "coffee" was stronger than she thought.

"I knew Lilly. She came over to our house regularly and was very nice to me and to my brother, who could be a bit of a nuisance. He would spy on the older girls and their dates, or the neighbor families, or people in town. He'd make a big production of sharing his hard-won knowledge with others, but after a while most of the adults tired of his stories. The one time he had something really important to share, no one believed him." She sighed.

Drawn completely into the story, Dani felt more than knew that Mrs. Swenson had more to say. She hoped the older woman had seen enough of her by now to know she was a careful steward of whatever she encountered—the letter-snooping notwithstanding. Dani had learned a lot since moving to Crestview by keeping her eyes open and her mouth closed. She crossed her fingers that Mrs. Swenson would trust her with what she knew.

The tiny wrinkles that creased Mrs. Swenson's eyes relaxed; her shoulders dropped. She took a big breath, a loosening, perhaps, of the tight and heavy load she'd carried alone through the years. She'd been careful to keep the secrets she'd been entrusted with, and now it seemed, through the passing of years and the deliverance of witnesses back to the soil, that it was time to unburden herself.

"Stevie was a great font of information, however it was gleaned." Her eyes teared up. "He died in Vietnam, the same year I started working at the library." She fumbled in her pocket for a tissue. Pressing a crumpled Kleenex to her face, Mrs. Swenson took another deep breath and tried to continue.

"This must be hard for you." Really, Dani had no idea whatsoever about the pangs of loss an older person felt, finding herself the last of her generation, the last of her family line. The last keeper of stories that, frankly, no one else would ever find amusing or memorable or poignant.

"I remember one late summer night the summer that Lilly left *particularly* well, because that was also when Elaine got engaged to be married. It meant that I would be the oldest child in the family—an esteemed position to be in, at eight years old. That night, Stevie came racing into the house to tell us he'd seen Lilly with a Mexican. This was a big deal at the time, you know, because we didn't mix with the workers who came by each spring."

She looked for a place to put her crumpled tissue; finding none, she tossed it into the leggy, overgrown bushes next to the steps. She shrugged, her gentle, wrinkled lips forming a quick smile. "Let Jacob deal with that!"

Mrs. Swenson leaned forward and clasped her hands atop her knees. "He'd gone to the garage earlier, to get his baseball cards from Elaine's bike bag, but Lilly had borrowed the bike again. It was evening, soon turning to dusk, so Stevie had to hurry in order to get his cards and get back home again before our father got angry." She raised her eyebrows and looked at

Dani. "Things were different then. We children were told to stay away from the farm workers. I don't know if it was because they were exotic or strange, or because our parents were truly put off by their ways of doing things; but, as they do, the stories about Mexicans sacrificing children to the gods turned into a 'ghost story' for us kids." She chuckled, but it didn't sound like she was amused. "We did like to scare each other with our stories."

"What happened with Lilly and her . . . ?" Dani's voice fell off. She didn't know how to bring up the subject of an illicit love affair with the proper, careful woman sitting next to her.

"What Stevie told my parents that night was that he'd seen Lilly Bradstreet kissing a Mexican man. They were by the old tree that stood between her father's property and the acreage beside it, past the work shed her dad used for his plants. I'd been listening to the radio—I'll never forget it, because the show I was listening to was not nearly as exciting as the story my little brother was spinning to my parents."

A semi full of hogs for the market chose that moment to rumble past the old Swenson place. The noise cut off their conversation for a few moments. Dani pondered what she'd heard so far, her mind leaping ahead to what might have happened next.

Finally, the roar died down and the story continued. "Stevie said that Lilly had never seen or heard him, even though he'd been shouting her name for blocks. He said he'd lost her at the stop sign, when a truck pulled through. By the time he got his bike going again, she was way ahead of him. That truck was right behind her."

Mrs. Swenson was caught up in her memory. "He almost caught up to her at the tree, when he saw her kissing the Mexican with the shiny boots and the blue truck. He didn't think that Lilly would have been too happy to see him, so he turned around and headed back home. He said he'd rather deal with our father's anger than have Lilly angry at him, but I don't suppose he thought that telling Father would, in effect, do both things at once."

"What do you mean?" Dani picked at a thread sticking out of the frayed seam of her jeans.

"He was probably thinking that Lilly would be upset, I suppose, if she'd caught him 'spying' on her, as he tried to do to her and Elaine on other occasions." She stopped a moment, gathering her next thoughts. "I don't think he knew that Father might pass this development on to Lilly's parents. I think Stevie thought they'd thrash him for being out after dark, but I don't think he imagined that Father might tell the Bradstreets what he'd seen."

She adjusted her plastic glasses more firmly over her ears. "After his confession, my mother took Stevie upstairs for a bath. My father left his newspaper and went out to the kitchen. I was still sitting on the braided rug in front of our radio, hoping to know what might happen next, but my mother reappeared and dragged me upstairs too. She said it was time for me to get ready for bed, though I knew it was far too early." Mrs. Swenson shook her head slowly. "Even then, I knew something was wrong, though I wasn't mature enough to put a finger on it. I knew that being seen with a Mexican man was a bad thing that a good girl wouldn't do."

She pulled on the rickety handrail to rise. "That same night, Stevie and I snuck out of our bedrooms to listen as our parents discussed downstairs what he'd seen. They talked quietly about what to say to Lilly's parents." She untied her faded, floral apron and removed it from her waist. "I don't know much more than that."

Her story and her energy level had both come to an end. Dani had more to ask, but thought she might be pushing too hard if she continued pressuring the older woman for answers. She couldn't help but add one last thing: "That hanging was related to Lilly Bradstreet and her situation, right?"

"I don't know for sure." Mrs. Swenson had gone back into the kitchen. She returned with several old towels and some faded kitchen curtains, handed them to Dani, and asked her to add them to the burn pile. "Perhaps we can talk more about this another time?"

Dani carried the items out back. Light slanting through the trees showed that it was near suppertime.

Returning to the house to say good night, Dani watched Mrs. Swenson through the dusty window: she stood motionless as a fence post, staring at the letters and papers that remained on the round dinette. She looked tired and small.

Dani climbed the back steps, stomping to announce her return.

Mrs. Swenson regained her composure. She asked Dani to come back the following day to finish.

She agreed, then gave Mrs. Swenson a quick hug.

Back in her truck, steering toward home, thoughts swirled in a jumble through her head. Sparse bushes of wild roses lined the far side of the gravel drive. Dani's imagination created and discarded "what-ifs" like the faded coral petals that dropped from the flowers in her wake.

Lilly

23

LILLY WATCHED FOR cars she recognized as she rode her bike back to the river. Orange and purple shades of dusk muted the edges of the darker shadows beneath the biggest trees. She pumped the pedals hard to get to the top of a ridge, then stood to coast down the middle of the gravel where car tires had smoothed a path. There were no plans or messages goading her on, only the nagging need to see him.

Lilly had told her mother that she and Elaine were spending the evening listening to a new record Elaine had gotten, and that she'd be home before ten. She hoped she would be.

Her heart pounded as she pedaled the road. Fresh-cut hay permeated her thoughts with its vibrant aroma. Turned and drying in the hayfield, the blossoms and stems were heavy and sweet, like perfume in the air.

The night grew darker more quickly this time of year, the days shortening as the sun set earlier each day. Children in the streets made the most of the remaining kickball and chasing games left before school and winter set in again. Lilly grinned to herself, thinking that this fall she would be in a completely different world than the kids who were staying home after graduation.

She wondered what that would be like, and how she might spend her winter evenings: perhaps studying in a cozy library nook, or meeting new friends for a late-night snack. Crossing County Road 8, she created imaginary versions of her future roommate. When they had both planned to attend Iowa State, she and Elaine had each agreed to take new roommates with the intention of making at least two new friends right away. In a way, this foresight was a blessing: it meant she'd already had time to plan for the adjustment and was used to the idea of living with someone other than her best friend. Even so, it was going to be hard, no doubt, not having Elaine on campus or in her dorm. The road blurred a bit in front of her before she blinked.

Her mood buoyed as the bike's single headlight ran a silver ribbon down the side of the tidy blue pickup parked next to the road. Starting not quite at the bottom of the hill and the migrant camp, two grass-lined paths ran from the gravel into the trees adjacent to the river. An old fishing shack leaned its weathered boards away from the river, the roof lined with moss and pocked with holes.

Lilly pulled her bike to the side and snapped off its silver headlight. The evening was quiet except for a few late-nesting birds and the whispering of some brittle leaves settling down for the night. The earlier wind had given way with the sunset to calm and peace. One lonely star shone from above; soon, it would be joined by its sisters, but for now it sparkled alone in the deepening dusk.

Lilly sat on her bike without dismounting it, watching the star, feeling rather than hearing the comfort of the evening like a blanket around her. She didn't realize, as she stood with her eyes aimed upward, that other eyes were focused on her.

Cisco quietly called out her name. It sounded decadent, slipping between his lips. He came toward her on the darkened path, his dark blue gaze fixed on her own. "I hoped that you would find me here," he said, stopping to stand before her. He waited for her to speak.

"I don't know what draws me," Lilly began.

His brown face creased into a smile; his teeth flashed in the twilight.

"When I see you," she continued, "I don't want to step away. It's like—like I'm coming home." Becoming aware that he had not yet responded, she lowered her head but kept trying to explain what she was feeling. "There is something about . . . being with you, that makes everything stand still." She looked up again.

His eyes had not left her. "I feel this warmth for you as well, Lillian." His smile, however, dimmed. "But you must know: as much as I long for us to grow to know one another . . ." He put his hand on her shoulder.

She felt its weight and warmth and, observing the act as if she were a stranger, saw herself settle into his grasp.

He finished his thought. "You must know that I am bound to move on, when everything is harvested." He removed his hand from her. "I cannot stay."

Lilly plucked it up and returned it to rest on her shoulder. She leaned closer. "But I'm not staying, either," she responded. She kept her palm over his calloused fingers. "I'm going away too, much sooner than you are."

He gently brushed her chin, turning her face to his. "Then we haven't much time after all, do we?"

His touch was so gentle; his eyes, so welcoming. Entrancing. Lilly felt connected to him by the slimmest and strongest of bonds. Every caress caused an uncontainable reaction, one which made her simultaneously weak and desirous of more: she was attuned to this man, his gestures, the scope of all he drew in with his gaze. He quieted her. He tamed the racing thoughts and worries that were her usual partners.

Gently, he reached for her hand. Unfurling her clenching fingers, he slowly bent down and placed a whispered kiss on the inside of her wrist. He paused there for a moment. Her eyes closed involuntarily. She leaned her head back and breathed in, slowly and deeply.

Stepping closer now, Cisco pushed back the hair from her shoulder. He continued to hold her hand so that it felt weightless against his warm skin. Leaning in, so close she could smell his clean, warm scent, he brushed a gentle kiss along her exposed collarbone. He paused to bring her hair to his lips. She heard him inhale slowly, felt his fingers as they gently caressed a tousled lock back to moor it behind her ear.

Lilly opened her eyes. Face to face, eons and mountains and cultures between them, she stared into him—his skin the color of rich earth, of warmth and acceptance; his cloudless eyes not asking but simply waiting, black lashes unblinking.

She drew in her breath and touched her lips to his. Soft, undemanding, but nonetheless a question. His mouth was still, waiting. Waiting for her decision, for her desire to go on. With the slightest pressure, a current of answered questions, of magnetic intuition, passed between them. The pressure between their pressed lips intensified. Lilly thought she could feel his heartbeat and stood from her bike's seat to press her body more closely against him.

Cisco pulled back first, trailing his fingers through her hair as he let it go. He squeezed the hand he held, just once, but then released her.

Her eyes flew open. He was smiling at her, his gaze unwavering. A promise had been made. She'd sealed this promise and, for once, wasn't afraid to go forward to where it might lead her.

Cisco dropped her hand, allowing her the freedom to make her own decision. He turned and moved without hurry down the path to the cabin in the pines.

His was an invitation, not a demand.

She chose to accept.

Dani

24

DANI DIDN'T SLEEP well that night. Her mind ran relentlessly through the information Mrs. Swenson had confided, the story's trail twisting against what she'd learned from the men at the café into an untidy, unruly mess. Somehow, she was sure, there had to be a clear path through the events. She couldn't keep from picking the snags that so stubbornly blocked her way.

Though the sky was still dark, Dani got up from bed and made a strong pot of coffee. The dawn's earliest hues hadn't scrambled to the earth's edges yet; she could see her reflection in the dark window pane over her kitchen sink as easily as looking straight into a mirror. She pulled one side of her hair back and away from her face—she needed a haircut. Looking closer, she thought she'd best ignore the gray hairs peeking out around her temple.

Before the pot finished brewing, Dani grabbed the carafe out of the way to poke an empty cup beneath the dark, fragrant stream. She brought the coffee back with her to the table, where she'd placed a spiral notebook and two ballpoint pens. She wanted to write down what she thought she knew, before she forgot the pieces.

Quite some time later, she pushed back from the notebook. Morning had fully bloomed, the butter-colored sunshine heralding another hot summer day. Dani retraced the timeline she'd sketched across the long side of the front page in her notebook, both the dates she knew and ones she'd guessed at. On the next page, she'd listed the names and locations of the people in the story's web, and through these activities thought she'd made some connections. She was still missing pieces of information, but the general picture was beginning to show through.

No use sitting and sifting any longer. Dani was late to rejoin the demolition work she'd helped with the day before. She showered quickly, grabbed a sweat-stained ball cap from the back of the sofa where it had been left the night before, and drove out to see Mrs. Swenson at the old farmstead.

"Stevie and I were there, you know," she stated.

When she didn't go on, Dani pressed her, gently. "Where? Where did you go?"

Her eyes looked tired. "We saw a man, hanging from that tree. Stevie and I."

"Wait," Dani interrupted. "You saw who hung himself on the Dorns' tree?"

Mrs. Swenson, in turn, patted Dani's hand as if to rein her in. "Let me continue." The two were back at the old farmhouse's dinette, continuing their conversation from the day before. In Dani's absence, the table had been cleared; Elaine Swenson's letters, along with the miscellaneous cookery items, were gone.

"Stevie told me that he'd been out to play by the river, near where the farm workers kept their camp. A truck like old Mr. Dorn's almost ran him off the road." She shook her head side to side. "Stevie had quite a temper! He followed the truck—at a distance, of course—to find out who'd cut him off. It parked next to where the double-headed tree used to stand."

Dani's insides froze. She could hardly draw a breath. "Then what?"

"When he got home, it was well after dinner. He was in trouble and had to go to his room without eating." Mrs. Swenson smiled a bit. "I felt bad, so I brought up a dinner roll and asked him what had happened." The warmth disappeared from her face. "He said he'd seen Mr. Dorn and another big man there with Lilly's Mexican. There was some trouble between them, so he hid until the truck drove away. When he thought he was safe, he stood up from the weeds. He said he saw the body of a man, in the dusk, hanging from the witness tree."

The women looked at each other. Neither one blinked.

"Did you believe him?"

"Of course not! He told stories all of the time, and was forever getting into mischief." Mrs. Swenson responded. "But he was so, so unsettled, this time. Something wasn't right." She wiped a tear from her jawline. "I heard him crying, that night. And I promised him that I'd go back there with him, the next day, so that he could prove that he was telling the truth."

Dani could not get enough air into her lungs. Her senses strained to pick up the last threads of Mrs. Swenson's explanation.

Her gentle smile returned, but her eyes remained sad. "He was telling the truth," she confessed.

Lilly

25

LILLY TRIED TO relax her breathing as she watched the passing road signs for the Ames exit grow close. She blamed her agitation on not being able to say goodbye to Cisco. He hadn't showed up to their last meeting, nor had he forwarded any explanation for staying away.

That last night, waiting for Cisco to show, she'd stayed out late enough to cause her mother to question her whereabouts; Lilly's explanation was that she'd been taking advantage of her last few days at home to bid farewell to high school acquaintances heading off on their own paths. Lilly didn't think her mother had believed her, but she hadn't questioned her daughter. If she had, Lilly didn't believe that she'd have been able to lie—and didn't know if she was ready yet to face the consequences of sharing her truth.

And that truth was this: despite the warmth and love that had grown between them, Lilly knew her relationship with Cisco had come to its end. Walking through the dusk next to the quiet river or lying together beneath the stars, they had shared a sense of wonder for the land, for discovering nature in all her strength and varied beauty. While they'd agreed on important values like trust and respect, they knew they would never be acceptable in either her town or his if they were to declare their commitment to each other. There was too much against them. They talked about meeting the following summer to renew their acquaintance, but Cisco couldn't promise that his obligations would allow him to return to her father's fields.

After tasting freedom and exploring the forbidden with him, Lilly was eager to continue her quest of independence. She knew she'd been rewarded for taking this chance. Despite her sadness, she felt she was better for knowing such a man, even for such a short time. Cisco had provided certainty and support for Lilly's new definition of her future. His way of listening to her thoughts, of refining her scattered ideas into possibilities, had helped her to see herself as a separate and capable person, not as someone's daughter or friend or fiancée.

Mr. and Mrs. Bradstreet reacted differently to their approaching destination: her mother became quiet, while her father's animation increased. She sighed and gazed out her window; he bounced the unlit pipe between his lips with more energy, eyes growing brighter. "We'll park first, to get the lay of the land," he said, carefully pulling off the highway and entering the campus from the Ag and Sciences side. "Once we know where you'll be situated, we can bring your things right to your new front door." In his element for the first time in a while, he spoke confidently.

Mrs. Bradstreet refreshed her lipstick and patted her hair into place beneath the summer hat perched over one eye. "I wish you wouldn't wear those silly dark glasses," she remarked to Lilly through the compact's mirrored reflection. "I daresay other young ladies will be more modestly attired."

Lilly cringed, but only to herself. Ignoring the critique, she fastened her thoughts on the days ahead—filled with the scents of crisp book pages and notebook paper, with chilly mornings walking under glorious leaves to stone buildings filled with people like her, yearning to both break free from the familiar and jump feet-first into new lives.

The contents of her purse had spilled out during the ride; Lilly did her best to collect them, stuffing her short white gloves in at the top. She noticed through her side window that other young women on campus weren't wearing their gloves either and wondered what her mother would have to say about that.

Her father situated their car precisely between two similar vehicles in the parking lot reserved for teaching staff. He shrugged on his lightweight jacket, tucked his pipe into the breast pocket, and smoothed back his pompadour before reaching out to help her mother, erect and unsmiling, from her seat on the passenger's side. His face softened when Lilly came to join them from her side of the car. "Are you ready, Rabbit?" he teased, his eyes crinkling at the corners.

I'll miss him! The thought burst through her brain. Tears welled up behind her dark glasses; her throat grew clogged and dry.

Not too long after they'd left the car, her mother pulled to a stop on the sidewalk. A tear of her own trickled down next to her carefully powdered, patrician nose. Mrs. Bradstreet snatched out her monogrammed handkerchief to dab it away, but Lilly noticed. Perhaps her mother's stoicism wasn't so immobile, after all.

The family took a sidewalk that angled toward Old Main under a canopy of leaves woven from a garish autumn plaid. New ornamental shrubs had been placed along the path, Lilly's father explained, by members of the Ag engineering department, and he was very proud of the result. He continued to expound upon the genetic background of a certain drought-resistant varietal when her mother interrupted.

"I see the placard for new student orientation ahead. Let's go there first to learn which dormitory Lilly has been assigned to." She tapped smartly up the marble steps and waited at the top for her husband to open the heavy wooden door.

Raspy metal hinges scratched gashes across Lilly's confidence: suddenly, she had the strangest, unbidden desire to run back to hide in the car. Instead, she took a breath, squared her shoulders, and followed her mother into the cool, dim interior.

Dani

26

DANI LISTENED TO the bag of letters sliding across the plastic floor mat behind her as she turned onto the gravel of her own driveway, pulling up to park without remembering how she'd gotten home. The secrets that bag might contain fired her imagination. She wondered what reason Mrs. Swenson's sister had for keeping the letters so long.

Before Dani had left for the second time, Mrs. Swenson handed over the parcel of letters the younger woman had seen her reading the day before.

"I want you to have these," the older woman said. "You're becoming part of our town, now. What you do with them is up to you."

At first, Dani had politely declined the gift. "Maybe the historical society would want them?" she put forth, half-heartedly.

"Not likely!" Mrs. Swenson laughed. "They hold their meetings at my library the first Monday of every month, and their agenda runs more along the lines of knitting patterns and winter vacations. They wouldn't know what to do with them." She grew more serious. "Besides, there's something similar between the two of you, you and Lilly," she added. "You're both explorers; adventurers, even. I think she'd like knowing that her letters had found a safe home with you."

Dani sat in her truck and thought about the conversation until sticky perspiration started to trail down her spine. Grabbing the bundle from behind the driver's seat and tucking the letters under her arm, Dani left the truck and climbed her worn porch steps one at a time. She reached out for her screen door, noticed that it was open, and tried to recall if she'd left it ajar in her hurry to return to the Swensons'.

She crossed over the wooden threshold, then froze—there was noise coming from her kitchen. A woman's voice cursed softly, then a cupboard door snapped shut. "I hear you out there."

It was Donna. Relieved, Dani tucked the letters under the telephone table as she made her way back to the back of her little farmhouse.

"Hope you don't mind, me letting myself in," Donna said when her unwitting host came into view.

"I'm a little surprised," Dani replied. "But no problem." She seated herself and waited for Donna to finish pouring a second glass of iced tea. Ice cubes fogged the glasses; the brew was dark and smelled like lemons and gasoline.

Donna sat across from her and took a sip from her own glass. Her pink lipstick smudged its rounded edge. "I got to thinking about what we were talking about, last week." Her shoulders hunched, but not because she was afraid or chilled: she was protecting a secret, holding it in until the right moment. "I called my Aunt Ellen after we talked last. Asked her if she remembered anything about that family her momma worked for." She returned her glass to the table. "She didn't—that would've been too easy— but she did remember that their name was Beadstreet or Bradstreet, same as what I thought." She tossed her curled bangs to the side and looked directly at Dani. "So I did some looking on my own."

Donna began to get up, but Dani gestured for her to stay seated.

"What?"

"I'm just back from Mrs. Swenson's house," Dani started.

"The old library lady?"

"The same. She asked me to help round up some of her sister's belongings before Jacob Dorn takes over, and—"

Donna interrupted. "How do you know her?"

"From here and there." Dani's smile was relaxed. "Crestview's not all that big, you know? Anyhow, her sister was friends with the Bradstreet girl, Lilly."

Donna jumped up to rummage through her tote bag which hung from the back of the kitchen door. She pulled out a leatherette photo book, the kind that used tiny triangular stickers to adhere square snapshots onto its pages, and settled it in front of Dani.

The waitress opened the cover. It cracked, several black-and-white pictures tumbling out along with a missalette from someone's funeral Mass. She shuffled the loose photos into a stack, pushed this aside, and turned to the middle section of the album. "Look!" Donna's excited voice rose as she pointed at one picture. "See here?"

Dani saw a collection of elegant adults gathered around a rectangular table adorned with silver candlesticks, gleaming plates, and sparkling crystal. Two men, one older and one younger, wore dark suit coats and slim ties. The younger one's hair was slicked back from his forehead; his eyes were dark and vulpine. The older man, shorter and rounder, sported horn-rimmed spectacles and held a pipe. The women across from each corresponded in age to their partners: the older one, marcel waves perfectly arranged, looked down her nose at the camera. Her right hand rested at the edge of the table as if she'd been captured in the act of gathering or distributing. The younger woman sat back, her arms self-consciously posed across her chest, eyes angled down and away from the photographer. Two dark barrettes trapped her blonde bob on each side of her thin face.

Dani didn't know what it was that she was supposed to be seeing.

"Look," Donna pointed. "Right here." Her sharpened forefinger, pink as her lipstick, directed Dani's attention to the two apron-clad women standing stiffly in the shadows at the back of the tableau. "That's my momma, next to my Aunt Ellen."

Dani looked. "Okay, I see them." She waited. "What am I supposed to notice?"

Donna snorted and stood up, exasperated. "Not them, hon." She tapped the photo again, more forcefully. "Next to them, under the table. See?"

Dani saw. The young man's hand was placed on the young woman's knee, under the table, out of view by the parents or the serving staff. His hold on her was tight and clawlike. "Who are these people?"

Donna turned over the photo and read from the back. "'Christmas 1938, Lillian's young man Ned joins the family dinner' is what's written." She flipped it back onto the table. "Why do you suppose the guy's so possessive of her?" She dug through her purse and pulled out a crushed box of Virginia Slims. "Can I smoke in here?"

Dani didn't bother to answer, her focus flown far away. The snap of Donna's Zippo lighter brought her back, and she stood. "Can you stay for a while? There's something I'd like to show you."

"I don't have to go in 'till four today." Donna blew a lazy stream that wended its own way out the door behind them. She bent one leg up to rest on the vinyl seat underneath her. "Whatcha got?"

"I don't know for sure." Dani returned to the front entry, replying over her shoulder. "It's something I think is important, but I don't know how, or why." She strode back into the kitchen, dropped the bundle of letters in front of Donna, and sat across from her again.

"What are these? Where'd you get them?" Donna spoke from the corner of her mouth while she untied the yellowed kitchen string that was wrapped around the papers. The fibers fell apart easily.

Dani couldn't keep still, standing once more to be able to see what Donna unfolded. "Wow, those things look pretty fragile." She gestured for Donna to pass some of them over; Donna handed the bottom half across the table, then settled back onto her chair with the rest in her lap.

"Keep your ashes clear, okay?" Dani felt slightly abashed when Donna narrowed her fake eyelashes at her, but continued anyway. "Let's try to see if they're in some sort of order."

Donna pointedly raised the saucer she was using as an ashtray, mashed down the remainder of the butt into a tiny square, and slid it over to the far side of the tabletop.

Dani hardly noticed, her attention arrested by the first letter she'd removed from its envelope. It was addressed to Elaine Swenson, 236 Maple Street, Crestview, Iowa, postmarked January 16, 1940, and sent through

St. Paul, Minnesota. The slanted cursive handwriting inside was bold, and numerous portions had been crossed out. It was easy reading, though: Dani was carried along by the voice of the writer as she described working at a factory with other young women. She described a gimpy boss as "limping along with half a brain and more responsibility than he knows what to do with." The author closed by asking Elaine to consider coming to visit, writing that there would be plenty of room at her lodging, and that it would be good to see one another in person again in order to "mend broken fences."

Donna broke in. "What's the date on yours?"

"I've only read one so far, January 1940." Dani carefully folded the letter back into its envelope and began scanning through the rest of the pile, looking at the postmarks for the dates. "These are from September '39 through . . . through May of 1940, then the one I read." She looked up at Donna. "How about yours?"

"These here start in September of 1939 and go through the end of 1940, as far as I can tell." She neatened the stack by bouncing it lightly against the table. "I got six in all. You?"

"Seven."

"All to Elaine?"

Dani rifled through the stack again. "Yup, all to Elaine."

Donna looked up. "They were best friends, right? Isn't that what her sister told you?"

Dani placed the first envelope at the back of her stack and opened the second. "That's what Mrs. Swenson said."

"Why're you so concerned about these girls, anyways?" Donna asked. She'd shaken out a new cigarette and brought it to her lips, but hadn't yet lit it. Her attention, intense, focused on Dani.

Dani searched for words to explain her interest. "I'm curious. I want to know what happened, what was so . . ." She struggled for the right word. ". . . so *terrible* that a whole community would buy into what, to me, sounds like nothing more than an old fairy tale."

"You mean the tree?"

"Yeah, but more than that." This pause lasted long enough for Donna to light up. "I want to know what would make a young girl, a young woman, leave her hometown forever," Dani mused, her voice trailing off to a mumble.

Donna placed the Zippo next to her ashtray and returned to her own pile of letters. "Well," she countered, "what made you want to leave your people to come here?"

Dani wasn't finished talking about Lilly, though. "What happened back then, to make the people who lived here so, so, superstitious?" She waited for Donna look at her. "Is that the word? You can't deny that they were pretty judgmental."

"Maybe it was that time," Donna suggested. "It was during the war, right? People were afraid then. They didn't know if the Japs or the Heinies would be landing their soldiers here." She blew out another cloud. "They didn't know who to trust. Not so different from folks today, really. Think about those Tallybans, or whatever they call themselves, bombing us here last year."

"Agreed. But wouldn't you think . . ." Dani paused. She held another old letter but hadn't yet started to read it. "Wouldn't you think that the farmers here would've been happy to have the extra help? Wouldn't you get to know someone, be friends with him even, working alongside him?"

"Maybe they didn't all think the same way, but who can know?" Donna replied. "You have to remember, most of the men were in the service already. There wasn't no police force or able-bodied men around, just the old guys and the hired help." Donna waved the next letter from her pile. "And you never answered my question, before." She waited for Dani's explanation.

"I came here because I didn't fit in anymore, where I was. I had a good job, you know, but things weren't right."

"Got into a fight with an old boyfriend?" Donna joked, but stopped immediately when she saw the stricken look pass over Dani's face. "Oh, hon, I'm sorry; I don't mean to pry." She shut up for a moment. But only one moment. "You know you can tell me. There isn't anybody around here who'd care what two old spinsters like us talk about, anyhow."

Dani sketched a bare outline of how she'd come to live in Iowa. She hoped she wouldn't regret telling so much about herself to Donna, even though they seemed to be cementing a friendship. Depositing the letter back on the tabletop, she finished: "Things between us fell apart. Then 9/11 sort of shocked me into deciding that it might be better to try what I'd always dreamed about doing. So I quit, started looking online for a little place to rent, and, well, I moved here."

Donna's face reflected the sadness Dani felt, but not the kind her mom or her work friends had displayed, that "Oh no, I'm so sad for you" look that immediately turned her stomach to acid. Donna's face showed acceptance but not pity. Dani's wall of composure started to dissolve.

She decided to change the subject. "I want to know what made this Lillian leave Crestview. It seems like she had all she could want here."

Donna used a minute to form her reply. "Maybe it wasn't that she didn't want to come back. Maybe she couldn't come back."

"Do you think it had anything to do with what happened to the guy at the tree?"

"It has to. Two strange things, both at once?"

Dani nodded. "You're right. They have to be related."

Donna got up to refill their glasses. Dani waved her away. "No thanks, I don't need any more caffeine." She ran her hands through her hair, standing it on edge. "How about you, Donna? Did you ever want to leave Crestview?" Dani was genuinely interested. "Have you ever thought you'd like to live someplace else?"

"I think you get to be known somewhere like here, and it's . . . well, it's hard to break away from that." She took a drag from her cigarette. "There's a comfort in knowing your neighbors, even if what they 'know' ain't always true." The waitress struggled to be perfectly clear. "That's what's different, between me and her. I don't want to leave. I want to stay here and I want to buy Susie's Café and try a bunch of new recipes I've been collecting. You know, like a Mexican night one night, or Italian," she tried to explain, standing up to pace back and forth. "I get bored, the way things stay the same. Like she must have. But I have some really good ideas to mix it up;

all's I need is a little more cash." Donna's eyes sparkled, her hands flying around like frantic birds, detailing for Dani where she'd restructure the kitchen and adjust the layout of the tables. "It could really be something."

"It sounds great," Dani grinned at the animated descriptions. "I'll come and help. I'm really good at washing dishes. But as far as cooking? My mom used to say that I could burn water."

"Aw, thanks, hon. You can be the first to try out the samples!" Donna collapsed back into her chair. "But let's finish up these letters. I don't have much time 'till my shift starts." Donna nodded toward the letter Dani held. "I really want to know what made our Lilly leave."

Lilly

27

"LILLY!" A PRETTY coed named Trixie knocked a second time on Lilly's door. Her sparkling earrings swung back and forth, reflecting the overhead hallway lights. Trixie was the only girl in their dorm with pierced ears. Some of the other girls on floor two referred to her as "fast," but Lilly found nothing in that gossip to believe. Trixie's big laugh and open personality just automatically placed her at the center of attention in most circumstances, whether in class, at the cafeteria, or at a mixer.

She gave up knocking and poked her head into Lilly's room. "Are you ready to go?" An all-girl dance band from Illinois had come through Iowa on a tour of the Midwest, and they were playing at their campus tonight.

Lilly was at her desk, head in one hand, book splayed open beneath a gooseneck lamp. "I don't know. I haven't really decided yet."

Her days had settled into a satisfying routine. She enjoyed the Early Civilizations class best, mesmerized by the way Professor Donnelly wove together the impact of early people on modern life. Most days, she greeted this new existence with energy, but tonight, after another long week of classes, she felt a little tired. Maybe she should stay in and catch up on her sleep. "I don't have anything to wear, anyways."

"You can borrow something of mine! Or of Sandy's. She's always asking to doll you up." Trixie sounded determined to get Lilly up and out the door.

Lilly groaned and relented. "I'm coming, I'm coming."

Some young men in the audience guffawed and catcalled when the first set began, but after a swinging version of the Count Basie hit "Jumpin' at the Woodside," the naysayers moved to the back corners of the Student Union. There wasn't a spot left on the dance floor.

The girls danced with a number of young men, most of whom might be labeled the "fraternity type" with their loud jackets and wide ties. After a while, Lilly was happy to just sit to the side and listen as Trixie continued to dance, accepting a splash of something Joey Larson poured from a silver flask into her ginger ale.

The evening passed quickly. The band closed with a sultry blues number before the girls escaped the sweating walls of the Union to gulp in cool breaths of night air. They traveled in a pack back to Oak House, visiting and comparing notes about who had danced with whom, and how Tommy Oleson had disgraced himself once again by drinking far too much.

"Did I see you with that dashing football player?" Trixie asked, looping her slender arm through Lilly's. The walking paths between buildings were paved, but most of the girls had taken off their heels and were enjoying the cool lawn instead. The dark provided cover for them to ignore the "stay on the path" signs posted every hundred yards; their tired feet welcomed that delicious, dewy grass.

Lilly laughed and bent her head to answer Trixie. "He's not really my type." Her heart gave a brief pang. Her type—would that be a dark Lothario bringing with him sweet caresses and stolen moments, or was that entanglement a fond memory that would never be repeated? "Anyways, I think Joey's more into sport than girls."

Trixie let out a guffaw. "I think old Joey would consider catching a pretty girl as a type of sport too, wouldn't you say?" she teased.

Lilly could see her point. A lot of the young men she knew were competitive in every area; competition for a pretty date was probably one of their chief opportunities to try to outscore one another. "Anyhow, I'm not really here to get a date," Lilly confided. "I want to get a degree. I want to have a career."

Trixie's voice became serious. "Aren't you afraid of ending up all alone? Everyone knows that career women end up being old maids."

"No, I'm not afraid." Lilly recalled the feelings of freedom she used to get pumping her legs to swing up to the treetops on a muggy summer's day, or playing the bold conqueror striding home from Elaine's in the twinkling starlight on a frozen, snowy evening. "I want to be someone," she said, squeezing Trixie's hand. "I don't want to be attached to a name that's not my own."

They slowed to let a group of tipsy girls pass. They were singing quite loudly, oblivious to their house matron's glare from the front door of Oak House, about ten yards ahead. Trixie pulled Lilly into the shadows of the Arts Hall. "What about the war? What will happen to us, if this war continues?"

Trixie had lost her father to World War I. His picture on her bedside table showed a gallant man with a solid, square jaw, wearing a uniform and a smart officer's hat. Trixie had the same cleft in her chin that her father did and the same dark coloring, though her facial structure was much softer.

Her earrings stopped swinging. She whispered, "I know my brother will enlist as soon as he's old enough. And that will leave me to take care of Mama." She looked down, her eyebrows knit together. "I want to stay here, to stay in this little world of safety and learning and fun." She withdrew her arm from Lilly's to hug it against herself. "If I go back home, I won't ever be able to leave again."

This was news to Lilly. Judging Trixie's ebullient exterior like the others, she hadn't guessed the depth of feeling that ran beneath her jaunty behavior. Evidently Trixie had her own reasons for coming to Ames.

"I don't want to go back, either," Lilly confided. She dropped her shoes and placed herself next to them, not caring that the dew would wet her skirt and she'd have to spend time cleaning and repressing it before she could wear it again. "There's nothing there for me. My parents are swell, but they expect me to marry a man they've known, that *I've* known, forever." She sighed and reached back to run her hand over the top of the mown grass. "And I've known for just as long that I can't do it." She looked up at Trixie. "I won't."

Trixie settled on the lawn next to her. "Do you think they'd make you?" she asked.

"If my mother had her way, I'd be Mrs. Ned Wagner already." The dread she'd tamped down when confronted with the situation clawed its way back. "She thinks I'll get this 'college business' out of my head after one year, and that I'll meekly return home in time to be a bride next June." She flung her upper body backward to lie on the lawn. Stars shone dimly through a haze that enveloped half the night sky—someone had been burning leaves. The comforting aroma wound its way to campus on a breeze that had begun creeping in from the west.

Trixie's voice reached her ears as tears filled her eyes. "They can't make us, can they?" she spoke with passion. "They'll have to find us first!"

Without warning, she jumped up from the ground, pulling Lilly onto the path. "We're going to be late for curfew!" she sang. "Ha ha! What should we do next?"

Careless of the shoes they'd left behind, the girls ran barefoot under the dark trees toward the campanile at the center of campus.

HALFWAY ACROSS THE state, Ned Wagner was having a hard time concentrating on the details of a plan he'd begun to devise. Timing this event was difficult, and Ned was frustrated by his lack of progress, not to mention the hours of rest he was missing as he schemed instead of slept through most nights.

A timid knock sounded on his office door, followed by a girlish voice. "Mr. Wagner, Jesse Dorn's here to see you." The secretary was about to enter, but stopped short when she spied Ned's frozen glare.

"I'm busy, and I don't have time for any appointments today. You'll have to ask him to come back. And close the door behind you." He didn't even pretend to couch his words in sugar, as he usually did to avoid a meltdown from a secretary who was gorgeous to look at but as manageable as unspun cotton candy.

Bobbie pouted and turned on her pointed, black heels with a huff. Ned could still hear her pass on his excuses through the door, though, her voice miraculously retaining its girlish charm.

He propped his arm up on the desktop, rested his chin on his upraised fist, and considered his best options. He wasn't without those who owed him favors, and he also knew of some he could press to help, given a certain incentive.

His office door flew open. A volatile, formidable presence aimed itself for his desk. Bobbie's frantic whine assailed his ears from her position outside. Ned stood so suddenly that his chair crashed back against the wall behind him. "What's going on here?" he barked. "Bobbie?"

"I'll tell you what's going on," Jesse Dorn spat. He'd reached the desk and slammed his hands down on it, his breath heaving, his eyes grim slits. "We got trouble, that's what."

"Mr. Wagner," his secretary's kitten-like voice continued, "I *told* him he couldn't come in, but he—"

"That will be enough, Bobbie," Ned interrupted. He didn't bother to look at her. "Shut the door on your way out."

He smoothed his tie and forced his feet toward the credenza. It held a cut-glass decanter and matching glasses. Pouring himself a hefty dose, Ned tried to control the tremor in his hand. Tossing back the liquid gave him time: time to consider the problem, and time to regain the composure he wanted to display.

Ned turned back to find Jesse exactly as he'd left him: grit-lined paws on the desk, cap pushed back over his high forehead, mouth a heavy slash set in solid concrete. "What's the big deal?" The banker put down the empty glass, keeping his desk between them. "Something come up?"

"You could say that," the angry man snapped. "We've got a situation that I ain't got time nor money to handle." He pushed himself up off the desk but did not sit. "Those boys I got working for me? They ain't gonna be around again next year. What with Roosevelt grousing about taking more of 'em for the war effort, I ain't going to have enough manpower next season to make payment on my land. If they ain't coming back, I won't be able to plant; if I don't plant, I don't harvest. And you know I won't have your money unless I do." His words spurted out like steam escaping from a heated pot. "I won't be able to make ends meet. I won't be able to keep up. I was counting on those guys to get me back above even next year."

Ned watched the normally composed man struggle not to disintegrate. "What do you want me to do about it, Jesse?"

Jesse's voice flattened. "I don't know how I'm going to do it, Ned. I need those workers." His bloodshot eyes didn't blink. "I can't afford the rates of the regular Joes passing through, and I ain't about to employ no Mexicans!" He rubbed his pale, whiskered face with his dry, veiny hand. Ned couldn't remember ever seeing him so unkempt or disturbed.

Suddenly, the banker's confidence swelled. He shifted lazily to the front of his desk, holding Jesse's half-crazed gaze with his own. "Now that I think about it, Jesse, there might be a way that we could help each other out," Ned disclosed, leaning back to rest against the burled mahogany surface. "Here's what I need you to do."

Dani

28

THE REST OF the afternoon dissolved while Dani and Donna read and compared letter after letter from Lilly Bradstreet to Elaine. It was astonishing, how quickly the time passed. Dani glanced up at her clock and saw that the hands had shifted to four—Donna would have to get going if she wanted to make it to work on time.

"If you come up with anything else, let me know," said the waitress, throwing her purse over her shoulder and shoving her feet into beaded sandals. "I'm going to leave the picture book here; maybe you can match up some of the people with the ones Lilly wrote about." Donna gave the black leatherette album a pat. "You know, I get why you're so interested in this, now," she added. "It's like a mystery."

Dani smiled, rose to her feet, and accompanied Donna to her car, parked behind the house. "I'll let you know if I come up with anything, I promise." Dani wasn't wearing shoes, and the way her tender feet caused her to tiptoe across the ground embarrassed her. She moved to the grass, hoping Donna hadn't noticed.

"Sounds good to me." Sunglasses perched on the tip of her nose, Donna rolled down the window with one hand while adjusting the rearview mirror with the other, an unlit cigarette bobbing between her candy-pink lips. She backed out using her knees to steer, then shoved the gearshift into "drive" and waved to Dani. The horn tooted twice as her tires spun in the gravel, aiming toward town.

Dani used the edge of the lawn to return to her kitchen, her thoughts miles and decades away. Lilly had found herself to be pregnant, and she'd been scared to let her parents know. In January of 1940, her envelopes had been mailed from Minneapolis instead of Ames—Lillian had moved to a home for unwed mothers. One thing was clear in her letters to Elaine: she didn't want someone named "Ned" to know anything about her location or her condition. She later wrote about disappointing her mother and father, and how neither of them called or visited her at the home.

The girls here are nice, though not the kind I'd call my friends, she wrote in January.

If not for their obvious conditions—oh, do I have to include myself in that description?—you'd think they were a group of regular gals from anywhere.

There was no way to know Elaine's response. Dani wondered if she'd sent a reply and, if so, what she had written to her childhood friend about her situation. Would she have supported Lillian? Shared news about Crestview, the friends they'd had, the places they liked to be?

She wished she could have known to ask some of this before she'd left Mrs. Swenson, and wondered if her older friend could have answered. There had to be a reason her sister Elaine had kept the letters for so long. What might that reason have been?

Back inside, Dani organized the letters by date, noticing that around July 1940 the postmark changed to "Rosemount Minn." There were only two left to read. She opened the next envelope.

In this letter, Lilly described an interview she'd had for a factory worker's position at a new munitions plant in a little town outside St. Paul. She wrote that she was hesitant to move there because the foreman couldn't promise how long he could keep her. As long as the war went on, he said, he'd have a place for her, but once the men returned he couldn't promise her anything more.

For now, she wrote, she could be reached at the home of an older lady named Helen, if Elaine wanted to get in touch. Dani took that to mean that Elaine had probably broken off their friendship. She wondered how long Lillian had continued to write to Elaine with no return in kind.

Rising and stretching, she relocated to the living room and dropped herself onto the cradle of thin cushions that rested on her armchair. Feet on the green cassock in front of her, Dani pulled open the last envelope.

This letter, written in pale blue ink, asked Elaine to meet Lilly at the bus stop in Harmony, Minnesota. It was dated June 1940; the rendezvous was to take place the weekend before July 4th. Also included in the letter was a mysterious reference:

Have you, by chance, seen Ned? He has somehow located this address. I know better than to think that you'd give it to him, Lainey, but he's found me somehow. Do you think he may have seen it while visiting my parents? Perhaps he doesn't see them any longer. They, so far, are still reluctant to reply to me or to visit. I continue to attempt some reconciliation between us . . .

Speaking of reconciliation, I dearly hope that you—

This query caused Dani's imagination to skew off in a number of directions. She could imagine this Ned creeping about in the dark, removing mail from Lilly's parents' postbox or perhaps from Elaine's. Who was this guy, and why did Lilly seem afraid of him?

Tossing the letter back onto the pile, she stood and moved to put on her shoes. She needed to get outside and clear her head. She entered the shed outside and hopped onto the ancient four-wheeler that had come with the property she rented. It started with a cough and an oily sputter.

By the time she reached the river, it was nearly suppertime. She eased off the road and nosed the ATV onto a footpath that led to the water, the boxy front of the vehicle pushing between the dry grasses and weeds. Dani concentrated on avoiding any big stones or washouts that could pitch her off or, worse, damage the frame or axles. Bugs stung her sunglasses and cheeks as she drove through the slanting sunlight. Laughter and teasing voices shrilled up from the shallow ravine ahead; a boombox beat a tinny rhythm that wavered in and out of hearing. From the river, metal clanked and female voices screamed: a group of kids out tanking, Dani decided. In between planting and cultivating and harvesting, most of the county's young adults found a thrill riding through the slow current of Beaver Creek in metal animal feeders. They'd bring beer, sit in lawn chairs inside the tanks, and ride from the put-in to another truck, parked and waiting a few hours downstream. Red-faced and warm, they'd pop out, drag the tank and the empties up the dirt bank, and head back to the launch for another run.

Dani turned away from the river. She supposed there were at least a few hours of evening light left; she might as well drive up to that place where the tree used to stand. There was usually less drama in the quiet fields, and if she was lucky, maybe she'd spot a deer and her fawn foraging in the tender growth. She wanted to take some time to sit quietly, take in nature's peace, and convince herself that there was nothing to be afraid of.

Lilly

29

As the days grew shorter, so did the girls' tempers. Thanksgiving would mark the end of the first grading period, and the students of Oak House were nervous about their upcoming exams. Most girls practically lived in the study room around the clock. Lilly's letters home were punctual but brief. She didn't write to Ned. The missives exchanged between Lilly and Elaine weren't as regular or lengthy as they'd been in the beginning. So far, they hadn't been able to get together as they had hoped they would.

Elaine wrote that she was getting along well at her father's shop, and while she did mind the number of accounts she was tasked to keep in order, she was pleased that she'd gained some understanding of accounting principles through a mail-order course. One significant issue hovered darkly overhead: her Lonny had received his call-up notice. He was scheduled to report to base the week after Christmas.

Elaine also wrote that she'd run into Ned one day as she was making a deposit for the shop. He'd asked after Lilly, she wrote, and pressed Elaine to learn when she'd be back.

. . . I think I was persuasive enough to make him think that I hadn't heard from you. You just need to continue to avoid him until he realizes that you truly don't intend to marry him.

Here's a question: how is it that most men his age, like Lonny, have either already volunteered or have been drafted? How does a guy like Ned get so dang lucky? I wonder if it's luck at all! Why, I wouldn't be surprised to learn there's been trickery . . .

Elaine's elegant handwriting, tilted at a precise 45-degree angle, brought back to Lilly's insides that cold miasma which automatically accompanied any thoughts of Ned. There had to be a way to get it across to him, she thought, wiping a tired hand across her eyelids and brow.

She closed the study room door quietly and climbed the steps to her room. Her legs felt heavy; her eyelids threatened to close at any minute. Maybe she'd be better able to handle him, once and for all, when she returned to Crestview for the Christmas break.

Trixie knocked on the door frame and leaned into Lilly's room. "Are you coming back down to study again tonight or not?" she called, tossing back her pert, bobbed hair. The front section was held back with a wide band across Trixie's forehead, drawing all attention to the startling blue of her eyes—no doubt the careful intention of their owner.

"Don't think so. I should probably head back to the library before it closes, and I still have washing to do." Her voice waned, and she placed her head on the book she'd been perusing. "I'm just so tired."

Trixie came into the room and sat on the bed closest to Lilly's desk. "Are you all right? Are you feeling okay?"

Lilly's muffled voice wafted up from the piles of paper underneath her. "I don't know, I think so." She sat up. "I can't seem to get caught up, is all."

"Are you sure that's all?" Trixie questioned, narrowing her eyes. "Is there anything you want to tell me, honey? Anything at all?"

"What do you mean?" Lilly asked, her voice tight and her face still. "It's more work here than I anticipated, is all." Her shoulders slumped. "But you're right—I don't feel like myself, really." A thickness clogged her throat. "Maybe I'm more lonesome for Crestview than I thought."

"Is it Crestview you're lonesome for," Trixie asked, "or someone who lives there?"

Lilly took her time forming an answer. "Trixie, if I told you about this, would you promise, promise with your whole heart, not to tell anyone else?" Her face, which had lost its summer glow weeks ago, was pale. Her cheeks looked hollow, and there were dark smudges under her eyes.

"Who'd I tell?" Trixie patted her friend's arm, her touch warm and genuine. "What little secrets are you so protective of?"

"You have to promise me, Trixie, I mean it. No one can know." Her eyes sought Trixie's and held them, unblinking.

"Of course not. Not ever, if that's what you want."

Lilly's shoulders settled back down, but her eyes held firm. "There was a man in Crestview, a man I grew to love." She told Trixie the story of Cisco: of how they met, of how they continued to meet, to talk, to dream, to be together, whether in the cool shade under the old witness tree or along the gently burbling river. Of his warm kisses, his gentle eyes, his calm belief that Lilly's thoughts and feelings and opinions were worthy and import-ant and valued. She struggled to keep her composure as she shared what she'd come to understand. "I knew we could never be together—married, I mean—but there was something between us that, I don't know, made me feel that he *knew* me. That he cared about *me*," she added, emphasizing the last word. "I knew that our time together wouldn't last, but I guess I didn't believe, or let myself believe, that I wouldn't ever see him again."

"Did you sleep with him?" Trixie inquired, her delivery the opposite of delicate.

"I never had the chance to," Lilly answered softly. "When we spent time together, and kissed, and, well . . ." She seemed more reticent than ashamed to share private details. "I had a curfew, and my parents would have noticed if I didn't sleep at home at night."

"Silly girl," Trixie chided, "I don't mean 'sleep' as in 'pass the night away.' I mean, did you have intercourse with him?"

Lilly blushed. "I, I . . ." Her voice trailed away.

Trixie almost fell off the edge of the bed. "Do you mean to tell me that you don't know about the birds and the bees, Lillian? About how babies are made?"

"Of course I do!" Lilly ducked her head. Red splotches showed on her cheeks, right under the smudges beneath her tired eyes.

Other girls from their floor were making their way back to their rooms after dinner. Their tired voices bounced off the linoleum as they passed by the room. Trixie got up and shut the door with a quiet click. She turned and looked directly at Lilly. "This is no time to be shy and ladylike, Lilly. Think: did he put his thing in you?"

Lilly turned a paler shade, if that was possible, and nodded once.

Trixie knelt by Lilly's desk. "Honey, I think we have a different problem than 'just being tired' to worry about."

AFTER LILLY'S LAST exam was finished, her books closed and tucked away, she let herself think about what Trixie had asked, and what her questions that night had revealed. No longer able to hide from these thoughts, Lilly pulled her pillow to her chest and looked through the window to the darkness outside. Most of the other girls had gone home soon after their last exams, but Lilly had no desire to make her own arrangements to return to Crestview.

She scolded herself for getting into such an impossible situation. Her eyes were dry and scratchy; no tears came forth to ease the building pressure inside her head and heart. Instead of confronting her situation, instead of making plans, her inclination was to pull herself more tightly into a ball, to occupy the smallest space possible.

A quiet knock at her door pulled Lilly out of her shameful contemplations. "Yes?" She struggled to her feet and smoothed her hair before opening the door. Trixie, tapping her pointed toe impatiently, was dressed in a short swing coat and a smart, black hat. She wore short, black gloves too, but they looked dashing and sophisticated rather than matronly, especially with the two-inch rhinestone bracelet cuffed over one wrist.

"Come on, miss." Trixie's confident stride brought her to Lilly's side of the wardrobe. "We're going to spend Thanksgiving in St. Paul with my aunt, Helen." She rummaged through Lilly's stockings and shifts and added a few to her own valise, a mock-crocodile affair trimmed with metal edges.

"I can't." Lilly forgot for a moment to feel guilty. "My parents expect me to come home for the holidays."

Trixie closed a drawer and started removing dresses from their hangers. "You certainly can!" she asserted, folding two of Lilly's dresses into the top of her case. "We'll call your parents from the station. We'll tell them that you received this invitation and you couldn't say no." Trixie snapped the wardrobe door closed and whirled to face Lilly. "Where's your coat?"

Lilly gestured vaguely to her own wool overcoat, arranged to dry over the arms of a chair. "I think I'd rather stay here."

"You'll do no such thing!" Trixie lifted the coat and held it open. "We need to have a plan, and there's nothing here to help with that." She eased first one and then the other of Lilly's arms gently into her sleeves, then placed her hands like solid brackets on Lilly's shoulders to twirl the girl around. Face to face, Trixie spoke more quietly. "We have to face facts. You, my dear, are going to have a baby."

Lilly's chin dropped, along with two fat tears.

Trixie buttoned up her coat as she would for a child. Her voice became softer, more cajoling. "There are other girls who have faced the same thing you're facing. There's a home near my aunt's. A sort of hospital, for girls like you."

Lilly looked up at Trixie as teardrops coursed down her cheeks.

Trixie gathered Lilly in for a hug. "You'll be fine! You won't be alone." She tried her best to keep her voice calm, but knew they needed to hurry to catch the bus leaving for St. Paul. Patting Lilly again before hefting her traveling case, she gave what she hoped looked like a confident smile. "Come on, honey. Let's go now, before it's too late."

Lilly knew then that she wouldn't be coming back. Accepting the situation made her feel like she was looking up through layers and layers of water to wavy outlines of indistinct shapes above.

She crossed the small room to retrieve a slim packet of letters from beneath her pile of textbooks. She ran one gloved finger over *General Psychology*, slid that and her history book off the tabletop, and tucked them securely under her elbow. She took nothing else. Her parents' carefully arranged features smiled out to her from the silver frame next to her bed.

She briefly touched the image of her father's face, looking strange without his pipe nearby, then turned and left her dorm room.

Dani

30

EACH OF THE last three mornings of August, Dani watched Lloyd work through his new bus route, preparing for school's return the day after Labor Day. He drove for the county school district for extra cash, he said; Dani thought he just liked to get out of the house. She could still drink her first coffee on her front porch this early, even though the air had a snap and the shadows that summer had banished were creeping back around the corners. Her hooded sweatshirt felt good until about eleven or so, when she was able to shuck it and finish the day in short sleeves.

Around town, the talk was of harvest. Some of the crops were close, but others—Dani's corn, for example—wouldn't be ready for another few weeks.

She wondered sometimes about the future she might have if she stayed in Crestview for another season. The property didn't feel like hers, exactly, to do with as she wished, but it didn't feel right for her to pack up and head someplace new, either. Like the people who lived here, the land was stoic and private about things that mattered. Dani hadn't yet reached a firm decision one way or the other.

One thing she *did* feel strongly about was her need to investigate those letters Eleanor Swenson had found. After Dani finished with the harvest, her plan was to drive up to the Twin Cities for a few days to look into that

Bryant Avenue address from the envelopes and the old munitions plant where Lilly used to work. Those were turbulent times, both during and after World War II: if the soldiers returned to their jobs and families, many women went through a second uprooting as they tried to reclaim their previous lives. But things had so changed that many weren't as satisfied or fulfilled as they had been while working outside of their homes. It would be nice to know what had happened to Lilly—if her position had been reclaimed or if she'd gotten tired of it all and left. If she had ever heard from Cisco again. What had happened to her baby.

One positive change was that Dani was no longer as worried about the curse attached to the tree she'd helped to pull down. In hindsight, the accident with Bud's boys was, unfortunately, probably bound to happen, what with the way they tore up and down the roads. And while losing Geoff had caused heartache for Dani and for his family, his death too could have been predicted. Perhaps the curse was nothing but an old rural fairy tale, after all.

Still nagging at her was her need to find a job for the cold, dark winter months when she'd be kept inside by inertia and bad weather. Dani wasn't looking forward to it. The wealthier farmers, like Jacob and his wife or even Bud and his Connie, left the Midwest for short vacations to warmer climates in January and February. She couldn't afford that. But she didn't want to spend the first three months of the new year in her parents' basement, either. Maybe she'd send an email to her old firm to ask if they might need help for a short-term project. Her bank account and her sanity required that she find something to do.

She thought she'd also better confirm with Chuck how much he was planning to charge her to use his harvester. Her property didn't have one. Most guys wouldn't lend out a big machine, but he was open to the idea, he'd said once. She supposed he'd have to be the one to run it, but that was okay with Dani; she didn't have the know-how or the experience to do it herself. She could pull the wagon and haul her crop to the co-op, though.

She felt a pang of satisfaction, looking forward to that day. When she'd quit her job in the Cities and told her folks she wanted to try this adventure, she'd hoped they would understand. As a youngster, Dani had preferred to be on her own, to invent solitary games, to be the lone child spinning circles by herself in satisfied oblivion while her brother and cousins and neighbors, used to her ways, learned it did no good to ask her to play.

That independence was what had led her to her grandparents' farm in Windom every year. Dani had spent parts of each summer learning about cattle and chickens, riding an old horse named "Steve," backing up the old diesel tractor for practice. She wore dirt like a badge of accomplishment, her tan like "the wild Indian" she wanted to grow up to be. Dani had been free, but through the years her time there had started to dwindle. Finally, Pop-pop passed away and Grandmom was placed in the Lutheran home in town. The farm, mostly remortgaged and overextended, brought in enough money at its sale to send Dani and her family to Epcot Center. She'd hated every single moment of that vacation.

There was only one other vehicle in the parking lot in front of Susie's when Dani pulled in later that morning. Opening the metal storm door, she was surprised by the hush inside. The radio was off, the tables mostly empty; no warm tang of sizzling bacon wafted over to greet her. Donna did.

"Dani! Did you hear?" Donna, untying her apron, rushed toward her.

"No. What's up?" The men weren't at their round table. She saw their chairs, though, all pushed back. There were half-empty mugs of coffee haphazardly strewn across the table's surface.

"There's been an accident at Jacob's!" Donna darted behind the counter, snagged her purse from beneath, and headed straight back for her coat by the kitchen exit. "C'mon, you can ride with me." She held her purse strap between her teeth, stuffing her arms into her coat sleeves.

Dani followed Donna out back to her car. She had to push aside a pile of plastic curlers and a scarf from the passenger seat before she could settle herself inside. Donna started the Honda and lit a cigarette at the same time, somehow.

"What happened?" Dani fished for her shoulder harness.

"Lloyd came running in about five minutes before you did," the waitress puffed, shifting from reverse into first gear. They took the corner out of the parking lot at about thirty-five. "He said he was in his shed working when the sheriff came blazing by, followed by the fire truck." She shifted again. "He lives on that same road as Jacob, you know, and can see their place from his. He said both rigs pulled in there, but when he drove over to see what was going on, they wouldn't let him come up."

"Was Jacob hurt?" Dani gave up trying to snap the seatbelt into place; she held it tightly with both hands instead.

"He didn't know. He turned around and came down to Susie's to see if they could all go back together, said that they might be able to get in if they all pulled up in a group." They cruised along toward the Dorns'.

Donna was right: various pickup trucks lined the driveway on both sides from the road all the way up to the biggest shed. Idling there, the red county fire truck had its sirens off, but the lights on top circled shards of blue ice across the barn walls and the sides of the nearest vehicles.

They drove through the trucks to the house and parked on the concrete slab in front of the Dorns' garage. The garage door was open. Loud, hysterical voices carried through the empty stall and raised the hair on Dani's neck. The two women looked at each other; Donna's penciled eyebrows drew tight.

"I'm not going in there," Dani stated. She still hadn't let go of the seatbelt she'd been clutching. "Maybe we shouldn't have come."

"We're not going inside." Donna opened her car door and had one foot out on the concrete. "Let's head out back by the guys." She jerked her head toward the shed and the trucks. "Maybe one of them can tell us what happened."

Dani took more time to exit her own seat. Donna's little Honda seemed protective to her. Dani wanted to stay inside it and lock the doors. This ordinary day had somehow transformed into a tense movie, and the fear that traced its cold fingertips down her spine was no longer her imagination. She zipped her jacket up to her neck before trailing in Donna's wake to the edge of the yard.

It was much quieter here than it was by the house. The stones crunching under her feet sounded loud in contrast to the shocking stillness she neared. First Donna, then Dani stepped up to stand next to the others. Hands in their pockets, silent, their seed caps pulled low, the men were immobile, standing in a line to witness the activity in Jacob's field below.

Dani took a deep breath and looked down. Jacob's green baler was wedged at a sharp angle against the mannerly rows of hay he'd already cut. A harsh dark line, scored deep into the earth, marked an obscene connection between the idling tractor and the EMTs. Their fiberglass stretcher and yellow boxes blocked her direct view. Dani could not tear her attention from a man's legs on the ground, motionless, sticking out from under the heavy wagon where the fresh bales had been tossed.

Lilly

31

THE OTHER GIRLS at Harriet Walker, showing various degrees of roundness, were planning a campaign to be allowed to attend the movie *Gone with the Wind*, which showed the next week at the Varsity Theater across town. Several girls had movie magazines featuring the handsome Clark Gable and swooned over him like they were lovesick.

Lilly envisioned herself in a movie of her own—a slow, lethargic, cotton-wrapped version of daily routines like sweeping, vacuuming the hall, and planning meals for girls too picky or weight-conscious to eat. She woke up to the same movie set every morning, plunked smack into the center of it.

"You ask her. Old Jonesy will do whatever you say," a stick-framed girl with black plastic glasses said, pointing at Lilly. Her belly stuck out in front of her like a round balloon. "Ask her if we can go to the early show—no one goes then but old maids and perverts!" She laughed loudly at her joke. Her cat-eyed frames swept the room to see how the other girls responded to her humor.

Each young woman there was dressed in a loose-fitting smock of the same style, in the same basic brown hue. Any differences extended only from their necks on up, featuring smooth faces or plucked brows or hair styles copied from their magazines. Lipstick was not permitted, nor was jewelry of any kind. The only other difference between the housemates was in the footwear each girl chose for the day, though those in the later stages of their pregnancies mostly opted for flats.

"I don't know why you think she favors me," Lilly replied quietly. She'd kept to herself since moving to Bryant Avenue, responding when she was addressed but preferring to spend her free time with her books and letters.

The raucous ringleader pressed on. "Jonesy likes you because you do what you're supposed to do. You're on time, you don't miss your chores, and"—she glanced at her favorite sidekick, a mousy brown girl as plump as an acorn, and pitched her voice melodiously to a lower register in imitation of their house matron—"you aaact like a laaaaady!" Her voice rose at the end in a giggle. Two other girls on the floral sofa laughed with her.

Lilly smiled. They couldn't help it, they were all teenagers or girls in their early twenties, one as young as fourteen, and they sought levity as surely as an early flower seeks sunlight. Each was here because she'd found herself "in the family way" without a husband to claim her or her child. Those outside the walls of their small compound paid little attention to what went on indoors as long as the girls mostly stayed out of public sight. Their groceries were purchased by Mrs. Jones; they were driven to their appointments in a large black Chrysler by a quiet, old black man named Johnny; and a tutor from the high school came in twice a week to monitor their learning; but mostly the girls were left to their own devices to pass the hours as they waited for their times to come.

Lilly wondered what that time would entail for her. So far, there had been no preparation for the imminent delivery of her child, other than the cursory examination by a severe, white-coated doctor upon her arrival. She touched her swelling stomach as a little arm or leg squirmed by. She loved these quiet moments, the secret of a new life inside of her—she thought it might be a boy, and dreamed of the dark curls and clear, sky-lit eyes of its father. Lilly knew the baby had to somehow come out the same way it had gone in, but other than that, her knowledge and expectations were limited. There were no books around the house that could explain the procedure, nor were her requests for medical books from the library fulfilled by Mrs.

Jones. She planned to ask Dr. Alexander about this on her next visit to his office.

Bringing herself back to the present, Lilly finally replied to the girls. "I'll see. If I can catch her at the right moment, that is."

The girls cheered—a treat to look forward to, maybe—and then settled back down to their daily discussion topics of boys, hairdos, and gossip. Other than their large bellies, they might have been teens at a café or friends meeting at someone's house for a day's fun. They didn't speak much of their situations or of the babies they'd soon be giving up. The "boys" they spoke of, the fathers of these new, little lives, were never described as parents or spouses. Instead, they were portrayed by the girls as carefree, fun-filled fellas who were evidently waiting for their girls to get over their problems and return as their former selves, back into the frolic and freedom they'd had before—before the "situation" or "lady trouble" had mysteriously occurred, sending each girl to this brick home on Bryant Avenue in the first place. Except for the youngest housemate, who was so quiet as to be silent in both her words and actions, each girl at the Harriet Walker Maternity Hospital seemed to want to keep up her usual behavior and interests so that she could more easily slip back into her former life once her "problem" had been resolved.

Lilly left the others and climbed the staircase to her assigned bedroom, their words fading as she neared the second floor. They were heatedly discussing Mrs. Jones's insistence that they wear fake wedding bands whenever they left the property, ". . . as if a group of eight 'married' girls all happen to be pregnant at the same time," snorted the bespectacled ringleader.

She lowered herself onto the wooden armchair placed next to her window, her back aching down low. Lilly shared this small room with another girl who was a bit further along than she, and who'd spent the last nights groaning and tossing, up every hour to visit the lavatory. Her name was Jane and she was from Wisconsin, Lilly had learned from the luggage tag beneath her bed. She called herself "Sandra," however—every girl was required to use a different name and was instructed not to tell the others about her home life or family. Evidently this procedure was to ensure their privacy, but the secrets they chose to keep and those they chose to tell were the only things over which these girls had any personal control. In the still, late nights, most of the girls shared their secrets and fears with their roommates, able in the dark to truly communicate their worries about what their futures would hold.

Lilly had last seen her parents in December. Her mother had taken one look at Lilly, her eyes narrow with suspicion, and asked her if she'd been eating enough and sleeping well, but, uncharacteristically, kept her other observations to herself until later that week. Trixie had borrowed Aunt Helen's car to drive Lilly back to Crestview but stayed only one night, bristling at Mrs. Bradstreet's obvious disapproval of her clanking bracelets and heavy rouge.

Elaine had met her at the café that Saturday between Christmas and New Year's. After receiving their coffee and slices of pie, they'd hesitantly looked up at one another. Taking in Lilly's drawn face and quiet demeanor, Elaine had waited for her friend to begin.

Lilly had started, in words that were clumsy and large in her mouth, to explain how it was that she learned she was expecting a baby.

"How could you let yourself in for this?" Elaine had hissed, drawing herself erect, away from their whispered conversation.

"I didn't know," Lilly had moaned. "I didn't think this"—she gestured vaguely at her midsection—"would happen."

Elaine's mouth was grim. "What did you expect, then?" she'd asked, rather sarcastically. "How could you not know that you might become pregnant?"

"How did you know?" Lilly had countered, a spark of her former steam reignited. She'd sat herself up more firmly. "It's not like it's a topic of acceptable conversation."

"Hush!" Elaine pulled her everyday overcoat more firmly around her shoulders. "Aunt Doris told me. She got pregnant right away after she married, remember?"

Lilly did remember, but hadn't wanted to talk about it now. "I don't know what to do," she continued. "My letters to Cisco have all been returned. He said he'd send me his address when he resettled, but"—her eyes glistened—"I haven't heard from him since I left for school."

Suddenly the pieces had fallen into place for Elaine. "Do you mean to say that this—this *child*—is not Ned's?" Anger and judgment seeped out from her narrowed eyes and tightened lips. Lilly had never seen Elaine this upset before, ever.

Lilly had pushed back from the table. Her ceramic cup had clanked against its ill-fitted saucer, spilling lukewarm coffee onto the white paper placemat beneath, little brown drops blooming on its scalloped, white edges. She hadn't answered.

Elaine sat quiet and still, but gazed at Lilly with such intensity that Lilly was forced to look away. Her friend's demeanor was like thunder claps sounding just moments away from a big storm. Then the tempest broke. "I would say that you're in some kind of trouble."

Lilly had gathered the remaining threads of her dignity: "It's not any trouble that other girls haven't faced." Snatching up her coat, she'd begun shoving her arms into its sleeves. "And it's not a 'trouble' as much as a new life," she said, underscoring the words with emphasis. "It's a baby, not a terminal illness."

"But it's a half-breed!" Elaine had hissed. "It'll never be accepted! You can't imagine you'll keep it, do you?"

She'd known Elaine would be shocked, but Lilly hadn't expected her best friend's words to cut so deeply. "I haven't decided." She'd folded her coat shut, then rummaged in her pocketbook for change to leave for the bill. "Call 'it' what you will, it's half mine too, and I'm perfectly acceptable!" A hairpin had worked itself loose during this last, causing the roll she'd arranged to fall over her angry eyes. This indignity notwithstanding, Lilly had stood and found her way to the exit, leaving Elaine to make her own way home.

Things got worse.

"How could you?" Her mother's voice, full of ice, had gusted like a strong wind past her daughter. "What were you thinking?"

I don't know, Momma, a little voice had grieved from deep within. Lilly hadn't bothered repeating the words out loud. She hadn't had the energy to do so, nor had she expected her mother would even hear her. Perched on the edge of her crisply made bed, she'd felt limp strands of her hair hang listlessly past her sallow cheeks. She'd kept her feet tucked beneath her, her hands clasped over her soft belly, barely swollen. Tears had pushed up through her throat, urging her to let herself cry, but she'd been determined to keep as much control as she could. At this point it was hard enough for her just to take another breath.

Mrs. Bradstreet had turned away from her daughter, crossed the room, and left without looking back. She'd closed the door behind her.

Lilly had penned a short note to Elaine a while later, an apology for her quick departure. She'd included the return address of "Harriet Walker" in the corner of the envelope. Four more letters had been mailed after that. Elaine had yet to write back.

She thought again about these events, sitting on the wooden chair. She held the letters she'd written to Cisco that had been returned to her, unopened. Carefully, she placed them into a cardboard hatbox at the foot of her twin bed. At the bottom of that same box were two other letters. They were from last fall, addressed to her at Iowa State in Ned's heavy hand. These were also unopened. Lilly covered the collection with her straw summer hat, closed the box, and slid it back underneath her bed.

Dani

32

The article in the Crestview *American* attributed Jacob's death to a freak accident. It also stated that the event was still under investigation. According to those at Susie's, he'd gotten off the idling tractor and, for some unknown reason, had gone behind the hay wagon hitched to it. Somehow, the machine had reversed and backed some 8,000 pounds of baled hay right over him. He might not have seen it coming; even if he had, there wasn't much he could have done to push himself out of the way.

After Jacob's funeral, well attended and somber, Chuck came by and pulled in her corn for her. He wouldn't accept payment. He told her to let him know next spring what she'd gotten for the crop. They'd settle up then.

A few weeks later, Dani steered her truck one-handed up Interstate 35 toward the Twin Cities. Over and over, she revisited the accidents that had happened since the witness tree came down. The details spiraled like a circus song stuck in her memory, one event blending with circumstances from a different occasion, until she had to start over again to get things right.

Cool, white fingers of snow tinted with brown road sand reached out and curled across the highway in front of her. The dark sky was a monochrome gray from one horizon to the other. Each side of the asphalt was hemmed in by berms of dirty snow edged in brown crust. The thermos of coffee at her side had grown cold, probably because her heater wasn't pumping out enough warmth to combat the frigid air outside. Winter had arrived earlier than predicted to the Midwest.

Dani was afraid to admit the reason for her flight north out loud: to escape the probability that she'd be the curse's next victim. She *had* used the chainsaw on that tree, after all, and though she'd initially protested about it, she'd been too proud that day to turn down Jacob's request, to seem like a scared newbie, a scared woman. Now she had lost track of the number of times she'd regretted it.

Across the Minnesota border, the wind picked up even more, howling through a gap in the rear window's rubber seal in a high-pitched whistle that made Dani shiver. Broken cornstalks jutted up in random places across the white, empty fields she passed. The trees lined up in windbreaks seemed to hold their empty branches close to their trunks. At one feed lot next to the highway, cattle bunched together on the side of a weathered outbuilding. Semis occasionally blasted past her truck, traveling south, but hardly any other vehicles were headed in her direction.

As she blew through the southern suburbs, Dani's cell phone rang. It was Donna.

"Girl, where are you?" Dani heard music in the background, but couldn't tell if the song was warbling out from the café's kitchen or from a radio playing at Donna's home.

"I'm almost to my parents'," she replied, signaling to the left to let an elderly couple in an ancient Cadillac merge onto the road next to her.

"What're you headed up there for?"

"I'm about to go stir crazy"—Dani laughed, trying to be funny—"and thought I'd give myself a little vacation, somewhere tropical and warm."

"Nah, you're not going to Mexico on one of them packages, are you? You should've asked me! I'd have gone with you in a heartbeat."

This laugh was genuine. "No, I'm visiting my folks. I need to check in and see how they're doing, since Dad retired."

"You should go to that Mall of America. They're supposed to have every kind of shop you could want to see." She had to be calling from Susie's, because Dani now heard plates being stacked together. Roughly.

"You know me, Donna. A mall is probably just ahead of a funeral home, as far as places I like to visit." Dani neared her parents' exit.

"You sure you're really a girl?" Donna delivered her jab with a snort. A male voice from her side broke in; he needed help in the kitchen. The waitress asked Dani to keep in touch before she hung up.

Dani turned into the driveway of a 1970s split-level located near the end of a cul-de-sac in an established neighborhood. The colored brick façade looked dated, but the drive was shoveled clean. The windows shone in the half-wan gleam of the frigid sun. A Christmas wreath over the door provided a bit of color.

The front door popped open as soon as Dani's wheels stopped turning.

"You're here!" her mom called out. The warm air rushing out from inside caused the glass storm door to steam over. "Get inside before you get cold. I'll send your dad to get your things."

Dani retrieved her bag from behind the seat and locked her doors. Before Jacob's death, she'd left all her doors unlocked and usually kept the truck keys right in the ignition.

Her dad waited his turn to welcome her. He took her bag when she reached the top step, a bit off-balance as he tried to hug his daughter with his other arm. "How long are you staying?" he teased. "This bag is sure heavy."

"You're enjoying your retirement too much." Dani relaxed into a smile. "You probably haven't lifted anything heavier than the remote, lately." She noticed that his hairline crept a bit closer to the crown of his head. He'd evidently started wearing glasses, too: they hung from a braided leather strap around the neck of his blue-and-green plaid shirt.

"I'm glad that you're planning to stay for a while, this time." He released her suitcase to the entryway floor. "I don't know that I'll ever understand why you moved to that little farm town, but I sure am proud of you for sticking it out. I'd like to hear more about what you've been doing, spending day after day playing in the dirt." His words poked fun, but the twinkle in his eye showed his genuine interest in his daughter's rural life.

"That would be great, Dad." Dani pulled off her coat and hung it in the front closet. "It's not only the dirt that's so interesting, either." Her smile faded. "For one thing, I thought that the people would be different—more open, or more trusting, or something . . ." She shut the closet. "After dinner, I want to tell you and Mom about what's been going on down there."

His chuckle undercut the intention of her introduction, but seeing that her words were meant to be taken seriously, he stopped.

"Really, Dad. Wait until you hear what I've found out. When I first got the farm lease, none of the farmers had the time of day for me. But some strange and awful things have been happening, and now? Now, they all have something to say about it."

Lilly

33

SANDRA LEFT HARRIET Walker Maternity Hospital the following night after dinner. She'd been complaining of cramps all day and, after the evening meal, was whisked from the kitchen sink into the back of Johnny's Chrysler. She did not return to the home again.

"She was rinsing the dishes," one of the girls whispered later, as they gathered in the large common room, "and she must have dropped or spilled something, because all of a sudden she was standing in a puddle and her skirt was all wet."

Another girl giggled. "That wasn't no water," she snorted. "Her time came. Her baby's on the way."

The room grew still. They all knew that once a girl had been taken to the hospital to deliver, she wouldn't be back again.

Lilly had been paging through an older edition of *Life* magazine, one she'd read so much she'd practically memorized it. It felt like the women in the slim A-line skirts and tidy heels, standing in front of new, gleaming ovens or behind fancy electric vacuum machines, were practically old friends. Her thoughts weren't entirely focused on the pictures in front of her—she worried about her roommate, and wondered what she was experiencing right now. She was curious to learn if she'd ever hear from her again. Before "Sandra's" belongings had been packed and removed from their room, Lilly had taken a moment to jot down the name and address she'd seen on the tag affixed to her roommate's suitcase. She kept that slip of paper in her hatbox, nestled at the bottom with her letters.

Lilly wasn't feeling all that well herself lately. Her ankles were swollen in the evenings, and she didn't feel like eating much because of the growing baby. While the April winds seemed softer and the snow that ringed the yard outside had mostly retreated, her heart remained heavy. Thinking of anything academic felt like swimming through murky water.

She struggled to her feet, said good night to the other girls, and heaved herself up to her room. The other bed had been stripped of its linens and waited quietly for its next occupant. One thin sliver of moon shone through the sheer curtains onto the polished floor. Lilly left the window open a few inches to let in the breeze and the songs of courting frogs and crickets. Her mind went back to something Jane (in the privacy of their own room, they'd used their own names) had whispered a few nights before, about how their lives would never be the same. Jane had wondered how she would ever be able to say goodbye to her intimate companion of the past months. Lilly had willed herself not to think too much ahead, but Jane's longing and fear were foremost in her mind as she struggled to sleep through the gentle thumps from the baby inside.

The following days brought new information about war developments in Europe. Mrs. Jones was adamant about restricting the news from the girls' sensitive ears, preferring that they read, play cards, or continue their academic studies. She told Cook that the less the girls knew about the world, the better, as these reports would only increase their anxiety for their boys and men from home. Her plan wasn't entirely successful, though—as each girl's delivery took her away, her absence was filled almost immediately by another young woman who brought fresh information and her own opinions from the world outside their doors. This cycle continued with the arrival of Lilly's new roommate, who called herself "Vivien" after the movie star. In breathless spurts, when Mrs. Jones or Cook was not in the room, Vivien told the others about how there were nearly no boys left in her hometown. She'd also heard that older men, men the same ages as the girls' fathers, would be next in line for the draft.

Lilly vaguely recalled the conversations between Ned and Lonny on the same topic. She brooded at the way time continued to march on. It seemed like only yesterday that she and Elaine had shared evening dates. That she'd met Cisco. That her life had changed, tilting away from the gentle meanderings of what she used to think was important to a world she never knew existed.

Lilly became more reticent as the days dragged past. Her baby stopped moving as often, causing Lilly to pause and hold her breath at strange moments, hoping to feel a movement or hiccup from inside. Perhaps the little one found the quarters too constricting and was passing time as well, waiting patiently to join the world outside.

On Tuesday, the week after Vivien arrived, Lilly woke with stomach cramps and a feeling of nausea. She found Mrs. Jones after breakfast and gave her the symptoms; Mrs. Jones told Lilly she'd best take a quick bath and get her hospital bag in order. Her response brought Lilly's fear back to the surface. She didn't know, exactly, what was about to happen, or how the baby had decided to come, or even what she was supposed to do. She didn't have anyone to ask.

Mrs. Jones was busy using the telephone when Lilly stopped outside of her office an hour later. The pangs had increased in intensity; she felt like she was being squeezed by a giant, wide belt.

"Better get you to the hospital, then," Mrs. Jones announced, hanging up. She'd seen Lilly pacing outside her office door. Lilly's hands were braced behind her hips, her eyes large and unblinking. So many young girls had endured the same routine during the last twelve years of Mrs. Jones's tenure, and yet they continued to come, one after the next, the war driving young people to make the most of a time that might be measured in fewer days than they'd expected.

Mrs. Jones laid Lilly's packed satchel on the seat next to her. Lilly hoped she'd impart some wisdom or instructions to get her through the next hours, but if she had any advice she kept it to herself. "Don't worry," she directed. "We'll get the rest of your things bundled up and ready for you, for when you're ready to leave the hospital." She shut the car door and Johnny drove off.

The hospital placed Lilly in a quiet room atop a cold, metal gurney with thin sheets. The pillow under her head might have been made of cardboard. She was washed and shaved, then left alone. Gritting her teeth through the waves of pain that came ever faster, she thought about her mother and about Elaine and wished that either one, anyone, could be with her right now. Her heart pumped wildly. Her pulse throbbed behind her eyes and in her throat. Perspiration streamed from her body, soaking the sheets.

A different nurse with short, dark curls under her cap came by later (whether an hour or a day, Lilly could not say). She took a quick peek, pronounced Lilly "ready to go," and wheeled her into a large, tiled room filled with lights on high stands and metal utensils atop a metal cart. The nurse transferred her unceremoniously onto a chair that somehow split under her seat. Her heels were strapped into stirrups in front of her. She dared not ask any questions; the green-gowned doctor was in a hurry and snapped in a bossy voice to the nurses who rushed to help him. Their eyes, quick and solemn, darted every place but Lilly's own.

The last thing Lilly recalled was a rubber mask being lowered to her face. She was told to breathe deeply, so she did.

Lilly woke up in a different room, covered with a thin cotton blanket, alone. It seemed to be twilight, judging from the scant illumination that ebbed into the room through the slatted shade. The bed next to her was empty, its stained mattress sagging in the middle. Her groin and lower stomach ached; her tummy was flatter but soft, like heavy dough.

She struggled to sit up. A wave of nausea hit her; she swallowed the burning acid back into her throat. There was no place to spit it out. Warm tears ran down her cheeks and pooled into her ears and hair.

Time passed; the shadows deepened. She heard no sound, infant or otherwise, from the hall. She was thirsty. She wondered how long she'd be forgotten and worried about what would come next. They would let her see her baby, she hoped, but didn't think she'd learn anything about his or her new parents, or where he or she would be taken to live their life. Lilly doubted the child would ever be told about her or about its father. She doubted that she'd ever feel happiness again.

She brushed at her eyes and struggled to sit, pushing herself into a reclining position with her elbow. There, the nausea wasn't so bad now. She used the metal tubing that supported the mattress to steady herself to standing. The cold linoleum slapped at her bare feet. Her threadbare gown gaped open at the back, sending shivers along her sweaty spine. Taking a deep breath, she pulled the cotton cover from the bed over one shoulder, then the other, like a robe. She began shuffling to the door. A thin trickle of red coursed down her right shin and trailed behind her, a silent betrayal. Lilly ignored it and continued her escape.

She made it out of her room and into the softly lit hallway. She was at the far end of a long line of doors, mostly closed. At the opposite end was a half-wall, beyond which Lilly thought she could hear voices and the clack of a typewriter. She pushed her feet along the cool floor, holding the blanket around her, intent on finding either her baby or any information about it.

A laugh escaped from the nurses' station ahead. A stocky nurse with glasses and short, strawberry-blonde hair shot out of the area, abruptly pulling up when she saw Lilly. Tiny pills in small, white cups quivered on the tray she held with both hands. "What are you doing out of bed, miss?" Her words were not unkind, though her eyes seemed to have doubled in size behind their lenses. She turned and placed the tray back on the counter atop the half-wall. "We need to get you off your feet and resting." She gently twirled Lilly back toward her room.

"I want to see my baby!" Lilly couldn't seem to get her own feet to stop moving, disobeying her struggle to continue in the opposite direction. Her voice, so loud in her head, sounded out loud like that of a young girl.

"There will be time for that," the nurse responded, her grip gently but firmly propelling Lilly back to her room. "We'll get some aspirin, too, and see if we can get a little broth into your tummy." Lilly's vision swam; the edges of the tile floor bulged and ballooned underneath. "You've had quite a day, after all," the nurse finished.

They shuffled toward the end of the hall and entered the last room. The nurse helped Lilly back to the bed when she noticed the soiled back gown. "Let's find you a new sanitary pad, honey, and get you cleaned up, okay?" Lilly had no strength to do anything but what the kind young woman directed.

It was like being submerged under the surface of something heavy and immobile, so lethargic and removed were the starts and stops of her thoughts, with virtually no continuity between them. Sponged and freshened up, a cool cloth on her forehead, Lilly suddenly remembered why she'd struggled to get up before. "Can I see my baby now?" she asked, removing the washcloth from her eyes to look at the nurse before she could leave the room.

"Sweetie, I don't know." She tilted her chin down and fussed with her wristwatch. "The county doesn't want you to get attached to it, you know," she began. "It's best for the baby and the new parents to get to know each other right off the bat, so they can be a strong family from the get-go." The words themselves, harsh and final and poison, were swathed in soft cotton and mild manners. "You aren't up to it right now, anyhow." The nurse shut off the room light and gently pulled the door shut behind her.

Lilly's tears, absorbed into her washcloth, made it warm; she let it slide off her face onto the floor. She pulled the thin blanket back up under her chin and hugged herself tightly under its meager protection. She felt scooped out and hollow, like the empty spot just beneath her heart.

Dani

_____

34

THE HOLIDAY SEASON passed. Before she headed back to the farm, Dani helped her mom sort through boxes in their attic: collections of colored pictures and report cards, dishes her grandma had acquired through stamp books she'd saved, trophies her brother had looked at once and tossed aside. Her parents were ready to "downsize," they said, and wanted the convenience of retirement living and the ability to travel. As far as snow shoveling, after helping her dad keep the driveway clear through the month's snowfall, Dani agreed that having someone else take care of the outdoor maintenance seemed like a good idea.

The evening sky grew dark early this time of year. During the drive back south to Crestview, Dani used the time to consider her plans for the year ahead. She'd enjoyed the time she'd had with her family, but little seedlings of discontent had gained strength through every day she'd spent inside, on crowded suburban streets, or in the artificial reality of indoor shopping and restaurants. Once more, she realized that she was at her best when she had space around her. As the miles unfurled and buildings and signs and lightposts faded away, Dani settled into herself, her scattered pieces knitting together again.

Maybe she'd needed the visit home to confirm what she already knew. It had been a blessing to be able to talk through the terrible events in

Crestview with others, to hear her parents' opinions about the strange and curious circumstances that, to their minds, were upsetting and unfortunate but most certainly unrelated. As her mom said, some old tree didn't have the power to impact human lives. Dani believed this now, she told herself, convinced that the sad incidents were simply quirky turns of fate, lined up in an unlucky, random row.

Before she turned onto County Road 27, Dani drove past the section that used to be the Swensons' farmstead. She slowed, leaning forward to see past the hills of snow the county's road grader had plowed up on each side of the road. Where the house once stood now rested an angular pile of concrete and stones, jutting up through the white drifts like a modern monument. The bushes and trees around the perimeter had been toppled and stacked to the side, robed in soft-edged mounds that disguised their former shapes. Only the shed remained, forlorn and abandoned in the night's chilling air.

She eased her truck ahead, deciding to make one more stop at the library before it closed.

Mrs. Swenson's Taurus wasn't parked in her usual spot beside the building. Dani checked her watch—almost eight o'clock—decided to take the chance, and parked in its place. She hurried up the steps and entered the vestibule at the same moment a man pushed through the door to make his exit. His smile was brief. "Sorry, I'm closing up for the night." He wore a tan Carhartt jacket and held a ring of silver keys. Something about him exuded a boundless energy that made Dani think of a large dog. And there was something familiar about him, too: the shape of his face, maybe, or the way his brown eyes tilted down at the corners, reminded her of someone she thought she knew. At any rate, he didn't keep still long enough for pleasantries: he'd already stepped outside next to her and was turning his key to secure the wooden door.

"I'm looking for Mrs. Swenson," Dani put forth, attempting to slow his exit.

"Are you a friend of hers?" The man hefted his backpack to rest evenly on both shoulders—broad shoulders, she noticed, tilting her chin up to see his face more clearly.

"I am, but I haven't been in town since before Christmas."

He started down the steps. She was forced to follow, if she wanted to learn where Mrs. Swenson was keeping herself. As far back as Dani could remember, the librarian's car had been parked outside the library every time she'd come to town. She knew that Mrs. Swenson took her vocation seriously; it wasn't like her to miss a day of work, even a snowy one.

The man reached the sidewalk ahead of her. The corner streetlight picked out the silver strands in his hair when he bent down to retie his boot.

"Is she okay?" Dani rejoined him. "I don't think I've ever known her to take a sick day."

He'd straightened up and was zipping his jacket closed. "She hasn't been well, lately."

Maybe it was his accent, Dani thought; there was something familiar about this person that she couldn't pin down.

"What did you say your name was?" He dug for something in his coat pocket.

"I didn't."

Two brown eyes flew over to rest on her.

"But it's Dani. Dani Holden."

He unwrapped a stick of gum and tossed it into his mouth. "I thought so," he replied, pressing the wrapper into a tight bundle before shoving it into his pocket. "I'm Pete, Donna's brother. I'm taking over for Mrs. Swenson for a while, 'till she's up and ready to come back." He squared up his collar. "Nice to meet you, Dani Holden," he finished, then turned the opposite way toward Susie's Café.

Dani stood on the sidewalk a moment longer, the streetlight carving a tent of light through the winter's early darkness and gentle snowfall. The confidence she'd carried back from Minnesota had faded after seeing the destruction at the farmhouse and now missing her friend's face behind the checkout counter. A quick check on the librarian might put things right again, Dani thought, returning to her truck. Her footsteps on the snowy path were a lonely sound. The town and its inhabitants had already settled in for another long, cold night.

SHE WAITED FOR Mrs. Swenson to answer her door. She didn't. Dani wiggled her toes, standing on the front stoop, listening for an invitation to enter.

After a long two minutes of silence, she quit waiting.

"Hello? Mrs. Swenson?" She turned the knob; the door wasn't locked. She tried calling out again from the threshold.

No answer. Looking down the long corridor to the back of the house, Dani saw a light in the kitchen. Heading that way, she called again, louder. Still no response.

Scanning the empty room, she turned and followed the hallway back to the front. She rushed up the stairs to the small home's second level, rapid heartbeats keeping time with her steps. Two doorways faced one another at the top of the steps, with a small bathroom directly ahead. The glow of a nightlight from within showed it to be empty.

Dani turned into the first room to the right and snapped on the ceiling light. Evidently, it was used as a study—a clunky, metal office desk took up one corner, a stuffed bookcase at its side. A large cardboard box sat in the center of the room, partially filled with papers.

The second room, the one behind her, was a bedroom the same size as the office. Light from the street streamed through the lacy window shade to speckle the bed's quilts and blankets like a snowflake cutout. The inert shape of Mrs. Swenson was tucked up like a child underneath.

Not wishing to startle the older lady, Dani whispered. "Mrs. S?"

Silence.

Dani crept closer and dropped to her knees. She pressed under the woman's jaw for a pulse. There was none. Mrs. Swenson's skin was cool; her lips, still bearing a faint trace of reddish lipstick, were dry. Her arms were drawn up against her chest, crossed as if she were hugging something. A small, silver watch on the nightstand ticked off the seconds like tiny grains of sand plinking into a crystal vial.

Dani sat back on her heels and dropped her hands onto the tops of her thighs. Her head sank down to her chest. She wondered if she should offer a prayer, though it was obviously too late to make a difference. Her pulse scudded against the bottom of her throat, but she didn't cry. The rationalizations she'd set up to separate herself from the curse snapped apart as if splashed in kerosene and set ablaze by a single, slender match.

She found herself back downstairs in the kitchen. A red, plastic phone hung on the wall by the back door. She grasped the handset out of the way and dialed. Reaching a human voice at the sheriff's office took forever. Finally, Dani explained to the dispatcher what she'd walked in on. The woman told her to sit tight: a deputy was on the way and would be with her in ten to twenty minutes.

The little house's silence pressed around Dani like dark, solid hands. Sliding her back along the wall to sit under the phone, she tried to think of things other than death while she waited. It didn't work. Mrs. Swenson must have been in her seventies, she guessed, and she'd certainly seemed healthy that last time Dani saw her. But then Dani remembered the stress of the auction, the heat that week when they'd cleared out her sister's home, the loneliness she must have felt spending the holidays by herself . . . she wondered if Mrs. Swenson had finally had enough.

Fifteen minutes passed, but no one arrived from the sheriff's department to take over. Dani returned upstairs and turned on the bedroom light for the deputy's arrival. She smoothed the top quilt over Mrs. Swenson, then wandered across the hall to the study, peering into the cardboard box placed in the middle of the study's floor. It looked like Mrs. Swenson had been sorting through the items within: several papers had been placed in folders, others clipped together. Dani sifted through the collection of papers Mrs. Swenson had carefully placed on top, telling herself that a little look wouldn't harm anyone.

Making her next decision took less than an instant: Dani removed the valuable documents, folded them into her jacket pocket, and pushed self-recrimination outside with her as she brought the package to her truck. She stowed it safely under the driver's seat, closing it in right as the sheriff's deputy pulled into Mrs. Swenson's driveway, blue and red lights blinking.

Dani faced the cruiser, then went with the deputy to the front door.

After the gentlemen of Crestview's only funeral home had calmly borne

Mrs. Swenson away, Dani stayed with the sheriff's deputy until he locked up.

"Don't suppose there's much of value in there," he declared, pushing his hat down over his short, bristled hair. "But I don't want to be accused of neglecting my due diligence." The radio at his hip crackled. After checking it, he became eager to get moving. "Why don't you go ahead now? I'll follow you to make sure you get on your way okay." He drove close behind her truck until they reached the end of her section, where he gave the two-finger salute before they turned in opposite directions.

She drove through the dark toward her own snow-covered lane. The unsettled fear she had managed to put away returned. Her palms grew sweaty, her face flushed hot, and she caught herself scanning her driveway for dark shapes that jumped out in the night. *Just keep breathing*, she told herself, and steered straight for her unlit garage.

Lilly

35

LILLY IMAGINED DRY corn husks left in the fields after harvest. The way the wind blew them across the denuded fields and over the dusty gravel on the roads. How their whispers were the only weight left to them, unsubstantial and untethered. Not quite free, but somehow still obligated to the tired earth they couldn't seem to leave behind.

The view from Aunt Helen's upper bedroom wasn't quite as bleak, though Lilly didn't spend time at the window. Trixie had returned to Ames after settling Lilly in St. Paul, assuring her that Aunt Helen could be trusted and would treat her kindly. Sometimes, though, Lilly didn't even bother answering Aunt Helen when she'd come to check on her. Twice a day, both before she left for work and upon her return, she'd delivered trays of soft food and tea for the girl; none of them, save for a few sips of tea, had been touched.

The cramps in Lilly's stomach area had ceased, but her breasts ached as though they would explode when she turned over in bed. The gentle nurse at the hospital had warned Lilly to wrap bands around them as tightly as she could handle, but so far she could barely even manage stepping from the bed to the toilet. Great, damp rings on the bottom sheet matched the wet pillowcase under her snarled hair. She wore the same sagging nightgown Trixie had pulled over her head when she'd brought her here to rest.

Late gray mornings merged with early gray evenings. She did not re-member sleeping but must have done so, evidently for quite a while, be-cause in what seemed like no time Trixie was there, tugging off her gloves and wagging her tongue, making Lilly's muscles jump and her eyes startle open.

"Are you telling me that you haven't gotten up all week?" Trixie bustled out of her swing coat and bent down to peer into Lilly's face. She snapped back to standing. "Let's get you into a warm tub, girlie." Her tone became softer; her eyes frowned at the corners. "There's nothing that a warm bath and a new outfit can't do to perk up a gal!"

Lilly wished she could roll off the other side of the bed, out of sight. Inertia bound her motionless. It felt like her brain was no longer able to strand together a thought.

Trixie grasped Lilly's forearm and shook the covers off her bed. Settling the mess onto the floor, she strode across the hall and started the tap in the bathtub. Her voice rang out over the splashing water—something about a new fella and an upcoming dance in Des Moines—and grew louder as she returned to Lilly's motionless form.

"You need to get yourself together, honey," Trixie crooned, smoothing Lilly's stringy hair from her forehead. "You have so much ahead of you! Don't let yourself just, just . . ." Words, for once, failed her.

Lilly's throat grew thick. Her closed eyelids swelled and her cracked lips wavered, struggling to hold back the choking, hot injustice that bloomed like acid from deep down in her chest. One more breath might cause her whole soul to collapse. She wanted to dissolve, to vanish, into a diminish-ing pool of grief.

Her feet were heavy, round stones stumbling over the braided rag rug next to her metal bedframe. Trixie's murmurs merged with gurgles of water cascading into the tub. Warm wisps of scent, dancing in the window, en-couraged her. The light outside, shaded by a thin, cotton curtain next to the glass, beckoned her to take a few more steps forward.

The cocooning weight of the bathwater embraced her without judg-ment. She slid beneath its surface and heard her slow, grave heart beating in her ears. Her swollen breasts became soft again; her spine uncurled. Lilly drank in shortened gasps of clean air, keeping her eyes and ears swaddled beneath the protective meniscus of the womb that enclosed her.

BEFORE TRIXIE RETURNED to school the next day, she guided Lilly downstairs to eat a quick bite with her and her aunt. It was a Saturday, so Aunt Helen had allowed herself to sleep in. She greeted the girls from a red-cushioned metal kitchen chair, wrapped in a thin, flowered housedress and reading the *St. Paul Dispatch*. A cigarette smoked from the green ashtray at her elbow; a half-empty coffee cup sat lopsided on its saucer.

"Girls, let me show you this!" She put down the newspaper and tapped her finger on a smiling woman placed at the center of the page. "It says here, 'If you can run a vacuum, you can do my war job at Gopher!'" Aunt Helen spoke with a gleam to her eye. "This'd be perfect for you, dearie. And the bus runs right by our corner, every day but Sunday."

So Lilly began working at the munitions factory. First she had an appointment in a big federal building in Minneapolis, a block off Lake Street, to assess her general intelligence. She had the impression that as long as she was smarter than a potato, she'd be hired. She was.

Her primary job was to measure out an ingredient needed in the production of cannon powder. She worked nine hours each day and made about ninety-three cents for each hour, a good wage. Over half the workers at the plant were women. After a while, Lilly found that they acted about the same there as they did in Iowa and at the Walker Maternity Home. Some visited when they weren't supposed to; some moaned about children left behind with begrudging mothers-in-law; some worried about husbands or special fellows serving in the war.

Lilly rose at 4:15 each morning. She grew accustomed to wearing her hair in a kerchief and sleeping on a moving bus. She carried a thermos of hot coffee and made three sandwiches to eat each day. It took a little under an hour to travel from Aunt Helen's corner to Rosemount, a bit longer on the return ride home. Aunt Helen insisted that Lilly stay with her and accepted ten dollars a week for her board. Lilly didn't make any friends at the Gopher plant, but she smiled when one of the other girls made a joke. She didn't joke, herself.

Her baby boy, gone within that first week, had been matched with a couple in Omaha who hadn't been blessed with a child of their own. She didn't see her son the day he was born, hastily wrapped and taken from the delivery room after the mask had been lowered and she'd drifted off to sleep. She'd spied him on the day he left. She'd been at the front window of the maternity floor's lounge, watching gray rain turn the puddles into tidal pools across the street, wind folding their surfaces into creases. Foggy as the weather, Lilly came to with a jolt that hit her from nowhere: she knew, she was certain in the center of her soul, that a little blue-wrapped bundle being carefully placed on his new mother's lap was her little boy. His dark curls ruffled in the wind. Before she could get out the door, though, his new family's sedan was gone.

This Thursday morning, Lilly followed a now-familiar-looking girl to the bus stop. The early spring brought early morning sunshine, and the sidewalks were dry all the way to the corner of West Seventh and Oleander. A cool, pine-scented breeze floated in from the northwest. Lilly pulled herself up the bus steps with the silver handrail, the smell of burnt coffee and the sound of "Jitterbug Blues" on the radio greeting her. She settled herself toward the front on an empty bench. The other girl paused, then asked if she could sit next to Lilly.

"Sure," she replied, but didn't allow herself to return the other girl's shy smile. Instead she looked over her shoulder at the neighborhood receding into the distance.

"Do I know you from somewhere?" the girl began. Her voice had a bit of a drawl to it.

"I don't think so." Lilly flicked her glance to the girl's face. Young, freckled, some blonde hair escaped her blue kerchief. Her brown eyes met Lilly's before she could look away.

"Are you from here?" the girl continued.

"No."

"I'm not, either." She hunched down into herself. They both turned to face the front of the bus. "I'm from Iowa."

Even though she didn't want to be interested, Lilly responded. "Whereabouts in Iowa?"

"Decorah. My folks have a farm there. Mostly wheat and corn, though Daddy says he may have to give it up. He's had to rely on the migrants for help, so he sent me and my sisters up here until things get better back home."

They rode through the edges of civilization toward the light-edged farmland beyond.

The bus's skimpy tires covered the miles to Rosemount, but Lilly didn't sleep. The absence of the other riders' clamor let her focus more clearly on her usual obsession. Here on the bus and in her bed at night were the only moments that Lilly could recall the downy forehead of her little boy, his soft folds and chubby cheeks, his dark blue eyes. She didn't know if she imagined the details correctly: she never held him, never touched his warm skin, didn't get to kiss him hello or goodbye.

She dreamed of him every night and thought of him every day.

Dani

36

DANI RETURNED TO the Crestview library the morning after Mrs. Swenson passed away. The man she'd seen the night before, Donna's brother Pete, was behind the checkout counter where Mrs. Swenson used to preside. It was strange not to see her there.

She hadn't slept after returning to her own place. She'd had to maneuver her truck through a month's worth of unplowed snowfall that blanketed her driveway. After dropping her suitcase twice on the hike to her porch, she'd given up the idea of unloading the rest of her cargo until the following day, thinking her chances would be better in the next morning's light.

Her furnace had grumbled before agreeing to put forth heat. She'd left the kitchen and bathroom taps dripping when she'd departed, in order to prevent her water lines from freezing; rusty smears garnished each white porcelain sink. The electricity worked fine, though, so Dani boiled water for a cup of hot tea, sorted through her bag for some leftover cookies, wrapped herself in the quilt she kept on the sofa, and unfolded the papers she'd taken from Mrs. Swenson's house to read.

What she'd found in the cardboard box shed light on one of the questions Mrs. Swenson had not answered. Her discovery added another development to the pile of secrets that a stunned Dani was still struggling to sort through.

Before she'd left Minnesota, Dani had used her parents' computer to email for information about the defunct Gopher Munitions plant. She logged into her email account from the Crestview library to check for a response. It was there. Dani squeezed her fist: a small victory, but one that gratified her. The reply reported that a database of former Gopher Munitions employees, if it still existed, was now under the auspices of the company that had purchased the old factory years ago. The email included a link to that company's headquarters with a suggestion to contact their human resources department for further assistance.

The information was good, but Dani didn't want to take the time to go through the whole email process again. She left her coat and notebook at the computer station she was using, took out her cell phone, and returned to the outer vestibule. She brought the phone number from the email with her.

She dialed, her voice ringing in the cold and empty corridor, and asked to be transferred to human resources. After six rings, a tired voice answered.

Dani gave her name, Lilly's name, and a short explanation of what she was looking for. The voice didn't respond.

"Hello?" Dani tried again.

"I'm here, I'm here," the woman replied. "Give me a minute." Dani heard a keyboard clicking and papers shuffling. She watched condensation from her breath form clouds in the frigid air of the vestibule's ceiling high above her.

The door to the library's upper level opened. The substitute in charge stuck his head out. He wondered if she was going to be awhile, as her call was disturbing a patron in the periodicals section.

"You're kidding, right?" Dani's short night of sleep must have disconnected her patience. Her snarl echoed around the empty air of the vestibule.

"What was that?" the woman on the phone asked. "Are you talking to me?"

"Oh, no. I'm sorry, ma'am," Dani used what she hoped was her most pleasant voice. "Someone on my side interrupted us." She glared back at the librarian. He winked at her and returned inside. "Are you finding anything?"

The voice from her phone cleared her throat and resumed. "Most of these people are probably dead, you know," she said.

Dani felt like she had been hitting the same brick wall over and over. "Yes, I'm sure that most are." Dani tried not to sigh. "But here's the thing: I've come across some information from her sister that I'd really like to pass on to her, if she's still with us."

At first, the representative didn't answer. Dani held her breath. The woman's voice finally returned. "I see here that there's a roster of names, and even some phone numbers." But her voice trailed off again.

"Is there any way at all that you could help?"

The voice gave in. "I don't see as it makes any difference now, one way or the other. Do you have a pen? Here's what I have." And with that, the woman listed the last known address of Lillian J. Bradstreet, once of St. Paul, Minnesota, most recently of Huntington Beach, California. She didn't have a phone number, but repeated the address for Dani twice.

"Thank you so much!" Dani's exuberance made the glass chandelier overhead quiver. She didn't care. She'd had to endure so many changes that she couldn't control this year; receiving this unexpected information was like a reward for her persistence. Dani hung up, then pumped her fist into the air.

A tiny flame of possibility reignited inside her: maybe she could put things back to rights by returning the letters back to Lillian. It wouldn't hurt to try. With Mrs. Swenson's passing, Dani wanted to stay firmly out of the curse's wide shadow. She sat on a vestibule step crusted with snow-melting pellets, the torn paper with Lilly's address clutched in her hand, and let her tears flow.

The substitute librarian came all the way out of the library's upper section this time. He hesitated for a moment at the top of the stairs, then stepped down and sat next to her. "Did you get some bad news?" His voice, like the soft flannel shirt and faded jeans he wore, was gentle.

She laughed, which made him look bewildered. Her cheeks may have been wet, but her smile was wide. "I got some fantastic news," she blurted.

"Huh. That's something." The man's voice seemed a shade less gentle than before. He stood up. "Do you think you'll be out here much longer? I don't want you to be the first patron I have to blacklist."

Dani got to her feet and followed him back upstairs. "I'm sorry," she explained. "But I've been working on this puzzle for so long, I thought I'd never get the pieces together."

He waited at the glass door for her to continue. "What's it about?"

"It'd take too long to explain." She was anxious to get back to a computer. "I'll finish up and be on my way. Quietly," she added. They went through the doorway together.

Back at the workstation, Dani entered the street address she'd gotten over the phone. A number of hits led her to a newer address for Lillian Bradstreet. It was still in Huntington Beach, and there was a phone number attached.

Dani

37

MUD AND SAND clogged every surface. Early spring runoff breached the ditches and drainfields, spilling liquid back up onto waterlogged roads. The mess reached past the edges of the field Dani had committed to farm for another season, clinging to her boots and the knees of her work jeans. She trudged through it slowly, inching back to the house. Though spring planting was around the corner, Dani had a different task at the top of her priority list.

Beeping the horn repeatedly as she slid past the shed, Donna managed to stop her car before smashing into the front of Dani's porch. Her engine pinged and coughed, competing in volume with a Rick Springfield song blaring from inside. The driver's door screeched open and Donna's newly colored hairdo sprung out from behind it. Swearing to herself, she looked for a dry spot to land upon.

By now, Dani was sitting on the top step of the front porch, observing her friend's dilemma as she shucked off her boots. In dirty, stockinged feet, she followed Donna down the hall into her own kitchen. Donna threw two mugs of that morning's coffee into the microwave to reheat and shuffled through the cupboards, still cussing to herself.

"Look in the cabinet by the stove," Dani suggested. "Unless the mice ate them, there should be some cookies there."

"You're disgusting! Why don't you get yourself a cat? Or set a trap?"

Donna plunked the half-empty package onto the table in front of them.

Dani collected the coffee from the microwave and sat. "Donna. I did something the other night that I shouldn't have."

"Oh goody," Donna replied in a tart, exaggerated fashion. "I can't wait to hear it."

"I'm being serious now." There wasn't any laughter in Dani's reaction. "I found something, the night I went over to Mrs. Swenson's."

Donna sat, but not before Dani had to continue.

"Before I found . . . her, I was searching for her, you know, all around her house."

"Hadn't you ever been there before then?"

"Yes, but I'd never gone upstairs, where her bedroom is. Was."

Donna dipped a stale cookie. "So, go on."

"In that other room she has, the one she uses as an office, she'd been packing or unpacking a bunch of papers." Dani shifted in her seat. "It sort of changes how I feel about her."

"What do you mean?"

Dani explained that she'd found, and taken, some additional letters. They were signed by Elaine and Eleanor's father and were dated August, 1939. One was addressed to the Bradstreets, Lilly's parents; another bore the name of Ned Wagner, sent to him in care of Crestview Bank.

Donna perched on the edge of her chair. "What did they say? Do you have them now?"

"I have them," Dani confirmed, "but I feel strange about them. I think they should be saved for Lilly, if I can find her." She paused. "Basically, Mrs. Swenson's parents pulled the rug out from under Lilly. They wrote that their son, Steve, saw her 'consorting with a foreigner,' and that they were obligated to let her parents know."

"How could they!" Donna spat out the words. She jumped up to pace in the tight space between the table and the back door. "Didn't they know Lilly for ages? Why'd they think it would help anything, telling her folks? And her boyfriend too?" Abruptly, she stopped. "But why did Mrs. Swenson have the letters, if they'd already been mailed?"

"I don't know—maybe Mrs. Swenson found them first, or maybe she got them back afterward, somehow. Remember how she told me, last summer, that she and her brother overheard their parents' conversation about this? Maybe she felt bad for Lilly, or guilty about her brother's nosiness, and retrieved the letters before they could cause any harm." Her tone calmed. "But think about it, Donna: the man Lilly was involved with was found hanging in that tree. Someone had to have seen something. Maybe it wasn't Mrs. Swenson's family that told, but would you want to admit that your family could've had a hand in what led to that death?"

"That's what I wondered," Donna agreed. "Her, her family, they would've been shocked! Maybe they thought they'd get in trouble. But for the love of God! She knew how hard you were trying to figure out what went on, back then." She sat again, but her right foot jiggled as she tried to make sense of this new layer of information. "So what do we do next?"

"Here's what I think: I want to call the number I found for Lilly. I want to tell her about Mrs. Swenson, and—"

"Are you going to tell her what happened to Cisco?"

Dani frowned. "I don't know."

Lilly

38

TRIXIE SLID TO a stop in front of Aunt Helen's house on two wheels, or so it looked to Lilly, sitting at the front window. Dressed this warm Sunday morning in a green, flower-print dress, she also wore ladylike heels in deference to the upcoming visit with her mother. She carried her flats inside the woven bamboo purse at her side. Thankfully, she wasn't required to wear hose: despite the shortages, the heat alone made this choice easy.

Lilly jumped up and gave Helen a hug. She thanked Trixie's aunt once again for her hospitality.

"It was nothing, honey," the older woman emphasized. "I'm happy to have been able to help." She looked like she wanted to say more, but instead she pursed her lips together, patted Lilly's shoulder and handed her a cool thermos, condensation slicking its metal sides. "Here's a little lemonade for your ride," she said, adding, "and don't let my niece add anything to this, you hear?" Aunt Helen smiled and crossed the room to open her front door. "Want me to carry this for you?" She'd picked up the cardboard hatbox from the floor next to Lilly's other bag.

Lilly tucked her purse into the crook of her elbow and grasped the suitcase handle in her other hand. "Thanks, but I've got it." She accepted the box with her free hand and followed Helen outside.

The summer rays bounced off the metal of Trixie's sedan like lightning, streaking directly into Lilly's eyes. Moving toward the street, she noted the black-and-white outfit Trixie wore: slim pencil skirt with a sleeveless blouse, no collar. Her bright-red lips and oversized, black sunglasses made her look like a model in the magazines. Trixie teetered on her high heels to the back of the car to fuss with the trunk, calling out greetings to her aunt and Lilly in her loud, cheerful way.

"Here, let me," Lilly interrupted, dropping the suitcase and holding out her hand for the keys.

Trixie's glossy lips smiled and then puckered up to deliver a kiss, which Lilly was only able to avoid by placing her hand between the red lipstick and her own cheek.

"You and your lipstick!" Lilly clucked. "I don't look as pretty as you do in that color; better keep it for yourself!" She settled her items into the trunk and closed the lid.

Trixie laughed. "Well, look who's back!" She gently squeezed Lilly's arm.

Aunt Helen, after fussing with a young neighbor girl over the safety of her metal roller skates, met the girls at the curb. "Be careful driving now, miss," she scolded her niece. "Don't stop anywhere that looks sketchy for fuel. And mind the fellas asking for rides: you drive on by."

Trixie lowered her chin to wink at Lilly over the top of her sunglasses. "We'll be perfectly fine, Auntie dear," Trixie replied. "And we need to be on our way!" She gave the older woman a quick hug and resettled herself behind the steering wheel.

Lilly opened the passenger-side door. She caught Aunt Helen's glance before sliding into the car. The older woman looked apprehensive but brightened up when she saw Lilly looking at her. She gave an energetic wave in response to Lilly's raised hand.

Blue-tinged gusts spurted out of the car's tailpipe as Lilly hopped in. She tried to arrange the skirt underneath her to prevent wrinkles but gave up, grabbing for the dashboard, when Trixie hit the gas. They flew down Aunt Helen's street, trilling the horn and trailing smoky fumes.

BY THE TIME they neared the Iowa border, the lemonade was gone and the gas tank gauge was very near the 'empty' mark. Trixie was all for pushing for Crestview. Lilly wanted to stop and get herself arranged and neatened before surprising her parents at home.

"It's my turn to pay," Lilly asserted, "so I should get to decide where we stop." She pointed to a fuel station road sign on their right.

Trixie sighed and signaled their turn, her slim arm riding the waves of hot air out her window. "Fine. I could stand to powder my nose, anyhow."

The still air seemed many times warmer than the breeze from the moving car's open windows. A young man with greasy dungarees and a dingy shirt strolled out of the service station to fill their tank, his glistening curls arranged just so over his forehead.

"Cliff?" Trixie purred, somehow deciphering the name embroidered over his soiled shirt pocket. "Would you also check the oil? We still have a long way to go."

He nodded and grinned back at her, expertly flipping up the hood. "Sure will," he consented. "Though I don't know that you two might not do better staying here a while!"

Lilly kept moving toward the service station and the ladies' room inside. Trixie wouldn't pass up an opportunity to flirt, despite the obvious age difference between the two—Cliff's rounded chin looked like it hadn't yet felt a razor. She heard the tinkle of Trixie's laughter before she stepped inside the station. It smelled like oil and cigarettes but was cooler than the day outside.

About twenty minutes later, after Trixie had blown a kiss to her young admirer and promised that she would be sure to stop again the next time she drove through, they were back on the road heading south.

Lilly rolled her eyes. "Why did you tell him you'd be back?"

"It'll give him something to look forward to!" Trixie replied, snapping a fresh piece of Doublemint gum. "He'll be bragging to his friends that he once knew me after they see me on the silver screen." She tooted the car horn for emphasis.

They were on their way to California. Lilly had put aside most of her earnings from the Gopher Munitions plant. She figured she had enough to cover expenses for the next three months, enough time for her and Trixie to find a small place to share and jobs to keep them there.

"Are you nervous about seeing your folks again?" They were the only car headed south under the bright midday sun. The fields on both sides of the highway looked full and lush, their green lines running with military precision up and down the contours of the land.

Yes, she was nervous. She hadn't seen or spoken to them since Christmas time, when she'd told her mother about the baby. She'd gotten a few letters at Aunt Helen's, but they were brief, full of crop news, and written by her father. She didn't hear much from Elaine. "I think they'll be surprised that I'm moving to California instead of going back to Ames," Lilly ventured. "I don't suppose they'll say much, though." She thought a bit longer, smoothing the hem of her skirt between her fingers. "After all that's happened, maybe they'll be relieved not to have to avoid the neighbors anymore."

"Do the neighbors even know?"

Lilly laughed. "The neighbors in Crestview know everything." Her words were barbed with sarcasm. She added, "And I suppose there was some talk after Ned and I broke up."

They took the next exit off the highway. "Have you heard anything from him?" Trixie asked. The heat of the day ballooned as the car slowed to turn.

"Not a word; that is, nothing since Iowa State."

"Does he know about the baby?"

Despite her determination to keep her head high and her emotions hidden, Lilly's gaze dropped. "I don't think so, but somehow he seems to get information the rest of us don't." She made herself sit up straight and tall and took in a deep breath, scented with a tinge of spearmint gum and road dust. "I'm trying to tell myself that he, that the neighbors, don't matter. All I want to do is to say hello to my parents and let them know that I'm going to follow my lucky stars to a new life in California. What happens after that, well, that's up to them."

"Good girl!" Trixie cheered, clapping her hands against the steering wheel. "You keep that chin up. It'll all turn out, you'll see!"

THE PHONE RANG, four, five, six times before a recording kicked in. A mechanical voice recited the number Dani had dialed and asked her to leave a brief message.

She gave her first name and her cell phone number, adding: "If this is Lillian Bradstreet, please call me back. I am, or I should say I was, friends with Eleanor Swenson, in Crestview, Iowa, and I have some . . ." She paused to remember the words she'd rehearsed, but before she could finish, the recording disconnected. A combination of dead air and embarrassment pressed down on her.

Dani thought about calling back and trying the message again to sound more knowledgeable, less tentative, but leaving a second message might make her sound desperate or even a bit unhinged. She told herself to let it go. If Lilly wanted to call, she'd call. Dani needed to get back out to the field. She could check for a message at dinnertime; maybe Lilly would call by then.

She didn't.

The week that followed found Dani and the other land-tenders out in their respective fields, tilling their plots to receive the seeds they'd sow when the right moon phase drew near. Her days were full. She slept well at night. She paid Chuck for taking in her corn last fall.

The men at Susie's invited her to sit at the center table. Dani said she would, but only if Bud's wife and Barbara Dorn were invited, too. She had short conversations with Donna's brother Pete, both at the café and in the library's vestibule, but their chats didn't seem to get anywhere.

Dani's cell phone rang when she was driving into town some days later. She glanced at the number before picking up; the caller listed was "Unknown." She answered anyway.

"This is Lilly Bradstreet. I'm returning a call from Dani. Is this she?"

Dani's heart stopped. She pulled off to the side of the highway. A semi behind her honked as it streamed by. "This is Dani."

They began to speak at the same time.

Lilly's laugh broke through first. "Go ahead!"

Dani breathed deeply. "Miss Bradstreet. Thank you for returning my call."

"It's my pleasure. I haven't thought about Crestview for a long time." Her voice sounded both energetic and serene. Cultured. "What can I do for you?"

"I don't know how to start," Dani began.

"First of all, why don't you call me Lilly?" the older woman prompted. Then, "You mentioned Eleanor. How is she?"

There wasn't an easy way to say it. Dani plowed ahead. "Mrs. Swenson passed away, Miss, Lilly. I'm sorry. She passed away after Christmas, a few months ago."

"Oh, my," Lilly reacted. It sounded like this wasn't what she'd expected to hear. "I suppose it's not a surprise. She was—we are—that age, after all." She took some time before speaking up again. "Your message said that you had something for me? I have to confess, that sounded mysterious!" The older woman's joking tone sounded a bit forced.

Dani straightened herself in her seat, switching the phone to her other ear. "Mrs. Swenson showed me some of her sister Elaine's letters, letters that you sent to her from college and . . . and afterward."

"My, my," Lilly said again, softly. "It's a wonder that she kept those for so long." Dani heard a quiet sniff, then Lilly cleared her throat. "Do you know what she did with them?"

"I do." Dani's mind raced. "I have them." Caught between wanting to know more and fearing that her intrusion would be rejected, she sought her way forward. "She found the letters in Elaine's attic. We talked about them, about you, a bit before she died."

"You have questions, don't you?" This time, another emotion had crept into the older woman's voice, one that Dani could not identify.

"Yes. Yes, I really do, but I also want to respect your privacy," Dani confessed. Another semi swooshed past, tossing wet, spring slush and dirty gravel onto the side of Dani's truck. She flipped on her red hazard lights and hoped no one would rear-end her truck. "I moved to Crestview last year, myself. It's been sort of . . . hard, trying to become part of the community here." Dani's face warmed. "Mrs. Swenson—Eleanor, I mean—passed your letters on to me. She told me that they were mine now, for safekeeping. I'm sure she never thought she'd hear from you again." She shut her eyes. She was really off-script, surprised by Lilly's call, and tried to remember the speech she'd planned during the nights she couldn't sleep. The conversation points she'd carefully rehearsed were abandoned. Plowing ahead anyhow, she continued. "I probably don't have to tell you, since you grew up in Crestview, how they like to tell their stories here. After reading your letters, though, I wondered if, maybe, you were part of a story yourself?"

Dani didn't know if Lilly would answer. When she did, it was with an apology. "You know, your call is such a surprise to me. I'm finding myself a bit tied up with thoughts and memories I haven't visited for a while." Lilly cleared her throat. "Would you mind terribly if we continued this conversation later? I think I'd like some time to think about things."

"Sure!" Dani promised, admonished herself for pushing too hard. "Absolutely! Why don't you give me a call when, or if, you feel like visiting again." Now she felt ashamed for prying. She should have taken it slower. She'd obviously overstepped another invisible boundary in her hunt for answers.

But Lilly had the last word. Before she disconnected, she asked the favor Dani had hoped to avoid. "Would you send those letters Eleanor gave you on to me?"

Dani

40

THE SUN ROSE earlier each morning as spring came back to visit the Iowa farmland. At full moon, the field crops were planted; as the moon waned, a soaking rain washed down. Farmers, including Dani, were quietly optimistic, busy from before the sun rose until the last rays kissed the new earth good night.

On her way to a late breakfast at Susie's, Dani saw the season's first robin singing from a pale-green lawn. Its trill warmed her, but she didn't have time to stand there in the parking lot and watch the birds: she hadn't been to town in over a week. She knew she'd better tell Donna about the phone call before she found herself in trouble.

Only one customer was in the café. He was busy turning the pages of the morning paper in the far corner, a coffee mug labelled "Big Mike" in front of him. Donna stacked dirty dishes together like castanets at the front counter. "Hey, you," she said, smiling. "Long time, no see!" She waited with the dish tub for Dani to sit down.

Dani chose a revolving metal stool. "Good morning! I'm sorry I've been out of touch, I've—"

Pete interrupted, sticking his head out from the kitchen. "I got that book you wanted, Dani. You'd better stop by and get it before it has to go back again." His words and movements were brisk and businesslike, his smile like warm, buttered toast.

Dani, more important things on her mind, nodded and turned back to her friend. "I heard from Lilly last Tuesday."

Donna's smile froze still.

"She said she was caught off guard, when she first spoke with me. Hearing about her letters to Elaine. I guess she thought they'd been thrown out or lost in time." Dani spun a bit on her stool. "After she got the letters back, she said she started thinking. She remembered that she had some old letters hidden away too. Some letters that, 'till now, she had told herself to forget."

"Don't just sit there!" Donna barked. "If you're going to wait a lifetime to finally tell me, spit it out, quick! What did they say?" She dropped the full dishpan with a clank onto the counter in front of her.

"The first one she opened was sent to Lilly by her old 'boyfriend'"—here, Dani drew little quotation marks in the air between them—"but it was written by Cisco, supposedly, and signed with his name. Lilly didn't know who wrote it, but she said it wasn't Ned's handwriting, or Cisco's, either."

Donna's eyes couldn't have grown any larger. "Oh my gosh! Why didn't she open them 'till now? Were there more?"

"The second letter was written by that Ned. He hinted at 'fixing an injustice,' and wrote that if it weren't for some information he stumbled upon, he'd have never known what kind of trash he'd almost married."

"Is that what he wrote to her?" Donna fumed. "Really? Couldn't he leave that girl alone?"

"I guess he wanted her to know what she was missing by not marrying him. He wanted her to feel bad. He wanted to hurt her, because she wouldn't have him."

The café door dinged open. Two of the regulars made their way in and sat themselves at a table, continuing the conversation they'd obviously begun outdoors. Donna asked them to hang on a moment, then turned back to Dani. "Did she say anything about Cisco, or about Elaine, or her sister?"

At that moment, Dani's cell phone vibrated in her back pocket. She looked at the phone's screen, then held it up to Donna: it was Lillian Bradstreet. Donna leaned forward, whirling her finger at Dani. "Answer it!"

For a moment, she hesitated, then jabbed the button to answer. "Hello?"

"Dani, I'm calling with a favor. Are you free to meet with me, later today?"

It was her, all right. Dani was glad that she was sitting down. "Sure," she answered. "Are you here in town?" She held out her phone so that Donna could listen in, too.

"I am back in Iowa," Lilly explained. "I'm grateful to you for finding and returning my letters. That means a lot to me. They helped to me to put together the missing pieces of a story I'd given up on."

In the midst of the old woman's subsequent pause, it seemed to Dani that the world had come to a stop. Neither she nor Donna took a breath, waiting for what would come next.

"I decided to come back to Crestview, to say goodbye for the last time," Lilly continued. "I'd like to meet you, and say thanks, before I head back home to California again. I'm sure things have changed since I've been away. I'd like to pay my respects to Eleanor, and I have a few other places I'd like to look in on. I'd welcome your company," she added.

Dani, still not entirely convinced this was real, agreed. They chose Susie's Café as their meeting spot.

Lilly bade goodbye; Dani disconnected. She and Donna stared at each other. "What I wouldn't give to ride in the back seat!" Donna remarked. "But I've got enchiladas to get started for tonight. You have to remember every detail, so you can tell me later." She hoisted up the dish tub. "Thanks for setting up the meeting here," she added. "At least I can get a good look at her."

After driving home for a quick shower and change of clothes, Dani returned to Crestview. As she pulled to a stop in the shade to the side of Susie's, she noticed a slender, silver-haired woman heading her way from the café. She could only be described as elegant, from her short pixie hair-cut down to her low-heeled, open sandals. She wore a sleeveless top with a slim, flowered skirt. *This is her.*

She held out one hand and smiled as they neared one another. "You must be Dani." The woman's tanned face was open and kind. "It's so nice to meet you!" Her eyes reflected the green of summer fields, flecked with gold. Creases from years of laughter radiated from her tanned face. She seemed altogether perfect.

"Hello, Lilly." Dani gently took the other's cool hand. "I'm so happy to finally meet you, too."

"I hope you don't mind," Lilly said, "but I've been into the café already, and I think I'd like to drive by my old home, and then see what Lainey's old house looks like. And, if there's time . . ." As her voice trailed off, she fished in her handbag for a pair of brown-tinted sunglasses and put them on.

"Of course. Would you like to ride together?" Dani asked. "I'm here to chauffeur you wherever you'd like to go."

"Let's do. We can take my car; it's a rental." Lilly suggested. "But would you mind driving?"

"No problem. Where would you like to go first?"

They toured the middle of town on an indirect route to Maple Street. Lilly remarked that the big trees she'd loved growing up, the ones that stretched over the street like umbrellas, must have died out. The light was different now, she noticed; the newer, smaller trees were lovely, but their sparse shade made the houses look paler than she remembered.

They pulled to a stop in front of Lilly's childhood home. It had undergone some remodeling, and the siding was a different color. The garage in the back had an apartment of sorts built on top. Her father's big garden was now a big, lush patch of lawn edged with colorful bushes and flowers. Lilly smiled, scanning the property with her gold-flecked eyes, and said she was pleased.

Next, a short trip to Elaine's. This house hadn't fared as well. The sidewalk in front was broken and tilted from the roots of an overgrown hedge. A car without a passenger-side door sat on concrete blocks next to the garage, where Stevie used to have a play fort. The front porch sagged; the lovely double swing was long gone. Lilly shook her head, then suggested that they continue on.

"You know . . ." Lilly's voice sounded more tired than when they'd started. "I wonder if my father's workshop is still standing? Would you mind driving there next, to see?"

"Of course. Can you tell me where to go?"

They headed back through town, avoiding the main section, and turned toward the creek. A group of Holsteins clustered together at the top of a hill, enjoying the sun and the breeze that kept the flies and bugs off their black-and-white, patterned hides. They blinked their large eyes and chewed thoughtfully, watching the car drive by.

"I never thought I'd come back," Lilly murmured. She stared straight ahead through the windshield and didn't blink. "Once I left, that last time, I knew there was nothing here for me to return to."

Dani snuck a quick glance to her right. The older woman had closed her eyes. Gathering her courage, Dani asked what she'd been pondering for so many months. "Why did you leave, Lilly?"

Lilly turned to her window. The fields they passed were dark and rich with turned earth, recently planted. Sunlight struck a pyramid of rocks and boulders some farmer had collected at the corner of his section. "My dear, I was that girl who wanted more," she began. "I had a wonderful childhood, and parents who loved me, but my imagination and my dreams kept tempting me away." She smiled at Dani. "I wasn't able to settle inside the plans others set for me."

"Are you talking about that man you were engaged to?"

"Yes, he was one of the biggest reasons," Lilly admitted. "Ned had determined that I would make the perfect wife and hostess." She adjusted the window on her side by flicking the button back and forth until the air streaming in moved to her satisfaction. "My mother agreed. And my father—well, my father was content to let things continue without having to pay much attention to them. He was mostly concerned with his work. He loved me, truly, but he—he became *aware* of me, of what I wanted, when it was too late and too inconvenient to stand up for me against my mother and Ned."

She directed Dani to turn right at the next corner and to follow the dirt road past the first crossing. Her father's workshop would be next to the road on the right, if it was still there. The fields flipped by, organized as neatly as a stack of playing cards. Her small smile reappeared. "I met someone, that year before college. A man who was born in a different place, someone traveling through. We became friends. His support helped me to understand that what I was offered through a marriage to Ned would be more servitude than a partnership. And this man—Cisco was his name—he knew what partnership was, whether partnering with the land, or with his family, or . . ." She stopped and coughed into a tissue. "But he left. He left, without saying goodbye to me. And that, I didn't understand."

By this time, Dani had turned through the crossroads and slowed to a stop. Next to the car was a flattened area ringed with old hardwood trees and weedy bushes. Nothing remained on this piece except for a cracked slab of asphalt that looked worn and broken.

Dani keyed off the ignition after lowering the two back windows. Though the air outside wasn't hot, the sun beating down on the car was stifling. "Did you find out where he went?"

"After I talked to you, I finally opened those letters he'd sent to me—Ned sent to me." Lilly lowered her sunglasses and turned to look at Dani. "Ned and another man, a man who owed Ned money. They were the ones who took Cisco away."

"Do you know how they found out about him?" The words escaped her lips before Dani knew she'd even formed them. She hadn't decided if she should tell Lilly about the letters Mrs. Swenson had held back, the letters she had found in the open box.

"I can only imagine. But he found out somehow—Ned did, I mean—about my . . ." Here, she stumbled. ". . . My relationship with this other man." She opened her car door but did not step outside; she seemed to be trying to catch a breeze.

Watching the older woman, Dani wrestled with herself about whether to expose what she'd gleaned from Mrs. Swenson's hidden letters. Before she could decide, Lilly went on. "You have to understand, Dani, that people didn't treat everyone fairly back then. Cisco wasn't from here." She stopped, then tried again. "Cisco was a migrant worker. He wasn't white. He wasn't from our class." Her smile turned bitter. "But he had dignity. He was smart. He knew the earth; he knew people. And he showed me, in that one summer together, what was important. And I learned what wasn't."

At that, Lilly pulled herself up and stepped outside into the streaming sun. "Dani? Could you please give me a moment?"

She made her way to the corner of the flattened lot, to the edge of the trees, and disappeared into the shade between them.

Dani, concerned and uncertain about what to do next, waited and peered into the shadows until she couldn't take the stillness any longer.

Pacing along the stretch of road that bordered the woods, she listened to cicadas drone like buzz saws; counted round, purple clover tops; told herself that she must find the right time to share what the letters Lilly didn't yet know about contained. When the older woman reappeared, looking refreshed and calm again, Dani ducked back into the rental car like she'd been waiting there all along.

"Would you have time for one more stop?" Lilly asked. "My, I wish we would've thought to bring a cool beverage. I'd forgotten how hot these Midwest springs can be." She climbed back into the passenger seat without waiting for Dani's answer.

Dani started the car, closed the car windows, and flipped on the air conditioner. "Where would you like to go next?"

"There used a be a big old tree," Lilly said. "It was a ways further along, between two sections—maybe a bit to the west from here?"

A pang sprung up from her gut. Dani knew which tree the older woman referred to.

"It was a strange old tree, even back then. It had two big tops to it, both the same size," Lilly continued explaining. "I used to like to sit underneath it, sort of hide there, you know?"

Dani gripped the wheel. "Lilly, I don't think that tree is going to be the same way you remember it," she cautioned. "Maybe we should head back to town, try to find a cool drink instead?"

"I don't think it's too far from here. Why don't we drive back to town that way, and see what we can see?"

Dani obediently turned west at the next junction.

Meanwhile, Lilly returned to her story. "My friend Elaine and I drifted apart, you know. She didn't approve of my friendship with Cisco from the beginning. The last time I saw her was when I moved to California. I stopped to say goodbye. She'd been married and was expecting her first child, but her husband, Lonny, was away fighting the war, so she'd gone to stay with her parents. When I arrived, she was sick with nausea and very surprised to see me on her front steps." Lilly drew up her skirt to catch the cool air blowing up from the floor of the car. "Ah, that's wonderful, isn't it?"

She settled her skirt back to a more modest level. "Elaine told me that Ned was upset by my refusal to marry him. He'd driven over to see her, that same day I turned him down, thinking maybe she could help talk some sense into me. She said that he became incensed, even crazy, and stormed away from her house."

"Did she tell him about your . . . other relationship?" Dani asked.

"I don't know if she did or not, but I think she was as upset as he was, to tell the truth—she didn't like the migrants, either. But that's not the worst of it. She told me that the following Sunday, after Mass, Ned stopped her and Lonny on their way to their car and told them that there was nothing more to worry about, that 'the problem had been taken care of.' I realized then why Cisco had never said goodbye.

"I left Elaine, went back out to the car, and drove away. But before I reached California, I opened my suitcase and dug out the letters Ned had sent me, months before, when I was still in Ames." She paused, but only for a moment. "I hadn't ever opened them. I didn't want to open them. I stood on the side of a road, a road like this one, and tried to find the courage to uncover what he thought he needed me to know."

Dani could hardly keep her eyes on the road. "What did the letters say?"

Lilly blew out a short breath and shook her head. Looking to her hands, clasped tightly in her lap, she answered. "I don't know. I couldn't do it. I put them back into my suitcase."

Dani had to pull over; she wasn't able to see the road, for her vision was pinned on scenes ten thousand days, a million heartbeats, away. Words weren't big or wide enough to capture the pangs that dried her throat and squeezed her breath from her lungs. "After I contacted you, Lilly, was it then that you finally opened those envelopes?"

Lilly nodded. "I told myself for many years that I'd forgotten it all, everything that happened back then. I became a whole different person—that the love affair from so long ago hardly warranted another thought. And it did fade, through the years." She chuckled. "Interesting, then, that I was able to locate the letters so quickly when I got your call after Christmas."

"You told me over the phone that you opened them. Would—could you tell me more about them?"

"One letter wasn't even from Ned. It had streaks of dirt on the back side. I don't know who wrote it. It said that the author took full responsibility for ruining the life of an educated, cultured lady; that he deserved punishment for taking liberties he had no reason or right to expect; that he accepted his fate with full responsibility for his damnable actions."

Dani reached over and patted the older woman's soft shoulder.

"It was signed *Cisco Martinez*, the name of my lover," Lilly whispered. "But it wasn't his handwriting." The pain she'd endured leaked out with the smallest of sighs.

Leaning a bit closer toward Dani, Lilly continued: "The other one, that was from Ned. He'd changed his mind and had found another, 'more suitable' woman, I think he wrote." She actually giggled at that. "He had such an ego! I think he thought he was breaking off with me." And with that, she continued to smile but said nothing more.

Dani was stuck. She knew she should hand over or at least tell the old woman about what she'd found in Mrs. Swenson's study. She also knew that the person next to her, so lively and capable and lovely, had already suffered so much. She said she'd let Cisco go—Dani couldn't decide if knowing this last part would help Lilly to heal or would harm her more.

They sat together in the still afternoon until a pickup hauling a bunch of kids skidded through the crossroads ahead. It looked like Tot, the boy who'd been in the four-wheeler accident, was at the wheel, but from this distance Dani wasn't quite sure.

The commotion startled Lilly from her memories. She swept both hands down her face. "Dani, I'd really like to see that tree. Then, I think, it's time to go home again."

Dani put the car into gear. They drove to the edge of the field. Some yards ahead, the shorn edge of a stump poked up like a grave marker through the foliage that surrounded it.

Lilly gasped. "It's . . . it's like the last piece of that world has gone," she managed. She fumbled with the door lock, unable to wrench it open.

Dani got out, opened Lilly's door, and helped her out of her seat. Tucking the woman's cool hand into the crook of her elbow, she began walking with her through the paths of dirt that separated the rows of corn. The stalks' newborn leaves, grown tall enough to wave in the breeze, beckoned the women forward with graceful encouragement.

A few feet from the stump, Dani stopped and freed Lilly's hand, letting her go the rest of the way on her own. When Lilly reached the site where her tree used to stand, she bent her head and sunk to her knees in the rich, black dirt. She placed both hands on the soft, gray bark, caressing the whitened marks where the saw had hacked through. Then she opened her fingers and plunged both wrinkled hands as deeply as she could into the earth.

Dani turned away.

IT WAS FULL-ON dark and moonless when she was able to return to the café, clouds obscuring whatever starlight struggled to shine below. The café's outside lights were doused, but Dani could see Donna busing tables, backlit by the bright kitchen. As usual, the front door hadn't been locked. Dani entered slowly, her body strangely heavy and tired. The aroma of fried onions and strains of mariachi music greeted her, wafting through the air along with the sound of Donna harping at someone to put that last load in the dishwasher.

While she didn't mean to, she startled Donna when she thumped herself onto a stool near the kitchen doorway.

"Hell's bells, girl! You're about to give me gray hair, sneaking around like that."

Dani didn't reply.

"Pete!" Donna yelled again. "Can you finish up in there? I got something I need to tend to." She dropped the salt shaker she'd been refilling and came around the counter to sit by Dani. "You doing all right?"

"I'm good, Donna. Just sad."

"Sad? Why? Tell me about Lilly."

Dani tried to find the words. "I admire her," she started. "She has every right to be bitter about what she went through. But she isn't. She isn't angry." Struggling to encompass it all, Dani finished: "She seems to accept what happened."

"Did she see—did you give her those other letters, the ones Mrs. Swenson held back?"

Dani's eyes crimped shut. Her lips pursed together. "Yes, I did. But it was awful, Donna. I handed them over, thinking that they pretty much proved that her best friend's family went behind her back, you know? But I—you and me—we didn't know the writer wasn't one of the parents."

She turned to Donna, her eyes brimming and her face ashen. "Lilly recognized the handwriting right away. Her best friend, Elaine—Elaine was the one who gave her secret away." Her tears finally fell. "Elaine wrote those letters and signed her dad's name."

Some of the sorrow Dani tried to contain was mirrored on the waitress's face. "My God."

They sat in the gloom, listening to Pete and the dishes and the music in back.

Donna had one more thing to ask. "So the younger sister, the librarian, she took those letters that her big sister wrote?"

Dani took her time before she replied. "She must have. But I don't know—we'll never know—if she took them before or after the Bradstreets or Ned had seen them."

Covered from the waist down by a dirty, folded apron, Pete ambled into the dining room. He picked up the last load of dirty dishes and returned to the kitchen.

Donna lit a cigarette, despite the "No Smoking" sign she had hanging in front of the counter. "How did she take it?"

Head slumping into her hands, Dani replied, "She was troubled, even devastated, when she figured out that Cisco lost his life saving hers."

"What do you mean, 'saving hers'?"

"It seems like she found her place, eventually. She probably wouldn't have had the life she'd wanted if she'd stayed here. Without him—without her having him to love and him loving her back—she wouldn't have taken the steps to free herself. To be herself, I guess."

"So, was she ever happy?" Donna persisted. "Do you think she had a good life?"

"I think so. She said she worked for a long time at Boeing, the airplane company, and she met another man. A widower. They didn't marry, but they spent the rest of his life together." Dani smiled. "She seems content. Happy, even."

She reached forward and gave Donna a hug. "And now, it'll be all I can do to get myself home and into bed. Whew!" Spreading her palms on the counter, she pushed herself to her feet. "I think we did a good thing, Donna. I think we had to give those letters to her. That secret wasn't ours to keep."

Donna stood too. "I hope so." She shook her head. "I just wish there wasn't so much trouble involved in the process."

"We did what we thought we were supposed to do, right? The things that happened, the accidents, Mrs. Swenson—those things would've or could've happened anyway, don't you think?"

Donna nodded, but didn't look convinced.

"Besides, what does an old tree have to do with it?" Dani smiled and began her return to her truck outside. "What are you serving tomorrow for breakfast? I think I'm going to need a big one, after the day I had today," she teased over her shoulder.

"I'll have the coffee hot and waiting," Donna said, following behind her at a distance. "Be careful, now; it's late." She blinked the café's outside lights on and off, twice, before closing the front door.

Dani backed out of the gravel lot and turned toward County Road

8. Leaving Crestview behind, she drove through the dark toward home, searching one-handed through the pile of jackets next to her for a CD she'd gotten for Christmas. She couldn't locate it. Grumbling to herself, she flipped on the interior lights. The illumination brightened the dashboard but cast a shadowy shroud around her shoulders. It hid the road ahead from her sight.

THE EVENING SILENCE was shorn to pieces: a screech of brakes, a jarring crash, the wrench of ripping metal tore the night apart.

Near the shoulder where the road curved, a thin sheet of steam blew up from the ditch. Tiny cubes of shattered glass littered the wayside. Dani's pickup truck lay upside down in the gully next to the road, its muddy undercarriage glinting dully in the wavering reflection thrown back by its feeble taillights. From the truck's cab, crumpled to half its original size, the horn continued its offended scream, piercing holes into the darkness. From the east, a pack of coyotes out hunting joined their ghostly wails with the cacophony.

The discordant concert and eerie lights robbed the country of its final threads of peace.

Dani

41

THE PIERCING BLARE became muffled, dampened, the way things had sounded long ago when her ears sealed swimming in her grandparents' pond. Dani rode the waves through disjointed dreams, over swells of scenes that could have been memories, connected by tunnels of gray silence. She wasn't aware of *being* aware; it felt more like she was cushioned in some swath of soft consciousness that didn't connect clearly to what was real. She didn't fight this. She floated on her back, her chin pointed to the sky, resting in a safe oblivion.

What finally poked holes through the gauze of her immobility were pricks of light—white needles that burrowed into the rolling loops of her dreams. Dani tried turning from them, but her head refused to comply. Its rigidity forced her to battle for a grip on some solid surface. Her shoulders, weighted like concrete blocks, disobeyed her growing intentions to get up, get out, move away. An ache wedged its way up and into her left side. She heard a solemn hiss of air and felt its cool rush over her upper lip.

She couldn't figure out where she was.

A cool hand startled her as it applied a faint pressure to her forearm— she hadn't heard anyone approach. A new sound inserted itself in between the layers of her awareness: a woman's calm voice, her words and their meanings indistinct. Dani's eyelashes brushed against a cotton wrapping, any explanation for its presence lagging like a lazy thunderclap miles away.

Now another voice, strident and loud, broke in. "Is she awake? Can she hear me?"

Dani heard the syllables, the assonance, the drifting smoke in the words. She knew that voice. The cool palm lifted away, replaced by the warm, insistent patting of a rough hand used to doling out steaming dishes and hotter plates. *Donna.*

"How long before you take them bandages off her eyes?" Donna's voice barged through the haze again.

Dani struggled to track the reply. *Bandages.* She was wearing bandages. That didn't make sense. Nothing about this dream made any sense.

"Hey! She's moving! She's awake!" the waitress called, excitement pulling her voice up from its usual tenor range. Her scratchy hand leapt from Dani's arm to her shoulder.

Intense, shooting pain burst from that joint like lightning, electrifying the nerves behind her eyes and what felt like a solid plate behind her back.

Dani understood the nurse's voice, closer and insistent. "You'll have to step back, miss. We don't know the level of her pain, and we won't until she's able to talk." The gentle hands smoothed the cloth more firmly around Dani's eyes, then travelled to adjust the oxygen nozzles' clean flow into her nostrils.

"When do you think that'll be?" Donna inquired, her tone softened.

"It's hard to tell," the quieter voice answered. "With a head trauma like this, she'll take her own time to heal." The nurse's words grew indistinct and drifted away, taking Dani's attention with them, tempting her to return to the undulating clouds and soft whispers of her disjointed dreams.

It took a few more days for Dani to fully grasp where she was and why she was being kept there. The lights above her bed and at the window continued to drill into her, causing blinding jabs of intense pain that made her vomit and cry. She'd broken her left collarbone and cracked several ribs on the same side when her truck rolled. Purple bruises colored her hip, knee, and elbow; the skin around and below her eyes showed hints of muted yellow and green where it wasn't covered by the dark, wrap-around glasses she wore against the light. Fortunately, her brain scans showed no damage or swelling; her doctor explained her dreamlike travels as the result of a severe concussion.

Donna came daily to check on her, bringing news of the café and greetings from the locals who she said asked after Dani every morning. The waitress had also stopped by Dani's place to gather her mail and pick up a clean nightie and slippers for her. Meanwhile, Dani's only goal was to grow strong enough to be able to stand under the shower—she'd grown irritable and short-tempered with the sponge baths offered to her, and was determined to find her feet and her balance and get back to her farm again.

"Here, let me put this on you," Donna offered, draping a tie-dyed blue silk scarf up and over Dani's damaged shoulder.

"Ouch! Careful!"

"Sorry!" The waitress tied a jaunty bow behind Dani's neck; the patient was supposed to keep her arm immobilized against her chest. "I just couldn't stand to look at that dang old-man contraption they had you in anymore, for Pete's sakes." She went back to the doorway to retrieve a brightly colored, plastic tote bag. "Here, I brought you something else."

Dani tried to sound appreciative. "Thanks, Donna." She leaned back into the chair next to her hospital bed. "What were you saying about my parents, again?"

"I said they're at the house. Your house." Tugging down her top to cover her middle, she brought the bag back to the bed in front of Dani. "They're fixin' up a place for you to sleep downstairs, by the bathroom? That way you won't have to climb the stairs up and down every hour." She dumped a pile of bills, newsletters, the local weekly paper, and a few other items onto the coverlet. "Least we can get you caught up on your bills, now that you're up and able again."

The Crestview *American* newspaper, perched on the top of the pile, flopped open to present a picture of Dani's dented and ruined truck just above the fold line. Bold, black type burst out from the top of the page.

Dani gasped, folding inward like a ball, drawing her one good arm over her stomach as she turned away. Her stuttered breath sucked in with painful shudders.

"Oh, crap. S'pose you didn't need to see that, did 'ya?" Donna grabbed the paper from the pile and started stuffing it back into her bag.

"Wait. What does it say?" Dani's head had tilted downward; Donna could see her eyes pressed shut behind her dark glasses, from her pain or the picture or both.

Donna waited a beat. "Well, I guess your accident with the truck is a big deal, comin' as it did after Jacob's death, you know."

"What do you mean?"

"I don't know how much I'm s'posed to say." Donna shook her head from side to side like she was dislodging someone else's advice. "Mostly, there's talk about how you, how you and Jacob, and Bud's boys too, how you all took down that tree, and—"

Dani's head jerked up. "The curse." She winced at the sudden strain on her neck.

The waitress nodded. "Yup." She sat with one hip on the side of the bed, close to Dani's chair. "But they're sayin' it's over, with your accident. The curse is done 'cuz you all 'paid the price.'" She stopped talking and watched for Dani's reaction.

Easing her glasses off with her good hand, Dani considered. "I'm glad, Donna. If it's true, I mean." She massaged the outer corner of her bruised eye and swept away the moisture from underneath it.

Donna bent toward her and kissed the top of her head. "You're okay, girl. You're gonna be fine. Don't you worry." She stood. "And that shower can't come too soon—your hair smells like an old cat."

Dani's sniffles dissolved into a broken laugh. "Ow! Stop! Ow . . ."

DANI'S PARENTS DROPPED by for a short visit after lunch. Following their departure, she tried to nap but was fitful and unsettled. After a lukewarm dinner of soft, bland food, she moved back to the chair and tried to paw through the papers Donna had left in the tote bag.

She ignored the county newspaper; she placed her bills into a pile of their own. One item, a light blue envelope addressed to Dani in an arty, curious script, caught her attention. Frowning, she carved a slit through the top and pulled the contents out.

The letter came from Lilly:

My dear Dani,

I thank you for your time and kindness, driving me all over Howard County to revisit the places I thought I'd never see again. Seeing them brought many people back to life for me. And to think that you became friends with Eleanor, whom I remember as a little girl in a jumper and scuffed Oxfords! I guess it's a sign, after all, that some things are just meant to be.

So, I've decided, after you shared your story of uncovering the truth—my truth—that I need to take a page from your book. I cannot hide from my fear any longer, and I don't need to, for all those whom I knew and loved from that time are gone. You've inspired me, Dani, to do something I should have done years ago. I want to see if I can locate my son, Cisco's son. I want to find out if there's time left to reconnect with him, with that part of my life that never should have been taken away.

And about that tree? My dear girl, I don't know that I can judge for sure, one way or the other, the truth of that "curse" you described, but I do know that the old girl was always special to me. To me and to Cisco, really. When I put my fingers down into that soil, where she used to stand? It was as if I was able to re-connect with who I used to be: the girl who was, the last time she was there, just learning to be brave. Now it's your turn to be brave—put away those old stories about curses and live the life set before you. Don't be afraid, like I was, to make a scene or demand your own way. Trust the rhythm of your own heart, Dani.

Thank you, dear girl, for the gift you've given to me. I shall forever be grateful. Most cordially yours,

Lilly

P.S. Say a little prayer for me, would you, dear, that I'm able to find my son?

The blue letter drifted down to rest in Dani's robed lap. She closed her eyes, leaned back into the comfort of the chair's cushions, and smiled.

The Curse

August 1939

THE WAY THE cool air rippled through the corn stalks reminded him of her hair—how it drifted like silk through his fingertips, separating into easy strands, whispering secrets. Saw-edged leaves and gray branches almost blocked his view, but he could see past them to the gravel road edging the section beyond. Three blackbirds swept past like sprung arrows; the rounded warmth of the sun caressed his shoulders as it slipped over the horizon.

He paid no mind to the garrulous voices below, ignored the chafing of the cord that bit at his collarbone and twisted into his wrists. The tawny scent of rich, moist earth filled his lungs as he breathed, deep and slow, again and again. As the shaded hues of twilight crept closer, he felt the pulse of his strong, bursting heart.

When the ladder flew out from beneath him, he did not make a sound. Instead, he remembered the tiny gold flecks in her green eyes, the colors of tree shade and summer sunshine. He savored the tang of her lips, tasting of secrets and promises. His own full lips pulled upward into a smile.

FROM THE GROUND, the banker squinted through the dimming evening to be sure the body had stopped swinging. A single star shone right above the double-headed tree, a steely shot scarring the velvet overhead. Reaching into his suit coat, the banker brought out a folded sheet of paper. He thrust this at the dust-covered man leaning against the pickup's front fender, a few feet away.

"You need to climb up and put this paper into his back pocket," he directed.

The farmer remained where he was, impassive, studying the younger man who stood uneasily at the roots of the strange-looking tree. "You didn't say nothing about this part," he growled. "I thought we agreed that I'd be the one to find him, tomorrow. I didn't want nothing to do with the hanging."

The banker's chiseled features sharpened into a deeper frown. "There were circumstances that came up which were out of my control," he explained. "Besides, since you made yourself available, I'd be willing to consider tonight's work as interest paid. I'll deduct it from your loan."

The farmer thought about this a minute as he observed the dead man's body above. Reaching his decision, he stepped forward to take the letter, but at the last second the younger man snapped it away.

"Stop! You're about to mess it up," he snarled. "Whoever sees it will know it isn't his, if there's dirt on it."

Both men regarded the neatly trimmed fingernails of the man in front of them. From a few yards away, a starling cried out.

The banker's impatience overrode his caution. "Just get it into his pocket," he directed. "And don't forget to take the ladder when you're done."

The older man made a big deal of wiping both palms down the front of his shirt. Grasping the ladder's wooden sides, he climbed the rungs and placed the paper neatly into the victim's back pocket. He adjusted it so the edge could be seen from below.

Back on solid ground, he tossed the ladder into the back of his truck. From the passenger's seat, the banker urged him to hurry. The farmer got in and closed the driver's door. Safe in the truck again, he eased up on the clutch and yanked the transmission into low gear.

He was careful to leave the field using the same tracks they'd made driving in. The pickup's tail lights, a shameful red in the evening's cool twilight, bobbed awkwardly as they bounced through the ditch and turned back to town.

GRADUALLY, DARKNESS TUCKED itself like a blanket into the sides of the road and the edges of the fields. The night grew still, punctuated only by frogs calling out by the creek. None but the gathered stars and a sliver of the moon in the northeast sky were awake to witness the journey of a single candle, wending its way from the riverbank toward the big, double-top tree. It moved steadily, noiselessly, keeping to the edge of the gravel until it met the parallel lines of trampled foliage.

A soft crooning began, words that were sibilant and juicy and warm; a swelling of pain and hurt and injustice rode the notes into the inky darkness.

A gentle breeze from the west, redolent of fresh-cut hay and sunshine, fanned the leaves to dance and twist on their slender stems. The man's body turned on its string from the road to address the verdant field before it.

The candle flame went out.

The breeze quieted.

The night embraced its favorite creatures.

The tree, a silent witness, held the secret deep inside her, and promised to hold fast to the duty she had been given.

Acknowledgments

I'D LIKE TO thank these important humans for their time, suggestions, and support: Shar, Sue, Sanna, Michelle, Paula, Kati, Big Mike, Michael, and Melissa. Love yous!

Thank you to Lorna, Julia, Lori, Christine, Barb, and Greg, for the gifts of your time.

Christin, Genesis, Karyn, Ellie, and Kelly—keep fighting the good fight. Words win!

Thank you also to Dmytri, my best friend, riding partner, and my champion from every corner. Thanks for listening to my stories. We are blessed. I love you.

PHOTO BY MARY DUPONT PHOTOGRAPHY

AMY PENDINO, A Minnesota native, works as a middle-school English teacher by day and a horse midwife by night. Formerly a keyboard player for a local band, she's also waitressed, worked as a secretary, sung backup for an international star, and rides a new mountain range on horseback every summer. She belongs to the Twin Cities chapter of Sisters in Crime; her writing has been published in several magazines and reviews. This is her first published novel. For more information, please visit amypendino.com.